JANE LOVERING

CHRISTMAS SECRETS BY THE SEA

A Seasons by the Sea Romance

This edition published in 2018 by Farrago,
an imprint of Prelude Books Ltd
13 Carrington Road, Richmond, TW10 5AA, United Kingdom

www.farragobooks.com

ISBN: 978-1-78842-120-1

Chapter One

The incredibly scruffy small brown dog dashed out from behind me and raced across the beach like a toupee on a mission. Its paws churned the sand into gobbets which rained down around the retreating shape so it vanished in a shingly backwash as it bore down on the slender figure of the whippet at the waves' edge, like Dennis the Menace in hot pursuit of a paddling Claudia Schiffer. There was a moment of gleeful overexcitement, and then the two of them headed off towards the dunes, the whippet leading the way but not looking as though she was going to put up much more than a token resistance to the brown dog's increasingly frantic overtures.

A cloud of oystercatchers billowed up, presumably to avoid the X-rated events, and I watched them zoom overhead, tucking my hands into my pockets out of the wind and hunching my shoulders. The mid-December sky was a piercing blue and the shrill cries of the little birds ran down my nerve endings; it was as if the whole of nature was on some kind of sensory assault. Further out, the breakers boomed and pebbles rattled, a stadium of appreciation for the ฉunk performance of the seagulls screeching and wailing, first shouts were subsumed under the general ba' noise.

'Hey! Hey, you there!' The words gradually became audible. 'You there!'

I turned my head and finally saw the man who'd been shouting. He was running down the beach towards me, his duffel coat flapping open and swinging with each stride like a set of automatic doors. He had a black beanie hat pulled down to the bridge of his nose, which struck me as severe overkill – the beach was cold but hardly arctic conditions – and there were curls of dark hair poking out from underneath it and forming a ring around his face. The effect was that of a tiny person peering out from the middle of a black sunflower and the first hint of a giggle tickled the back of my throat.

'Can't you control your dog?' The man pulled up in front of me, panting slightly and shading his eyes against the low glare of the sun. He moved around, trying to see which way the dogs had gone, the toggles of the coat swinging and bumping. It was a surprisingly childish coat for a grown man and I found myself checking whether he had mittens on string down the sleeves. 'Call him off!'

Again the giggle rose. I didn't know if I should greet it or not. It was the first time I'd felt like laughing for a long time so the feeling was welcome, but not so welcome that I was going to let it out. 'It's not my dog. I've never seen it before.' My voice sounded cracked and underused.

The man was ignoring me, pacing angrily around, treading shapes in the sand. 'Seelie is a valuable pedigree dog!'

'I don't think mongrel is catching,' I said, reasonably.

'Are you trying to be funny?' Now the man's attention snapped away from its perusal of the dunes and the distant flocks of wading birds, and on to me.

'No. Are you trying to be rude?' I hunched my shoulders again. 'Because I'd say you're having a lot more success than

4

me.' The wind was strong enough to bend the thin grasses that dotted the beach and it was beginning to work its way inside my jacket. I wanted to get back to the van which, although not a great deal warmer than the outside, at least didn't have air that tried to assault you.

He narrowed his eyes at me. 'My bitch is in season and your dog is probably out there,' a wide-flung arm indicated the otherwise deserted beach, '*mating* her. She's...' he tailed off and I saw his jaw clench as though he was biting down on words he didn't want to say. 'She's valuable,' he finished.

Behind us a large wave sloshed further towards us. The tide was turning. In another hour, I knew this bit of beach would be under water, the sand getting a complete makeover, to re-appear brand new when the water receded again. 'Well, as I said, it's not my dog.' There was a certain ambiguity in my words. Whilst the dog wasn't actually mine, he'd turned up at the van last night looking cold and with his coat matted and I'd fed him a sardine. Did that count as ownership? He had no collar and I had no idea where the local vet was to have him checked for a microchip. 'And if you bring a bitch in season to a public beach, I'd have thought you would have kept her on a lead.'

The man did the 'clenched jaw' thing again. He looked me in the eye as he did it, and I had the feeling that I was supposed to be finding it attractive or, at least, being sympathetic. 'A lead wouldn't have stopped your dog from jumping on her, would it now?' An accent was seeping through his words, and I had the feeling that I was supposed to find that attractive too. The man had the air of one who is used to women being speechless with lust in his presence. Just don't ask me how that air manifested; it was more of a self-consciousness on his part, as though he was waiting for me to ask for his mobile number or something and was paused on the edge of a breath to turn me down.

'You'd better go and find her,' I said. 'Your dog.' And then I took the greatest pleasure in turning away and walking back off the rapidly narrowing strip of sand. However wonderful he thought he was, he was still a conclusion-jumping overbearing idiot in a stupid hat, and my interest in men was at some maths busting minus figure. Right now I'd sooner have dated the small brown dog, sardine breath and all.

I walked down to the little café that huddled in the shelter of the sand dunes. The door stood hopefully ajar, as though to suck customers in, and a woman was visible inside, sweeping the floor energetically. She had curly fair hair that bounced with each brush stroke, and a bust with a life of its own.

'Are you open?' I poked my head in and addressed her.

She stopped sweeping for a second. 'Well, don't like to talk about my ex much, oh, and I don't do political opinion – apart from that you're good.'

'What?'

'Take no notice. It's her version of a "joke".' A lanky teenage boy pulled the door wider. 'Mum, it's not funny.'

'Makes me laugh.' Sweeping woman straightened up and leaned against her broom. 'Let's face it, there's not much else to giggle at round here. Come in, love, coffee machine is on.'

I hesitated, half in the doorway, whilst the young man opened the door still wider, as though he thought I might be carrying an invisible large load that required more space. 'I really just wanted to use your Wi-Fi.'

'Ah.' She turned more towards me now and I could see she was wearing a black skirt and shirt with a nametag that said 'Jackie'. 'You must be the woman in the van down on the dunes? Come on in and get warm, I'll get you a coffee. On the house.'

The boy waved me inside. As I passed him I got a better look; he had mousy hair cut in an improbable style, very short at the sides and longer on top. It had been fashionable about two years ago, as had his untied trainers. With the speed of youth he saw me look. 'I know, right?' he said, and gave me a grin. I wasn't sure what I was supposed to know, so I shrugged.

'Here.' A mug of coffee steamed on the table nearest the door. 'Password is Jurassic, one R two esses, capital J. You must be freezing in that van. Why are you not stopped up at the caravan site over to Lyme Regis? They've got electric hook ups and everything.'

I stared into the dark depths of the coffee and tried to think of an answer that didn't make me sound pathetic. 'Well,' I began, but any following words were cut off by the sound of claws skittering over wooden flooring, and then a damp weight slumped down onto my foot, combined with a wet, fishy smell and a trail of dribble which stretched back towards the still open door. We all went silent for a moment.

'That your dog?'

'No.'

The dog looked up into my face, tongue flopping, and yawned. Then he scratched energetically behind an ear, and half a beach sprayed out across the newly swept floor. 'Really,' I said, although somewhat faintly because it was clear that neither of them believed me.

'Rory, get the bugger a bowl of water,' Jackie said. 'And there's some of those there dog chew things in the kitchen; he can have one of those.'

'Rory' turned out to be the teenage boy, who began shuffling in his untied trainers towards the door behind the counter, complaining that it was the holidays, he shouldn't be being forced to work and anyway there were several levels of Assassin's Creed that wanted getting through.

'Thank you, Jackie,' I said, still faintly because I actually was feeling a bit faint. The smell of the coffee made my stomach howl. It had been a long time since my last proper meal. In fact, when had it been? Three days? Four?

'Oh, my name's not Jackie,' said Jackie. 'It's Karen. But we haven't got a Karen nametag. I was Jill before this for three weeks. It's not so bad, once you get used to it, like trying on different people for size – I liked being Jill. There's a bit of class to a "Jill" I think. Here, put your head between your knees.' The back of my neck was gripped firmly and shoved downwards and I found myself staring at the wooden planks of the café floor as they swam and broke and crested for a moment. 'Rore! Bring us up one of them paninini things, will you? Poor girl's near passing out.' A moment's quiet pressure on my neck and then she half-whispered, 'it is hunger, isn't it? You're not pregnant or got one of them there nasty diseases?'

'No,' I said, my voice muffled by the table. 'I just haven't eaten in… a while.'

'Hurry up with that paninini thing, Rore.'

There were a few more moments of quiet, that was then broken by a slurping sound as the brown dog cocked a leg in the air and began licking his hindquarters. 'I think I can sit up now,' I said, when the sight of the dog's cleansing routine was starting to make me queasy. 'I'll be fine when I've had some coffee.' I straightened up slowly, to find Karen looking at me and Rory slouching up to the table with a steaming sandwich on a plate. My stomach howled again, and the dog jerked away from his ablutions and gave me side-eye. 'There's no way of cooking in the van.'

I hoped that nobody was going to start querying my washing or lavatory facilities. Both were so rudimentary as to consist of 'mainly outdoors' and I already felt bad enough.

'What's your name, love?' Karen asked. 'You know, in case we ever need to alert the authorities because the dog turns up dragging half your leg.'

'Mum!'

'What? Just being realistic.'

'It's not my dog,' I said again. I didn't know why I was bothering, since nobody, including the dog, seemed to believe me. 'And my name's Tansy, Tansy Merriwether.' I had a momentary shudder of shock as I said my name. Maybe they'd heard of me, even in this obscure corner of Dorset, or at least heard about my erstwhile business, but there wasn't even a flicker from Karen. Rory did a kind of one-shouldered shrug.

''S a funny name.'

'Rory!' Karen swung a hand which totally failed to deliver the presumably intended clip round the ear. 'You watch your manners, boy. Sorry, Tansy, I thought I'd brought him up better than that, but obviously not. It's a herb, for your information, Rory Osborne, not that I'd expect you to know that because I shouldn't think there's much call for herbs when you're shooting people and you're never in a kitchen for longer than it takes to pick up your plate!'

'Sorry,' Rory said, completely unabashed. 'Panini is cheese and tomato, by the way.'

I stared at the panini. My stomach, against all biological possibilities, stared at the panini. 'Oh, but I shouldn't. I can't pay – long story and very dull, and you can't be breaking even at this time of year.'

Karen leaned against the counter. 'Nah, you're OK. We're a community café and I reckon you living on the dunes makes you part of the community. Dunno what we're going to say about the dog, mind.'

We all looked at the dog, which had a back leg sticking straight up in the air and its head buried somewhere in the brown fur. There was a very off-putting chewing sound. 'He really isn't my dog.' The words sounded a little weaker every time I said them.

'Probably a stray.' Rory reached down and patted the dog then looked dubiously at his hand. 'Holidaymakers do that. They come down to stay in the caravan parks and it's too much trouble to get someone to look after the dog, so they bring it with them. Dog wanders off and they never bother to go looking, so there's always a few strays kicking about at the end of every season. Bastards,' he added, and then ducked to avoid his mother's arm which seemed to fling out reflexively at every other sentence he uttered. 'Well they are, Mum! Imagine having a dog and just leaving it somewhere when it doesn't even know where it is! *I* wouldn't do that.'

'No, because until you can look after yourself, and that means taking a shower more than once a month and not spending every spare hour playing Duty Calls or whatever that bloody game is, you aren't getting so much as a slow worm, Rory Osborne! Now, get in that kitchen and give that dishwasher filter a good scrub.' Karen picked up my now empty panini plate. 'And you can wash that up while you're at it.'

'Thank you.' I had barely even chewed, but my stomach received the hunks of bread, cheese and tomato gratefully, although my tongue had had something to say about my speed of eating very hot food.

'Like I said, community café. We can suck up the odd panini now and again, which is just as well otherwise Rory would have eaten a year's profits by now.'

'How does that work then?' I was trying to keep her from noticing how fast I'd eaten and drunk the coffee, keep her from asking questions I might not be quick enough to think of an answer for.

Karen shrugged. 'Place is owned by some local bloke with money. Anyone who's interested can do a stint working in here, helping run the place and learn stuff. That's pretty much just me and Rore at the moment though, since the caravan site opened and they goes up to there instead. Pays more on the hour and all the loo rolls you can nick, they says. Here now, it earns in the summer, not so much in winter, and he keeps it afloat if it looks like sinking. Nice guy, just wants to provide employment, for anyone who's seen enough industrial bleach and strange bathroom habits to last a lifetime.' Karen glanced in the direction Rory had taken in his untied-trainer-shuffle, and her glance spoke volumes about her worries for her son's future. 'And, you know, the caravan park, that's seasonal too. Plus, I've heard about the toilets up there and dysentery is no kind of future for a lad.'

I had a sudden mental image of the bloke on the beach, in his duffel coat and oddly pulled down beanie hat, and had a horrible premonition. 'Your local benefactor... he's not some guy with an accent that sounds put-on and dark hair, is he?' I could practically see the way this was going to pan out.

Karen picked up the broom again. 'Not unless he's been taking acting lessons and hair dye from Boots. He's in his seventies if he's a day. Nice bloke though.'

And then her words really sank in. 'So there's no work round here?' *Bugger. I'd barely got enough fuel to get me out of the dunes.* 'Not even temporary?' I looked around the wooden interior of the café, designed to look like a ship's wheelhouse, I presumed, although since I'd never seen a ship's wheelhouse it might really be the deck of a cross channel ferry. 'I can... sweep.'

The look Karen gave me was so pitying it was almost sarcastic. 'Panini we can do,' she said, leaning on her broom. 'Anything permanent that involves paying, not so much. There's pretty much hardly enough to keep me paid right now, it's only cos we've got someone paying the difference to keep us afloat.'

'Oh.'

I stared down at my hands and then further down to my feet, where the small hairy dog had finished chewing his underparts and was gazing up at me with a Battersea Dogs' Home look on his face. Never mind 'last puppy in the pet shop'; he was doing 'last sentient being on a world ravaged by war and famine'.

'What about that TV lot?' Rory had appeared in the kitchen doorway again. Our conversation was clearly more fascinating than cleaning the dishwasher filter. 'Ryder says that they'll pay cash by the day for people doing odd jobs for them. He says he and Spence are going to go up there and see what's going, he says they've been paying lads to go up and down for them, it being so steep and saves them from having to leave the beach.'

My head had come up when I heard the words 'pay cash', but Karen had obviously been listening more carefully. 'Well that Ryder boy, he's full of ideas like that. And who's "Spence" when he's at home, eh?'

'You know Spence! Remember that girl that got done for shoplifting, right, the one with the coat? Last year? Well, her mum is Spence's mum's sister's best friend, and his cousin is that there little lad that never speaks.'

Karen nodded. 'Oh. Him.'

'Can we go back to the bit about the TV lot? What TV lot? And, more importantly at the moment, do they really pay cash?' I sat up straighter in my chair.

'Some TV programme they make, up the bay there.' Karen pointed by shrugging a shoulder in the general direction of the door. 'Never watch the thing myself. Can't, *he's* always on it, him and his General Assassination Duty, or whatever you call that wretched game.'

Ignoring his mother's jibes, Rory bounced back into the room. 'It's called *Watch Tower*. It's about coastguards and stuff and they film it up to Landle Bay, only they call it Wake Bay in the programme and they pretend like it's all set in the village only they goes right over to Exeter for some of it.' He took on a stance of extreme pride. 'My mate Sam was in it once, when they did some filming in Dorchester. Well, his shoulder was. He was in a crowd, had to pretend they was raising money for a new lifeboat only someone thieved the tin and ran off through the crowd. Sam was the crowd. Well, not *all* of it, just his shoulder.'

I had a vague memory of seeing something – probably some newspaper headline where a TV programme storyline masquerades as 'real news'. 'And that's down here?'

'Well, next bay over.'

'Learn summin' new every day.' Karen did some pointedly energetic sweeping. 'Probably your best bet then, Tansy, if you want casual work, cash in hand, like.' Her body language harrumphed over people who avoid the tax man.

I felt terrible. I *didn't* want cash-in-hand, under the counter work. I wanted my old life back, where I'd been scrupulous about receipts. God, I even knew about working out VAT! But that life had gone. 'It's not really what I want, but I just need to get enough to buy enough diesel to move on.'

'You one of they Travellers then? Your van don't look as if it'd be much good for travelling far, mind, does it, Rory?' I took it that this was Karen's unspoken apology for harrumphing over my desperation for casual work. Rory had gone back to the kitchen, although, from the lack of noise, I doubted he was cleaning out the filter.

13

'I'm... moving around. Looking at my options.' *Hiding from the world, where my name was probably what accountants menaced their children with. 'Eat your greens or you'll turn out like Tansy Merriwether.' 'Go to bed, or Tansy Merriwether will get you...' A cautionary tale in a camper van, that was me.*

'You're not eating properly is what you're doing.' The pause after Karen's words was filled by the squelching sound of the dog licking his undercarriage again. 'Rore! You stop doing whatever it is you're doing on your phone in there, because I don't for one minute believe it's useful, and take Tansy round the bay. There might be some people down there who can tell her what's what.'

'Sick! Come on.' Rory was out of that kitchen and in front of me in what seemed an inhumanly possible time.

'And take your dog with you.' Karen shoved at the dog with the end of her broom.

'He's not my... never mind. Do we need to go by bus or anything? Only...'

'Nah. Tide's coming up but there should be enough space for us to squeeze round. Yeah, Mum, I'll be careful, I've known this beach all my life, remember? And how often have I got caught by the tide?'

'Twice,' said Karen, darkly. 'And that lot round the bay aren't coastguards, they're just pretending. Get caught again and they'll have to send up from Lyme again, so don't you get fooled.' She sighed. 'Good luck, Tansy. And you watch out for them TV people, they can be tricky buggers. We've heard about what happens when they're making that *Broadchurch*, no parking for three miles, they says.'

'We'll be fine, Mum.' And, at a speed not dissimilar to the whippet that the dog had brought disgrace on earlier, he was off out of the door, barely stopping to check that I was following.

Chapter Two

We walked in the opposite direction to the dunes, along a narrow – and, to my slightly nervous eye, narrowing – strip of
sand that ran underneath some earthy, slumping cliffs that grew
lower the further we walked, like shoulders relaxing.

'What are you going to call him then?' Rory eventually
got tired of throwing bits of seaweed for the dog, who would
scamper after them in an overexcited way, sniff them and
then either cock his leg or dribble on them. 'He needs a
name.'

'He's not my...'

'Yeah, you said.' Rory kicked a rock. 'How about Tarot? Cos,
only, there's this guy on YouTube, right, who does these really
amazing card tricks.'

We watched the dog for a moment. It began a small hole in
the sand and then dug frantically until it was down to its middle. When its head reappeared over the edge, it had something
decomposing in its mouth. 'No,' I said.

In front of us the cliff jutted out, a solid wall of rock and
slowly subsiding earth that ran into the sea. Waves were breaking over its tip, sending scatters of spray up into the air like
a bottle of champagne being opened in slow motion. In the
corner, where it stuck out from the mainland, there was a

diminishing triangle of sand about the size of a large tablecloth. The water was nibbling away at the edges. 'Is this safe?'

Rory, with a typically teenage attitude, assumed confidence. 'Course. I do this all the time. My mate Ryder lives over this side. Come on.' He hopped across the reducing sand and began scaling the crumbly ascent, grabbing hold of tufty grasses to haul himself up.

I hesitated, looking up at the face. It wasn't sheer, more sort of slumped, as though the land had become deeply depressed and was just giving up in the face of the sea, but at its highest point it stood a good fifty feet above the beach. A mountain goat would probably have called me a right wimp, but I'd been born and brought up in a town, where climbing had been something we did at school under carefully controlled conditions with harnesses. And helmets. Leaping up near vertical surfaces hadn't really featured in the curriculum, and life had been resolutely flat since then.

The first wave broke over my foot, and the dog nearly climbed up my leg. He was looking at me from under wiry black eyebrows and above a bearded chin that made him look a bit like Father Christmas before he went grey. 'What? I'm not carrying you. You've got four legs, you can do this better than I can.'

The dog's expression didn't change, but he reached higher up my leg, cocking his tail so that it didn't hang in the water. He was saying, about as clearly as he could without actually breaking into an operatic aria, that he wanted off this beach. Rory was a rapidly receding figure scrambling up the least steep side of the cliff just where it branched out from the land mass, and I heaved a sigh. 'All right. But just this once, understand?'

The two-tone tail wagged, and I bent down, picked up the dog and sort of slung him onto the cliff, where he immediately gained a grip and chased off after Rory, clinging to the crumbling surface like those toys that stick to windows. I sighed again and hoisted myself up, clutching on to grass stems that felt like plastic as they slid through my hands. The waves took the last of the sand from below me.

Keeping half an eye on Rory and the rest of my vision very firmly fixed onto the surfaces in front of me, I climbed upwards by a combination of digging my feet and fingers in, crawling and dragging. It was possibly the least elegant way to go upwards other than being pulled up on a rope with my nose scraping the surface. When I finally reached the top Rory and the dog were waiting for me, looking unfazed. 'Easy climb, yeah?' Rory said, setting out to walk along the cliff top.

'Er. Yeah.' I leaned forward and panted for a moment, scraping mud off my hands and trying to prise it from under my fingernails. My jeans were smeared from knee to ankle, my trainers had encrusted toes and the rest of me was sweat and panic. But I spared a moment for the view, which showed me where I'd come from, the dunes curving gently around to enclose the small bay and the waves now ferociously covering the beach to a depth I didn't want to think about. I had no idea how I was going to get back to the van. Ahead, the coast stretched like a set of stone dentures into the distance, giving the impression that the coast of Dorset was taking bites out of the sea, carved and whittled into dinosaur shapes by the implac-able water. The grey sky rose up from the horizon and arched overhead, the grey sea arched below; it was a bit like being at the bottom of a tin bucket that smelled of seaweed, and had a bunch of seagulls nailed to the framework.

The dog gave a peremptory bark and I jerked my vision back to the more immediate surroundings. The other side of the cliff ran gently down to touch the sand in a tiny bay which seemed to be largely occupied by caravans, trailers and lorries. There were no buildings, just a car park and a narrow track which vanished off up a vertiginous slope, and a sort of tank on stilts which jutted out onto the sand. From our vantage point I could see people dashing about and lots of cables and, for a moment, I was very homesick for London.

'The dog's got to have a name,' Rory resumed our earlier conversation. 'You can't keep calling him "dog", 's not fair on him. How about Wilberforce?'

We were scrambling down the slope towards the beach, the dog running in the lead. His spiky fur, truncated legs and over-large head did not inspire me with Wilberforcian vibes. 'Bit dignified. He's more of a…' I thought of that black-eyebrowed look and over-exuberant climbing, 'a Brian.'

'Like on *Family Guy*? True dat!'

I had no idea whether this meant Rory agreed with me or not. 'Er, yes, I suppose. But I just think he looks like a Brian.'

Rory stopped and we both looked at the dog, who had his backside in the air, head down what I supposed was a rabbit hole. His tail was held out stiffly behind him, and, with his front half invisible, he looked like a device for rodding drains. 'Think you're right. He's a Brian.'

The dog looked back at us, raising his head from the earth, jowls covered in sand and drool, and gave a 'hmmmph' noise, as though acknowledging the name.

'Come on,' Rory said, setting off at a leaping, tussock-hopping pace. I filled my lungs again with the mixture of old seaweed, salt and cold that was passing for air, and headed off after him, and although I was trying for a somewhat more decorous speed, the top half of me had already overtaken my knees and my speed was increasing as we lurched down towards the sea.

On the beach below us, three people wearing huge coats were walking up and down, two of them appearing to be listening to the third. Others stood around and there looked to be a phe-nomenal amount of equipment of various kinds stacked up on mats along the sand. Rory and I, plus Brian, plummeted down off the cliffside and dropped down, practically in front of the three walking people, one of whom shrieked, slightly unneces-sarily I thought.

'Oh my God! Who are these? Where did they come from?'

'It's fine, Larch. It's just the public. Lennon! Lennon, do your fucking duty as security and get these people off the beach! We're rehearsing here!'

In the interim, while we stood and waited for whoever Len-non might be, we all stared at one another. Inside the bulky coats were a woman and a man, and the third person, another man, seemed to be in charge. He was tall and greying, inclining towards being portly and wearing large horn-rimmed glasses that gave him the look of a slightly pissed-off owl. He was also familiar.

'Keenan?'

'*Tansy?*'

And then the remaining corner of the triangle spoke and I realised who *he* was. 'Great. It's a fecking reunion. And she's still got that bloody dog.'

* * *

Rory's eyes were practically falling out, but they'd been stopped up by a healthy helping of catering van sausage and mash. While he scooped up food and stared, Keenan and I sat either side of a laminate table and caught up.

'So, what on earth are you doing out here, Kee? I thought you couldn't exist without high rises, don't they funnel the air down into your lungs or something?'

'Very funny. I, for my sins, am directing the second series of *Watch Tower*.' And then, with a glance at the rapidly spooning Rory, he whispered, 'And a bigger bunch of neurotics, horror stories and general ne'er-do-wells you'd be hard pressed to find.'

I felt we were leaving Rory out of the loop a bit. 'Keenan and I knew each other in London when we were young. Young*er*, I added, because the presence of a teenager, his slang and general reaction to things was making me feel about a hundred. 'We were at college together, before he branched off into the wonderful world of TV.'

'And you went off to be all entrepreneurial. How's that working out for you?' Kee sipped a cup of black coffee. He was, apparently, on a diet and fooling no one.

I had a sudden vision of what I'd lost. The little range of shops, the meetings, the flat, *Noah*. Once again my nerve endings seemed to break through my skin, catching at me with little barbed hooks.

'Hey, sorry.' Kee pushed a napkin in my direction. Rory had stopped eating, open-mouthed. 'Last I heard you'd got your own brand going and you were all up with that marketing guy – what was his name?'

I couldn't say it. Could barely even *think* it. I just shook my head and wiped my face and tried to concentrate on my coffee.

From outside the van came a shout, then a series of shouts, a scream and then footsteps running up the metal stairs. 'There's a dog out here loose on set!' A girl wearing a headset and carrying an iPad came in. 'It's... well, we're going to have to clear the sand again.'

Keenan sighed. 'We'd have to clear the sand anyway, Jay, get the footprints out. Is it your dog?' He turned to me. 'Only I saw it arrive with you.'

Rory made a face at me over his sausages.

'I suppose he is. A bit.' I said slowly, glad of the opportunity to stop thinking about Life Before. 'I call him Brian.'

'What, like on *Family Guy*? You can't call a dog Brian.' Kee looked out of the window as two people ran past, pursuing a small scampering shape, which looked to have a microphone-shaped object in his mouth.

'That's what I said!' Rory, mouth full of mash, replied.

'He... looks like a Brian.' I followed Kee's line of sight and we all fell silent, watching the-dog-now-apparently-known-as-Brian gallop down the sand towards the sea, followed by a man in a parka and headset shrieking some quite earthy obscenities. I hoped Rory had had a broad education and I wasn't sure whether Karen would want me to put my hands over his ears at this point. I decided against it.

Keenan sighed. 'That's about par for the course for this shoot,' he said. 'Bloody thing's about damned. *And* they want me to scope out sites for a spin-off, reckon they're trying to turn Davin into a leading man. Like I've got time to look for places to film, I've barely got time to wipe...' he glanced at Rory, 'er, to drink a cup of tea.'

'*You* could do it though!' Rory said, through the last mouthful of gravy, 'Couldn't you Tansy? You wanted a job.'

I drained the coffee. 'I know nothing about this area. I only arrived a week ago. I know about the sand dunes in the next bay over, and the café, and that's about it. Anyway, don't you have people for that? Location scouts and that sort of thing? They'll have a much better idea of the sort of thing you're looking for.'

Keenan was looking at me with a kind of thoughtful gratitude. 'We *could* get someone down, I suppose, but I don't know if there's the budget for it, otherwise they wouldn't have asked me. Don't know what they think I do in my spare time, if I had any I'd be spending it sleeping and trying to get away from this lot, not driving up and down the coast. And I want to at least *pretend* that we're going to get filming done in time for Christmas. Would you do it, Tansy? If I give you the brief? I mean, I'll pay you…'

'Can I be in it?' Rory was sitting up straight, practically trembling with eagerness. 'I can help Tansy look for places, I was born here, I know *everywhere*. And I'd really like to be in a TV programme, my mum would love that!'

Events were getting away from me. 'Look, I'm not sure about this. I mean, yes, I want a job, but I was hoping it would be something I'm a bit more comfortable with. Something I'm good at.'

'What business was it you were in? Cakes or something?'

Handmade, personalised cupcakes. Actually. And then we branched out into chocolates… were doing really well, especially in the wedding market and birthdays, but people came in to buy the cakes as gifts, as party favours… And then.

And before I know it I'm living in a camper van in some sand dunes a couple of hundred miles away, and my business is being run by a man who wears red socks and uses words like 'going forward' with no sense of irony.

'Something like that, yes.' *Plus your man, the one with the accent, thinks Brian is a sex maniac and that I should be prosecuted for letting him go near his whippet.* 'I really don't think I'd be any good, Kee. I'll just move on, find somewhere else, maybe go to Exeter and get a job in McDonald's.' *If anyone can lend me enough money for the fuel to get there.*

'Oh dear Lord.' Keenan had glanced out of the window again. 'Sorry, but I think my two main characters might be trying to kill each other again. Davin O'Riordan and Larch Bessant. Pair of right numpties. I'd better go and try to sort things out. We are never going to run to a spin-off series if she's strangled him with his own bloody binocular cord.' And he leaped up and dashed out down the metal stairs and out onto the beach, where I could see the dark-haired man, now devoid of his ridiculous beanie hat and whippet, arguing furiously with the woman who'd screamed at our arrival.

'Sick! This is sooooo cool! I mean, you know the director of *Watch Tower* and he's giving you a job!' Rory scraped his plate ferociously and began eyeing up the cakes laid out on the counter. 'Cool squared! And I get to help out and be in it and everything!'

'Erm. I don't know if I...'

The metal steps clattered again and Brian was staring in through the open door at us. There was something made of black fabric in his mouth and an expression approaching a grin on his whiskery face.

'Five thousand quid,' a voice said, bitterly. 'That sound equipment cost five thousand quid. And he's eaten it. And what he hasn't eaten, he's dropped in the sea. And the stuff he hasn't eaten or dropped in the sea, he's buried.' The bloke with the headphones, turn of speed and ripe language flopped onto the next table. 'This series is bloody cursed if you ask me. Davin and Larch hate each other, script editor's got flu, half the team haven't got a clue what they're doing and now your dog's eaten the good mic.' He cast us a quick glance. 'You're not from one of those celeb magazines are you?'

'This is Tansy. She's helping to look for somewhere to film the spin-off.' Rory now had his mouth full of chocolate cake. 'I'm Rore. I'm her assistant.'

Oh gods, no. I mean, yes, I need a job, but my life seems to have taken off without me again...

'Oh, OK.' The sound engineer, who was lanky and had hair that stuck up, probably from putting on and taking off his headset all day, didn't even seem to find it odd that I'd have an assistant who was clearly still unacquainted with GCSE procedure. And 'Rore'? But then, I suppose Rory was a bit mainstream when you took into account a Davin, and a Larch. 'And the dog's yours?'

'His name's Brian and no, it's not a usual name for a dog,' I said, quickly. 'Sorry about your equipment. I'd offer to pay for it, but…'

'Nah, it's insured. Just a pain to replace. Neil McLintock.' Sound engineer guy held out a hand and solemnly shook mine and then Rory's. Rory clearly found this impressive, but then it was probably the first time anyone had shaken his hand, unless teenage peer greeting methods had come on a lot in the fifteen years since I was last one. 'I'll get a spare one off Chloe. She's second sound engineer,' he explained when I frowned.

Brian had a sense of decorum, clearly, since he hadn't burst into the metal catering van; he was lying down in the doorway, obviously waiting. I didn't know what he was waiting for though, possibly a few of the sausages to come marching out under their own steam. When Keenan came back, followed by his two troublesome stars, he had the good sense to climb down and hide under the steps.

'Tansy, I'd like you to meet our two leading actors. Davin O'Riordan and Larch Bessant.' Kee said, loudly and dramatically, from which I assumed that he was using meeting me to stop them fighting.

'I'm Larch.' The woman with the very blonde hair and the most beautiful bone structure I'd ever seen, gave a smile, which was ruined when she then said, very slowly, 'It's a tree.'

'I'm Tansy.' I wanted to say, 'I'm not an idiot, I know what a larch is', but settled for, 'it's a herb.'

'And I'm Rory.' He was clearly also getting 'antagonistic' vibes. 'It's a name.'

The man, who'd been looking anywhere but at us, turned his head slowly and gave me the kind of look that I'd imagine a very large wolf would give... well, Brian. 'And I'm Davin. Davin, not Gavin.' His accent was Irish, and had got a bit stronger since I'd last met him. He had brown eyes and the kind of cheekbones that gave Larch a run for her money. The hair that had been squashed under the beanie was mid-length, dark and clearly expensively cut to look 'messy'. He looked like the kind of man who calls hair gel 'product'.

'Tansy's going to be looking for the site for the spin-off,' Keenan said. 'You'll need to OK any possibles with Dav, Tansy, it's going to be his project and you won't be wanting anything too primitive, eh, Dav?'

'Dav' just grunted.

'Well, I haven't actually said I'd do it yet,' I said, carefully.

'Good,' Davin grunted again.

'Aw, but you'd need to be able to drive!' Larch was still speaking slowly and carefully to me. 'You know...' and she made 'steering wheel' motions with her hands. It made me wonder what the hell Keenan had told her about me. OK, I was wearing jeans and a cable-knit sweater, but I'd put them on because they kept me warm. I looked quickly at my reflection in the metal tabletop to reassure myself that I didn't look like I had the reflexes of a sloth on Valium. My hair was a bit frizzy, but apart from that I wasn't disgracing myself too badly.

'I've got a van.'

'Oh, you could use one of our vehicles.' Keenan waved a hand towards the car park full of lorries and equipment. 'You'll need Bluetooth.'

Rory looked as though he'd died and gone to a peculiarly specific heaven. 'Yeah!' Then he nudged me. 'Bluetooth, right?'

'Yes, thank you, I know what Bluetooth is.' I almost said 'I used to run my own business, you know,' but as that hadn't turned out exactly brilliantly for me, I kept quiet. 'Do you really think I could do it, Kee?'

Davin snorted. 'It's hardly fecking rocket science now, is it? Drive around a bit and find a bit of coastline that's fit for filming, and we get to turn Dorset into something like a *Poldark* theme park. Only without the fecking costumes.'

'We need somewhere with shops,' Larch put in. 'Cafés, you know the sort of thing. Sometimes one just gets so *tired* of the catering van!'

Rory pulled a face. 'Most of the stuff round here is shut down for the winter now.'

'There's your mum's café,' I said. 'Sand dunes any good to you?'

Davin scoffed. I'd never really heard it done in real life before. 'We're after filming a coastguard spin-off, not *Baywatch*. Sand dunes! And some cheap beachside café where they give you instant coffee and watered down coke. Tch!'

'Well, aren't you a peach?' I said, tartly. There was a moment of 'atmosphere', in which I judged that everyone generally bowed down before the greatness of Davin O'Riordan. Either stunned by his awesome eyelashes or just beaten down by his rudeness, and either way, I didn't care. I might be short of money but I didn't have to take that sort of thing, especially when it was directed at possibly the only friend I actually had right now. 'If you're too good for instant coffee, then can I suggest you get a bloody big vacuum flask and make it yourself, because I don't think anywhere round here will fit your ego through the door.'

The communal intake of breath was so strong that I was surprised it didn't blow the windows in. Davin stood up. 'I don't have to take this,' he said, and stalked off, stamping down the metal steps so hard that the front of the van shook. Without a word Larch took off after him.

Neil broke into slow applause, and Keenan looked impressed.

'Sorry,' I said. 'I hope I haven't really upset him.'

'No, no, it's good.' Keenan gave me a grin. 'You've stopped him from stropping with Larch anyway; the pair of them will be bitching about you instead. Good move. And you're right, he's a total tit, but the public love him, so... He won't walk, not yet, he's not *quite* big enough to be sure of getting other roles, but, my God, once he's got his own show he's going to be insufferable.' He put his head in his hands. 'What have I done, agreeing to this? Why didn't I stay up in town and carry on making wanky perfume commercials? Pardon my French,' he added, when he caught sight of Rory's grin.

There was a sudden outbreak of the kind of music you would more normally hear in the background at a fairground arcade – something loud, with more 'hey hey heys' than Debussy could have found a use for in a lifetime. Rory went a little bit red around the ears, and, because of the haircut, this was very visible. 'Sorry, better get this,' he said. 'It's my... agent.' He stood up, fished in the pocket of his jeans and drew out a mobile, which he took to the door of the van and started speaking into, rapidly. 'Hi. Er, no. Yes. I know.'

Kee raised his eyebrows. 'His *agent*? Isn't he about ten?'

'Ssssh. Poor lad's got an image to maintain. And he and his mum are being incredibly good to me. I'd never even have known you were here if it wasn't for them.'

'God. I thought we were high profile these days? There's usually a gang of people standing about on the cliffs with cameras, and I'm sure Larch did a "day in my life" thing for some woman's magazine only a few weeks ago.'

I threw a quick look over towards where Rory was doing his best placatory 'yeah, yeah, sure.' I bet it was Karen on the phone. 'Things have got a bit bad for me lately. I've not really been keeping up with the *Radio Times* and *Woman's Weekly*. Or the papers. Too busy trying to avoid seeing myself in them.'

Kee's glasses moved up and down his nose as he frowned and then widened his eyes. 'Oh. *Oh.* Surely you didn't get caught up in all that dodgy tax avoidance stuff? How the hell? You were always the smartest cookie on the baking tray – how did you ever fall for that "it's perfectly legal" thing?'

I picked at the edge of the table. 'Oh no, it was – well, it was something else. But I sold the company and there was a lot of speculation as to why, we'd been starting to diversify but it wasn't all going the way I expected. Hence this.' I waved a hand that, I hoped, indicated living on the beach in a camper van but probably made it look more as though I'd gone into amateur magic.

Kee reached a hand over the table and squeezed mine. 'The fuss will die down and you'll be fine,' he said. 'You'll not be the first to have fallen for a bloke who fed you a pack of lies and left you wondering what the hell just happened.' He rolled his eyes.

Kee was reading between the lines, and wrongly too, but I decided to go with it. 'You as well?'

'Yup. Benoit wasn't quite the knight in shining armour he portrayed himself to be. So he's currently moving out of the flat, and I'm down here on the Dorset coast, freezing my nadgers off, trying to keep Dav and Larch from committing mutual murder, and wondering where it all went wrong.' He sighed. 'I took the job to get me out of London. I didn't realise it was going to get me right into A&E with hypothermia and garrotte wounds.' Another squeeze of my fingers. 'So. If you don't mind driving around looking for sites for the new series, and if you can help me keep Davin and Larch apart for as long as it takes to get this one made, the job's yours.'

'What's the catch?'

'You have to drive around looking for sites and keep Dav and Larch apart.' Kee shoved his glasses further up his nose. 'It's not as much fun as I make it sound, believe me.'

'Um, Tansy.' Rory, looking even redder than before, held his phone out towards me. 'My mu… I mean, er, she wants to have a word with you.'

'It's fine.' Kee stood up. 'I'll get someone to give you a lift back over. Any volunteers? Neil?'

'Sure.' Neil, who had been eating his way through a lasagne while Keenan and I caught up, gave me a smile. 'As long as you keep Brian restrained.'

There was a tiny sound under the steps, as though Brian was trying to make himself invisible.

Karen just wanted to check that Rory hadn't abandoned me and gone off to meet up with his friend, who, apparently, he'd been banned from seeing over the Christmas holidays until he got his homework done. I reassured her that he was being a diligent guide, that we really *were* sitting in a catering caravan on a TV shoot and that it wasn't some fantasy of Rory's designed to make her forget his curfew time, and that we'd be back soonish.

Then, with the light fading, the sea flopping higher on the sand with a noise like a wet blanket being shaken and Rory with several cakes stuffed in his pockets 'for later', we climbed into the back of an old van, I grabbed hold of Brian, and Neil drove us back around the bay to the sand dunes.

Chapter Three

'Ryder and Spence are gonna be absolutely *cracked* when they see me! They are just never gonna believe this!' Rory looked around the inside of the car. It was a big, top of the range four-wheel drive thing, with heated seats and steering wheel, electric everything and some built-in gadgets that I hadn't even worked out yet.

Karen had been very understanding about me borrowing her son, to the extent of saying 'keep him as long as you want, no hurry to bring him back, honestly.' And Rory had, apparently, even done his holiday homework in record time in order to be allowed to come with me for a few days. So, here he was, bouncing around on the front seat of some car I couldn't even pronounce, spreading out maps on the dashboard and pressing a lot of buttons that made alarming things light up and ask me coded questions.

Unfortunately, we also had Davin O'Riordan in the back seat, sulking like a ten-year-old being denied a party. 'Just keep him off set for the day,' Keenan had pleaded. 'We're trying to do some pick-up shots with Larch; we can use his double. He just argues and won't work from the script, so if he's off-site we might get some actual work done.' He'd then patted my shoulder and muttered something like 'good luck,' but I'd been too busy trying to get the car to open to really listen.

So here I was, with a PewDiePie devotee in the front seat and Victor Meldrew's grandson in the back. Brian had chosen to stay at the camper van, where he was stretched out on my bed with his head under a blanket, like a sufferer from the world's worst hangover. Well, he hadn't really *chosen* to stay, but I couldn't bear the idea of having to drive him around the countryside and had shut him in there to stop him following me. I'd deal with the fallout when I got back.

Rory had taken selfies with the car, inside the car, out of the car window, and was busy sending them using the car's Wi-Fi. Kee had asked him not to take pictures of any of the cast and crew and so far he was sticking to that. They were, after all, old and mostly boring (apparently, although most of them looked about my age so I didn't want to ask too much about what he meant by that. I didn't need to hear that early thirties was 'oldie' land. I already felt about a hundred in the face of his relentless energy and enthusiasm) and his friends would, apparently, be more 'boomed' by the car. Although I did get the feeling that he wouldn't be averse to a picture of him and Larch, but we'd worry about that later. Now we were skipping out of the car park as I got the measure of the clutch, spraying gravel around very impressively. Rory stared out of the windscreen, unfolding the map of the locality across his legs, while Davin 'tch'ed in the back. I could see him, occasional glimpses in the rear-view mirror, arms folded and either staring at his knees or occasionally glancing out of the window.

'Are you all right back there?' I was not going to apologise for calling him, basically, an ego on legs last time we met. He wasn't doing anything to make me think of him otherwise. But I could exercise basic politeness on him.

'It's a bit small, but heated seats, so, y'know.'

I was going to take that as a 'yes'. 'OK, Rory, which way are we heading?'

We'd come to the top of the very steep track that led down to the beach, and, to be honest, it wasn't much of an improvement. A narrow lane branched in both directions, lined by autumn-bleached trees worn to stubs by winter winds, and stray leaves bustled past us as we ticked our way to a stop at the junction.

'Er.' Rory rotated the map and then turned it back around. 'I'm not sure where we are.'

'Don't you do map reading at school?' I had vague memories of D of E expeditions, where we'd learned to use a compass and lace boots correctly. I had also learned that Darren Williams was not to be trusted and Cleo Marks was a *lot* more involved with Nathan Shan than she'd ever let on. But none of those things were much use here.

'I dunno. I'm only in Year Ten.'

I took the map off him and thrust it into the back of the car. 'Can you find where we are, Davin? I just need to know which way to turn.'

The flapping paper sheets were shoved back through, quite aggressively. 'I'm not here to give you fecking directions.'

'Well, you're certainly not here to improve the atmosphere, are you?' I said, sweetly, spreading the map over the steering wheel and hoping no other vehicles came up fast behind me. I found our current location and tapped it with a finger. 'Here's Landle Bay.' I traced the lane, showing Rory our route. 'And this is where we are now.'

Davin sighed heavily. 'Great. It's like Bear Grylls does CBeebies.'

'Ignore him. So, we can go right, which takes us up towards Dorchester or left and track along the coast.'

We stared along the unprepossessing road. Left looked bleaker, narrower and more overgrown. Right was obviously the way most traffic, including the film crew's lorries, came. Most of the hedgerow was scythed smooth to vehicle-top height, the road didn't have grass growing up the middle of it and there were darker shadows at the edges where an element of pothole filling had gone on. The other direction looked like the lane had gone feral. The surface was broken into gravel-sized shards, a pubic ruff of growth marked the centre line and the hedge overhung it to the extent that a small flock of birds had put a white line down the middle whilst roosting.

'Dorchester's nice,' Rory said, eventually.

'We're making a programme about life by the sea, you...' Davin sounded as though he had been about to finish with an insult, but thought better of it. 'So not much point in going inland.'

As it was the first constructive thing he'd said, I ran with it. 'Good point. I think it's going to have to be left. Where does that take us, Rory?'

'Um.' Rory turned the map in both directions. 'Where did you say we were again?'

'There's a signpost.' Davin sighed. 'Why not, I dunno, look at it, or something?'

He was right. Buried in the hedge was a wooden post with something carved on it. 'Why don't you hop out and have a look, while we check the map?' I said, trying to spread the Ordnance Survey out sufficiently to see further down the coast. It was the largest scale they did, which I supposed was fine for locating little coves but bloody useless when you were using it to navigate inside a car.

'I'm only here to keep me out of trouble. You want a course plotting, that's what your man here is for.' Davin folded his arms more firmly and went back to staring out of the window. I knew it was an affectation because the window was currently pressed right up against the branches of a hawthorn bush, which were poked up against the glass as though we were being attacked by a pack of rogue Twiglets.

'It goes down here.' Rory had found us again on the map.

'OK.' I put on my best 'spirit of adventure' voice. 'Let's just follow it and see where we end up.'

'Somewhere with cappuccinos and a decent phone signal, please God,' Davin said. 'And croissants. Is it really too much to ask that Dorset learns how to provide proper food?' Since I'd been living off anything that Karen had been going to throw away for the past two days, I didn't have a lot of sympathy with the desire for French pastries and expensive coffee, and I just might have pulled off more suddenly than was strictly necessary for the pleasure of seeing his head wobble about in the middle of my mirror. 'And someone who can actually drive?' he added, but I was counting it as a small victory that he added it quietly.

We drove some miles in silence. Rory was busy WhatsApping all his friends with a variety of 'you'll never guess where I am!' messages and pictures of the inside of the car, Davin was staring out of the window as though Dorset was the Road to Hell, and I was trying to keep the car straight on the track so that the leaning hedges didn't graffiti the paintwork. On our left, occasional rises in the road revealed seascapes as we travelled the clifftops, but mostly the journey was just hawthorn and the odd gateway, with some sightseeing seagulls dropping in and out of view. The sun was slanting pleasantly through the windscreen, I'd been promised a bank transfer of enough money to feed myself this week and, apart from the black cloud of Irishness in the back seat, life was beginning to look more positive.

'Stop the car!'

The sudden words broke my concentration and we jaggled along some hawthorn tips with a resulting squeal for a few yards, before I pulled up. 'Davin? What's the matter? Are you travel sick?'

He didn't answer, just wrenched open the door and squeezed out, forcing himself a Davin-shaped passage along the side of the car and back the way we'd come, whereupon he vanished into the previous gateway. Rory and I sat in silence for a moment.

'I should go and make sure he's all right,' I said, reluctantly. 'He might have passed out.' And then a thought struck. 'Actually, you should go, Rory. He might be – you know. And not appreciate me pitching up.'

'Having a piss?' Rory looked up from WhatsApp. 'Maybe we should just leave him to it.'

'But what if he *is* sick?' We contemplated the various likelihoods in silence again, until I made a decision. 'Bugger it. I guess I have to check on him. Kee won't be pleased if we let his Big Star die in a ditch.'

I'd just opened the car door, when Davin's head appeared back around the hedge. 'Come on, I need a hand here! And bring the boy too, it's going to take a bit of work.'

Rory and I looked at one another. 'I *really* hope this isn't going to be piss related,' I said.

'He'd be calling for a doctor then, not us.' Rory put his phone down and started to clamber through to the driver's side, his door being pressed tightly up against the hedge. 'Let's just hope no other cars come along.'

'Great, thanks for that thought.' I headed back along the lane until I reached the gateway, where Davin was visible, head and shoulders thrust into the undergrowth. 'What's up?'

Davin's head popped back out. 'Sheep caught up in wire,' he said, a trifle breathlessly. 'I need one of you to hold her while I untangle her head and another pair of hands to help hold the fence clear.'

'I'll hold the sheep.' Rory plunged in behind Davin and I followed more slowly, to see a ewe, who'd clearly been opportunistic enough to try grazing from the ditch outside the field and had shoved her head through the sheep fencing, getting tangled in the process. Davin was straddling the sheep and trying to untangle the wire without success. Rory took over the sheep-straddling and Davin and I started trying to unwind sections of wire that had dug into her wool and were preventing her from moving either back or forwards. The ewe struggled a bit and Rory sat on her.

'How on earth did you manage to see this from the car?' I asked Davin. He was unspooling wire like a pro from the fleece around the sheep's neck, while I held her head still, not without some effort.

'She's crapped on me!' Rory complained from the business end and, to my astonishment, Davin actually smiled.

'They do that, sheep. Little feckers.' Then he looked at me. 'We did a bit of sheep farming. It gets to be second nature, you know?' His eyes had lost something of the antagonistic expression he'd been wearing all day so far, and there was a new capability about him in the way he untangled the wire from where it had bitten into the sheep's wool. 'Sheep's main intention is to try to die in interesting ways.' He freed the final bit of wire and ran his hands deep into the fleece, checking the sheep for cuts. 'Ah, you bugger, you'll live. OK, let her go boy.'

The sheep, released, pulled backwards and dashed a couple of metres into the field. By the time we had extricated ourselves from the needles of hawthorn and sloe, she was grazing unconcernedly, as though the whole thing had been a figment of our imaginations. I glanced sideways at Davin, who was running an eye over the flock with the air of one largely unimpressed, his dark hair raked by the clifftop wind. He looked different here. Capable and practical, miles away from the primped and glossy actor who stomped along the beach and sulked in the back of the car.

'They could do with some extra feeding,' he said, finally. 'They won't lamb well in that condition.' And then, without a word to either Rory or me, he climbed back over the gate and vanished from the field.

Rory was indignantly scraping his jeans with a dock leaf. 'These are my best ones. Mum's going to kill me,' he said. 'Nobody said you got crapped on by sheep doing this job. You should complain, Tansy. Sue them.'

'Your jeans will wash,' I said, firmly. 'I'll explain to your mum that it happened in the line of duty. Now, we'd better go and get that car moved, in case people want to get by.'

We walked through the muddy gateway and hopped over into the lane. 'He was funny there, Davin, wasn't he?' Rory said, as we headed back to the car. 'Like he was somebody else.'

'Not quite such a moody sod, you mean. Yeah, I noticed that as well. Maybe he's just got a thing for sheep?' And Rory and I exchanged a quick grin. 'And don't you dare put that on Facebook.'

'Nobody uses Facebook any more. Only girls.' Rory got back into the car, climbing over my seat and leaving a trail of sheep dung in his wake that I had to brush off before I could get in.

'Fair enough. Right. Let's get on.' I glanced back in the mirror to see Davin once more in his customary position, arms folded, staring out of the side window. 'Whereabouts in Ireland are you from, Davin?' I was hoping that his recent lowering of his barriers in the field might indicate a general loosening up in his attitude, but his body language wasn't giving me much hope.

'Just around.' He didn't even look in my direction. 'If you're so interested, have a look at Wikipedia.'

I made a 'give me strength' face at myself in the driving mirror and pulled away.

Davin – December 2018

By all that was holy this woman was annoying, Davin thought, once it was over and he was safely back.

He had to admit that he'd been playing up to it a bit, laying on the 'miserable actor' thing a bit thicker than usual, but so far she'd given as good as he'd put out. It was intriguing. Most women were so busy staring at him, in the case of the public that crowded around while they were filming – held back by barriers and film crew and, in one or two cases, the police – that they could hardly speak, even if he spoke to them. Or they were in the business themselves and obsessed with what they ate and what they wore and who they were seen with.

This woman – this woman had none of those preoccupations. And he had to admit that it had riled him a touch that she wasn't struck dumb in his presence, but then he gave his head a wobble. Feck's sake, he thought, I really am going native here. Starting to believe my own hype. Maybe I need this, a woman who doesn't care what I am, just sees me as some Irish bloke she's got to babysit for a while…

Was that what he wanted her to see? He sat in the trailer and looked around. The Winnebago was so far removed from where he grew up that it was a different planet. Still, essentially, a caravan, but so big you could have fitted most of his childhood homes in it three times over. The familiar twitch cramped his chest for a moment. Mam would love this. She'd love to sit in here and stroke the furniture and make toast in the hi-tech kitchen. But she refused to fly over, refused to leave Dublin to come and see what it was that he did that made the money that he sent her every month. She was proud of him, he was sure, but –

Tansy. That was the woman's name. Tansy. Seeing him as the boy from Cork – could she see what else there was? That it came with all the attendant insecurities about where he'd come from, what he'd left, to be here in a posh caravan with money to burn and women dribbling over his picture in the *Radio Times*? He wondered if she'd noticed him with the map. That he'd not even known which way to hold it, let alone what the words and symbols meant. Wondered what she'd say if she knew what he *really* was, underneath it all. Just this lost boy with his dog, waiting to be found out for the imposter he was.

Chapter Four

'How did it go today?' Keenan tugged off his headset, dislodging his glasses in the process. 'Everyone still alive?'

'Well, we didn't find anywhere yet, put it that way. Plus I nearly drove your leading man into the sea on a number of occasions. I'm going to take the map back tonight and try to make a proper plan. I really thought it would be easy to find somewhere; turns out that only one in three roads lead anywhere, the rest just sort of peter out on clifftops.' I climbed out of the car, shoving maps into my pockets as I went.

'And I got crapped on by a sheep,' Rory put in. This had clearly been the highpoint of his day.

Davin had wordlessly got out as soon as we had arrived back at the film site and headed off towards an enormous Winnebago, which was, presumably, his location home. He hadn't even looked back over his shoulder.

'And, ah, how was himself?' Kee leaned on the car bonnet. 'When you say you "nearly drove him into the sea" was it premeditated at all?'

'Only sometimes. He was, well, he was quiet for most of the time.' I didn't mention the sheep episode, nor how different Davin had seemed to be during it. Maybe contact with ovines glitched his personality or something, like a positive allergy. 'When he wasn't being sarcastic.'

'OK, well you didn't kill him; you get extra sausages for that. If it's any consolation, we've had a day with Larch and that wasn't a lot better, but they are definitely not so bad when you take them singly. Together they open some kind of portal to hell.' Kee stared out over the sea. 'God, I want to go back to London.'

Rory had headed straight for the catering truck and was now sitting on the top step eating a burger and watching some cables being unwound across the shingly sand. 'I'd better get him home. And sort out Brian,' I said. 'Can I take the car? I don't want to have to keep stealing Neil to pick us up and drop us off.'

'Course. It's yours for the duration,' Kee said, cheerfully. 'Thanks again, Tan. Even if you never find us a location, just keeping Mr O'Riordan out of my hair for the odd hour here and there is worth paying for.'

'It's like being an adult babysitter. An adultsitter,' I said and he laughed.

'Not so far off. Tell the truth, his agent's assistant usually comes with him and keeps him out of trouble, but she's off having something removed – tonsils, appendix, some bit of anatomy – so we've got him unattended. Come to think of it, he's been worse than usual this time round, maybe because she's not with him.'

On the other side of the car park, the door to the Winnebago opened slowly and then the whippet was out, looking like a piece of blue string being pulled across the sand towards the sea. There was something flapping from her mouth. A second later Davin appeared in the doorway, hands on hips.

'She's got my feckin' script amendments!' he yelled.

A couple of the men dragging cables made a dash for the dog, but she clearly thought this was the best game ever, dropped a shoulder and dodged between them, tail tucked in and ears firmly clamped down as she accelerated across the beach towards the sea. Pursuit was a little bit lacklustre, but maybe that was because everyone could see how fruitless it was to chase a dog bred to run at thirty-five miles an hour, particularly when said dog was heading into water.

'You'd have thought he'd have learned to keep the bloody door shut by now,' Kee said. 'That's got to be the third time she's done that.'

I was quietly being smug, since Davin seemed to think Brian was particularly badly behaved; at least he'd never run away with anything significant, apart from the actual whippet. Although, given it was his dog and his script amendments, he didn't seem to be straining himself to get either back. He'd stayed at the top of the caravan steps, the flapping door giving occasional glimpses inside, and I caught sight of a tastefully beige interior. Finally, the dog seemed to tire of streaking along the tideline, the paper in her mouth now either detached and scattered on the sand, or folded and saturated. She cantered a bit further, then stood up to her hocks in the sea, head raised and looking towards Davin. He gave a sigh that was audible right across the bay and a whistle that made my eyebrows rise. It was a proper shepherd's whistle, one designed to carry across acres of upland and bring a dog in from invisible mountain crags, driving a flock of wild-horned beasts with fleeces you could lose a small child in.

'Hoy! Seelie! Away!' he shouted and the whippet wheeled in the surf and bounded back to the Winnebago, the last bit of his script dropping from her mouth as she came, to float redundantly on the incoming tide. The door closed behind the pair, leaving nothing but some papier mâché scatters, a bunch of puffing crew members and Keenan and I staring like onlookers at a cricket match that suddenly got gripping in the last over.

'I'm going,' I said at last. 'He's your problem. But if he *ever* criticises Brian again I might just beat him to death with a rolled-up copy of *Dogs Monthly*.'

'That would be only right and fair.' Kee brought his eyes back to the iPad in his hand. 'Right. Guess I'd better get tomorrow's schedules sorted and try to find another set of scripts to give Davin. It's not the first time that dog's chewed up his work; you'd think he'd learn by now to keep stuff out of the way – it's not exactly a Great Dane, is it? See you back here tomorrow?'

'Am I really going to have to take Davin with me again? Can't you tie him up and gag him and leave him in the catering van?'

Kee grinned. 'Sorry, Tan. Oh, you could have Larch, if you'd rather?'

We looked over to where Larch Bessant, looking absolutely gorgeous in a filmy white dress that was blowing in the wind like one of Kee's 'wanky perfume adverts', was speaking very slowly and carefully to a girl unwinding cables from a spool, as though the girl was a hearing-impaired non-native speaker with a dramatically low IQ.

'It's not much of a choice really, is it?' I said. 'Either be patronised or sulked at to death. At least the sulking is quiet.'

'What can I say? Your choice.' And Kee went off to do something arcane with his iPad. I loaded the burger-munching Rory back into the improbable car and we drove back up around the headland. I dropped him off outside the café to walk back to the little house he shared with Karen, and popped the car into four-wheel drive to get over the dunes to where I'd left the camper van.

There was a marked absence of Brian when I let myself in. He certainly wasn't on the bed or in any of the corners I could see. I whistled, cautiously, in the manner of Davin. 'Brian? Oh, don't be stupid, Tansy; he doesn't know his name is Brian… Dog? Where are you?'

After a few moments a pile of laundry moved and Brian emerged with a sock in his mouth. He looked, as far as I could tell, a bit sheepish, but he didn't really have the face for it and so his expression was mostly his eyebrows touching and a droopy moustache. 'Come on. I'd better take you for a walk.'

A stumpy tail wiggled.

'So you know the word "walk" then?'

The tail wiggled again and I sighed, attached the front bit of Brian to an old belt, buckled it loosely around his neck, and took him outside the van, where the wind caught and tugged at my clothes and rearranged some of Brian's fur into interesting patterns. He sniffed around the wheels of the van for a moment, then his head went up and he took off along the beach in a purposeful way, tail up and arching forward over his back. On the other end of the belt I was forced to keep up or strangle him, so I trotted along, head down to stop the wind dragging tears from my eyes. The dunes provided cover from the worst of the wind, but once we got clear of them the wide stretch of beach just funnelled it all my way, and I realised why Keenan and the crew were filming in a small bay rather than on a wide stretch of coastline. Trying to get much done in a wind that took your breath away and then gave it back covered in sand and seaweed would have taxed Kenneth Branagh, never mind an independent company who were already stretched by events and awful stars.

Talking of whom, I suddenly realised where Brian was heading with such a determined tail. Two figures were rounding the headland that lay between this beach and the small cove where filming was taking place. The tide was out to its fullest extent and the cliff now rose and clambered over a sandy expanse, rather than from a heaving sea, and walking along the exposed stretch of beach came an unmistakeable tall figure with a small darting shape running ahead. The shape was lean, bounding through the shallow tide with a very distinct gait.

'Oh no, it's that bloody man again. Come on Brian; you can join a dating site like everyone else.' I pulled at the belt end, but Brian was having none of it and gave a bark, rather louder than I would have thought his suitcase-sized frame was capable of. 'Sssshh! We don't want them to see us! He makes Sherlock Holmes look like a party animal and I'm not sure I can take two doses in one day.'

Too late. The blue whippet had noted Brian's presence already and was doing little play-bows from the gently breaking surf. It was clearly more provocation than Brian could take. He did a little shuffle backwards, dropped to the ground, performed a 'duck and roll' that a gymnast would have been proud of, and, without a backward glance and now free of the belt, took off at a speed I would have sworn his short legs weren't capable of, towards the now joyously barking whippet. I had the feeling that the word 'cavorting' might come into use any moment now.

I had a very strong urge to go back into the van and close the door on the lot of them. Seriously? None of this, *none* of it, was what I'd intended when I drove down and parked in these dunes! I'd just wanted a quiet spot: somewhere to pick up some casual work, lick my wounds, work on a future plan for my life, without Noah, without my business. And now – I watched the dogs, cavorting was swiftly rising up the agenda – I'd acquired a small, scruffy dog, a job babysitting a teenager and Severus Snape and a predilection for catering-van lasagne.

I wanted to stamp my foot and shout 'this isn't my life!' My life should have planning meetings, design meetings, marketing meetings. It should have expansions and business plans and the words 'going forwards', and… and Noah. This stretch of sand – the heartbeat of waves breaking at a distance with the jutting nose of cliff at one end and a gradual meeting of land and sea at the other; this wasn't what I'd had in mind. Except, possibly, as a weekend getaway from the stress, with Noah and I spending most of the time in bed or pottering down little lanes in search of quirky ornaments. Eating in gourmet restaurants and checking out any likely bakeries for possible ideas for future designs. Not *this*.

Davin was running again. He'd got that duffel coat on too, so, from a distance, he looked like an overgrown toddler chasing a dog down a beach, with his hood flying like a windsock and his toggles moving in a sort of sine-wave fashion. He was shouting too, at me or the dogs – I couldn't hear at this distance – but his annoyance was obvious in the way he was waving his arms about. Neither Seelie nor Brian were taking any notice, so I decided to take a leaf from their books and ignore him too. Brian knew where the sardines were – he'd come back to the van when he was ready – and trying to catch up with a whippet was a sad hiding to nothing, I didn't know why Davin was even attempting it.

I was half way to the van when he caught up with me. I hadn't even realised he'd been behind me, so when he appeared beside me, I jumped. 'What the hell… oh, it's you. Why did you bring your dog back over here again?'

He spun round so that he was in front of me. He hadn't got the beanie hat on and the wind was parting his hair at the crown and pushing it down over his face. It was catching in the stubble on his chin and going in his mouth, flying around in front of his eyes like a cloud of large and determined midges. 'You signed the non-disclosure?'

Standing here, on this windswept strand, with the barks of happy dogs echoing from the clump of dunes in front of us, these words made no sense. 'What?'

He made an impatient sound. 'The non-disclosure? So you won't sell your story to the papers. Keenan made you sign one?'

He was looking at anywhere but me, I noticed. The wind was even in his eyebrows, giving him an expression close to Brian's. 'To be honest, I doubt *The Times* is going to be interested in five hundred words about driving fruitlessly around Dorset. But yes, I signed. So, for the record, did Rory, although he's only fourteen so I don't know how binding it would be on a minor.'

'Oh, it's binding,' Davin said, tightly. His eyes were still restlessly shifting; he wouldn't look at my face but his gaze would occasionally make contact with my shoulder or my chin, then go off again over the endless sea/sand interface and then back across the dunes.

'Well then,' I said, unnaturally brightly. 'That's all good. We both signed; it's binding, nothing to worry about.'

'Who said I was worried?' And then Davin O'Riordan gave me a smile. It was very clearly a smile he kept for magazine photographs; it practically came with a caption underneath: '*Davin's obviously enjoying himself filming his new series*'. It was almost convincing; it scrunched up his eyes and dimpled his cheeks, gave him an air of someone utterly overjoyed to be where they were. It was only in the depths of those ever-shifting eyes that the expression was shown as a lie. The tiniest splinter of another emotion wheeled around behind the grin, something that hadn't been reassured by my promise. I couldn't put my finger on it, but it made me uneasy. This man was very good at not giving anything away; so good, in fact, that I wondered why he worried about the non-disclosure agreement. Unless he was more worried that we might sell pictures of him looking less-than-perfect to the magazines. Although that seemed a laughable suggestion too; even here, in the childish coat and the gale-force wind, he managed to look rugged and solitary when he should have looked like an illustration in *Paddington Bear Loses his Hat.*

'Well then,' I said again, in my best 'closing down a meeting' voice. 'Good.' He needn't think he was going to charm me with his meaningless smiles. I had a sudden flashback to that last day with Noah, the slow realisation that my whole future was slipping away from me. And then my memory went on to when I'd signed the business over to him, given it all away in my sadness and inability to think straight. Now, oh, I could find myself a position in another company; go into marketing for one of my competitors, perhaps? But really? From heading my own, small but successful, empire to working for people who'd be watching me through careful eyes, wary of every decision I wanted to make? I'd rather live in this van in the dunes, thanks. Something would come up, something that wouldn't bring me back into contact with the business I'd loved and lost. Or with Noah and his twinkly, trustworthy smile, designer suits and spreadsheets.

The memories were stinging me like the windblown sand. I turned my back to the gale and let the grains scatter along the back of my practical coat. No more. That was the life I'd had. This was the one I was in now and its demands were more pressing. I only realised I'd gritted my teeth and closed my eyes when I opened them to see Davin was watching me. He'd dropped the smile, thankfully. He looked as though he was about to say something, when I was hit in the leg by a soggy mass, which shook itself liberally over both of us and then sat on my foot.

'Hello Brian.'

Davin peeled away without speaking and set off along the beach again. Seelie had reappeared and was dancing her fairylike way towards the lacy edge of the surf, sniffing and dawdling, and I wondered what Davin would do if she was in pup by Brian. He seemed, in his own and rather abrupt way, to really love the little whippet; surely he wouldn't cast her out like a Victorian heroine? I looked down at Brian, who was staring up at my face with an expression that seemed to be trying to draw out my inner sardine. Then I looked across the beach, to Davin greeting Seelie with a hand to her knobbly head. A quick stroke between her ears and then she was off again, running happily back the way they'd come, following the seething tide back round the headland towards the film site.

Brian gave a peremptory bark.

'Yes, all right, I know.'

And Brian and I climbed back into the van, which started to smell of seaweed and damp dog remarkably quickly.

Chapter Five

'OK, I've had chance to look at the map now. I think we should go…' I traced along the route with my fingernail, 'along this lane, then go this way, then turn for the coast here. There's a big old building up on the hilltop that's marked as a school so the village down here must be a reasonable size. I thought it might be worth a look.' I glanced back at Davin in the back seat. 'How does that sound?'

'Whatever.' He folded his arms again.

'Sick!' Rory said, but he seemed a little bit subdued today. Either that or he'd used up all his phone memory because he wasn't taking nearly as many pictures.

From the carefully plastic-lined boot of the car, Brian gave a yip.

'And why do we have to take that with us?' Davin spoke without looking up. 'It's sniffing at the back of my head.'

'Because it's not fair to leave him shut in all day again,' I said, sharply. Besides, I'd discovered what Brian had been doing when I'd left him yesterday and he wasn't getting the chance to do that again. 'What do you do with Seelie when you're out all day?'

I hadn't meant it to sound accusatory but maybe Davin had a bit of a guilty conscience because he raised his head and met my eye in the mirror. '*She's fine.*' And the words were almost fired like bullets. 'Neil takes her out with him when they break from shooting.'

According to Kee, they'd been filming at daybreak today, a touching scene between Davin and Larch as the late sun rose over the headland and scattered the sky with red clouds. Which was why we were taking Davin away again; apparently after the filming he and Larch had had another argument. These two took 'artistic temperament' and ran it right into 'psychological disorder'. Kee said he couldn't fire either of them, because they were being set up as stars of the future – hence Davin possibly getting his own series – and they didn't need to be nice; they just needed to look good on screen. He'd followed this up by saying that if he ever worked with either of them again he would see to it that they were killed off in the first episode and then he'd tutted and gone haring off after the sound crew, leaving me to load Davin into the back of the car.

So we drove up the steep hill, Davin doing his usual 'sullen silence' and Rory kicking the toes of his trainers against the underneath of the dashboard. I had no idea what Brian was doing in the back but from Davin's slightly horrified expression he was probably still licking his head.

'All right back there?' I finally thought I should check that Brian hadn't got his teeth embedded in the back of Davin's neck.

Davin 'hmphed' then said. 'It's not me you want to be worrying about. What about your man there?'

I flicked a quick glance in the mirror. Davin was actually looking through at Rory, now stretching and flexing his feet as though his shoes hurt. 'Rory?'

Rory shrugged.

'Are you OK?'

He shrugged again, then cocked a foot upwards and began picking at the rubber around the toe of his trainer. 'Dunno.'

I slightly lost my temper. 'Right, you two. There's so much "bloke" going on in this car that I'm about to start male-pattern baldness. Rory, what, exactly, is the matter?'

He dropped his head even lower and picked more energetically at his toe. Just when I thought he wasn't going to say anything, he muttered, ''s my mum.'

I hadn't seen Karen this morning when I'd picked Rory up from the café. The door had been open and there had been a smell of bacon in the air, but she hadn't appeared to tell me not to rush him back and not to let him spend the fiver she'd given him on junk food. 'Is she ill?'

'She was crying last night,' Rory said, adding, somewhat defensively, 'she *never* cries. She's wicked hard, my mum.' And suddenly he wasn't the near-adult he pretended to be; he was a scared little boy with a life that seemed to be getting out of control and I knew how that felt.

'Right,' said Davin from the back. 'Turn this car round.'

'*What*?' Rory and I said, exactly together, and together we turned to see Davin, arms unfolded as though he was about to grab the wheel. This was unusual enough, without him actually speaking to us.

'Car. Round. Fecking coast has been there a billion years – it will wait a day; your man's mum needs him. Or needs someone. Go.'

I couldn't have been more astonished if he'd suddenly recited Shakespeare and, from his expression, Rory couldn't either. I had absolutely no come back for this, although, in the depths of the night with Brian snoring on my feet, I'd practised some witty one-liners to use on Davin's apparent misogyny, so I steered the car into the nearby gateway and turned back the way we'd come.

We drove to the café, Davin silent in the back and Rory in a state of panic. 'Don't tell her I said, Tansy, will you? She wouldn't want me to hear her crying, was just that I woke up; Spence WhatsApped me yesterday and wanted me to take some pictures and I said I'm not allowed and he said I was being a useless wet... anyway, so I was thinking about that and I heard her.'

'We'll pretend we've forgotten something. And tell Spence that we won't let you take pictures,' I said.

'You signed the agreement,' Davin put in. He had practically reached conversation status.

'Yeah, but Spence, he's a bit, well. He thinks I should take secret pictures. Oh, he wouldn't show them to anyone; he just wants me to prove where I've been, sort of.'

Yeah, of course he wouldn't. I remembered boys like Spence when I'd been at school. The whole 'I'll never do anything you don't want me to,' swiftly followed by pushing, pushing to do whatever it was you'd asked them not to. At school it had mostly been sexual; I'd been assertive and discouraged them, and luckily they'd taken no for an answer, even if I had then got a reputation as a 'frigid, lesbian bitch'. I hadn't yet come to the realisation that there were other ways to be manipulative. And then I'd met Noah.

'Give me your phone.' Davin reached forward.

Rory hesitated. 'You won't break it or anything? Only, I had to work all summer in the café for that, and mum can't afford to mend it, plus, we have to go all the way to Dorchester to get it fixed and it's a pain on the bus, really 'spensive too.'

'Phone.' Davin held out his hand and I felt second-hand apprehension as Rory cautiously handed it over. 'Now, move over here.'

Rory leaned to the extent of his seatbelt, Davin moved over, and then handed the phone back. 'There. Send that to your man and then turn the feckin' phone off.'

Rory stared at his screen. So did I, with the result that the car swerved along the lane and nearly clipped the grass verge. Davin had taken a selfie of him and Rory, heads together, and him wearing an expression of amused tolerance as though he and Rory were best buddies exchanging a joke. 'Wow.' Rory clearly wasn't as stunned as I was, because his fingers moved, sending the picture to, probably, all his friends, never mind the pushy Spence. 'Thanks Davin.'

'Phone. Off.'

Rory complied and I found myself looking in the rear-view mirror, back at Davin, settling himself down into the seat again, his expression back to being sullen boredom. 'Thank you. You didn't have to do that.'

He grunted and stared out of the window. And I almost certainly imagined it, but there seemed to be the tiniest bit of relaxation around his features. Not that I could really look properly, what with driving the car and not wanting to kill us all, but there did seem to be the merest hint of a lightness around his mouth. Not a smile, that would probably have caused him terrible pain, but just – something. It gave me hope that Davin O'Riordan was a real human being under all that bad temper, argumentativeness and all round awkward soddiness, and not just a robot designed to make other people miserable. He was the poster guy for 'looks aren't everything', but then he didn't need to be nice to be a TV star; he just needed to be able to say someone else's words convincingly and walk up and down in an appealing way. Which, according to Kee, he was quite good at.

We pulled up in the otherwise empty car park by the café. Two people were just leaving: birdwatchers from the binoculars and sturdy clothing, coffeed up and ready for a day scanning the sands for migratory species. We sat in silence for a moment then Rory got out.

'OK, say I forgot my coat.'

'Have you got a coat?'

'Yeah. It's in there somewhere.' He gave a shoulder-nod towards the café. 'But nobody wears a *coat*, come on, I'm not ninety.'

Cautiously I got out too, and, to my surprise, Davin came as well. He saw me look at him. 'Coffee,' he said, shortly. 'And it better be good.'

So, trailing the two males and with Brian, watching us go through the prison bars of the dog guard, I went into the café, where Karen was clearing a table. The birdwatchers had clearly gone for the full-scale breakfast experience. There was a smell of baking mince pies in the air and a hand-chalked sign on the wall that told me I could have one and a tea or coffee for three pounds fifty. Karen had left the 'e' out of mince, but I felt it went against the spirit of the season to tell her that.

'Hey Tansy. Has he disgraced himself yet?' Karen said, only half looking up, and then catching sight of who I'd come in with. 'Holy hell. You've brought the cast list.'

'Karen, this is Davin O'Riordan,' I said, unnecessarily. 'Who would like a coffee, but I'd advise you not to speak to him unless you've signed away your life in triplicate.'

Davin sat down at a table, folded his arms and stared at the floor. Karen adjusted her uniform and tossed back her hair, clearly caught in the glamour-field. 'Well. This is a surprise.' She even licked her lips. I didn't know why; Davin was showing all the signs of a man who finds teak boarding more appealing than women. 'Has Rory been… Rore, you've not got yourself brought back for doing something, have you?'

'Cappuccino,' said Davin, apropos of absolutely nothing.

'Er, coming right up.' Karen stopped primping and headed slowly towards the kitchen. I went with her, while Rory perched himself up on the counter and started on an iced bun. I'd never really had much exposure to teenagers, apart from when I'd been one myself, and the fact that he treated eating as a hobby still made me raise my eyebrows. 'You never came all this way for a cappuccino,' she half-whispered to me as she took the milk out of the fridge.

I realised that I couldn't admit to anything without dropping Rory firmly in it. But Karen was giving herself away. Her eyes were reddened and she'd got the droopy lashed look of someone who hasn't slept much. 'Are you all right?'

'Better for having that in the café,' she whispered back, nodding towards where Davin was slumped. 'Do you think we could have him stuffed as a visitor attraction?'

'Only if I can personally do the stuffing. He's awful, but you never heard that from me.'

'The words "kill him slowly with a pitchfork" never left your lips.'

'I don't know whether the desire to do him bodily harm is covered by the disclosure agreement, but better be on the safe side. It's just that you look a bit…' I tailed off.

Under cover of making the coffee she seemed to be biting down a sob and struggling to keep her face neutral at the same time. It was giving her the expression of someone stifling a sneeze. 'I had some bad news.' Her voice was even lower. 'But don't tell Rore. I haven't thought of a way to put it yet that doesn't make it sound quite so bad.' The milk steamer hissed and fumed at us. 'And that there Mr O'Riordan doesn't need to be a nice guy, looking like that. Even if anyone did hear you saying it, no one's going to believe you.'

I ignored the bit about Davin. 'So what's happened?' I put a hand on her arm to slow down the coffee making. 'You're not ill?'

Karen gave a snuffly snort. 'Built like a dray horse I am. Illness wouldn't dare. I've not had a day sick since Rory was born. Bit touch and go with some of the stuff he brought home, mind – that boy was to viruses what I am to nice stationery – but there you go. No. I had a phone call yesterday.' And then she stopped talking and poured the steaming milk onto the coffee. 'Does he take sugar?' Her hand hovered around the bowl where sachets of brown sugar were propped alongside the rest of the condiments.

'I think he sucks whole lemons. Come on, Karen. The phone call.'

She busied herself fetching sachets and arranging them in the saucer. 'It's the café. Mr Beverley – remember I told you, the man who kept us afloat?' She didn't even wait for my nod. 'He died. Last week. Nobody told any of us and now his nephew is selling the café and it will probably turn into one of they burger places which shut down from October to May!' She gave another swiftly suppressed sob, then sniffed hard. 'It's Rore I worry about. We'll have to move; without this job I can't afford the rent and there's nothing else round here.'

'Oh dear,' I said. I was aware it was inadequate, but what else could I say?

'So.' She wiped the back of her hand over her eyes, shook her hair back and stretched her lips into a smile. 'Now. I hope he likes the coffee.'

'I'm fairly sure Davin came out of the womb criticising the hospital sheets, so don't take it personally if he doesn't.'

'I don't know what I'm going to do, Tansy.' And Karen's face was suddenly pinched and terrified. 'Rory's doing well at school – OK, he's doing as well as we ever expected him to at school

– I've got a place to live and I *love* my job. I've got no other qualifications – I worked in McDonald's up to Lyme before I had him – and moving costs a fortune!'

I gave her arm another inadequate pat.

'Oh, and I know he deserves better than this place, but it's something, isn't it? Something he can go to after he leaves school? He might not want it, but I've seen the world out there and there's precious little for people like us, just a load of moving every six months when the landlords want new people in and jobs where the best you can hope for is a laugh with your mates to get through the day.'

I felt horrible and awkward. I'd been raised by two doctor parents in a house they owned, with a sister who'd married a doctor. We'd both gone to university without questioning it, and earned enough to… OK, that was gone now. But still, I knew what it was like to have money and the privilege felt like a big stamp on my forehead right now when I was trying to sympathise with a woman who'd had none of it.

'Can the community raise enough to buy the café?' My business brain wouldn't shut up. Even in the face of its extreme humiliation it still ticked away in the back of my skull. Being on a TV set wasn't giving it a lot of overtime right now and managing Brian was simply not the same as a chain of shops, so it bit down on this new problem and started worrying it, like – well, like Brian with a bit of seaweed.

Karen snorted and led the way through to the seating area, where Davin was conducting a spectrographic analysis of the components of the floor with his eyes and Rory had picked up a Nintendo and was hunched over it in a corner, thumbs moving. 'Most of us haven't got a penny to scratch our arses with,' she said. 'Coffee. Cappuccino. Hope it's all right. I used the proper Jersey milk from the farm up the road.'

59

I had no idea why she was telling Davin that but it did get a reaction. He looked up as the coffee cup jangled onto the table and, to my astonishment that was getting a fair bit of exercise today, he smiled. 'Thank you.'

It was a proper smile, a smile that did things to his face that enabled me to see what the viewing public presumably saw in Davin O'Riordan. His brown eyes sparked and his eyebrows raised and some kind of mystical process caused a new kind of attractiveness to spread over his features, like a ray of sun hitting a previously unremarked natural landmark and making it stop being a rock in some undergrowth and suddenly worthy of a calendar photograph. Up until now I hadn't really seen what made him such a must-have star but this smile could have graced *Vogue*. Karen went a bit pink and even my heart, rusted into inactivity by Noah and his betrayal, managed a quick loop around my chest.

I had to clear my throat. 'So.' Karen threw a glance over to where Rory was clicking away, attention seemingly all on the tiny screen, and I took the hint. 'Any ideas where we could go looking for a film site? I looked at the map and there's a bay a few miles over the clifftop, that sort of way.' I pointed out of the café, but I think my arm had been affected by Davin's smile because it wobbled a bit. Maybe glamour has gravity.

'Oh, aye. Over to Steepleton, sounds like.' Her voice had also gained an unnatural cheeriness. 'There's a village out there, sort of goes down the cliff, bit like Lyme only smaller. Got a little harbour one side and a beach the other. It's a bit of a drive down, mind. And they lorries I've seen going down to Landle, they won't get down there.'

Having something to think about other than the impending doom of the café seemed good, so I went on. 'But it might be possible? Which way do I go from here?' I'd already plotted it on the map and the car's satnav, which despite all the up to date technology, quite often showed us as driving several metres out to sea. But Karen needed the distraction and the conversation our eyebrows were having, regarding lots of deep thinking to be done and absolutely no telling of Rory what was going on, was enough.

She pointed and gave directions that consisted mainly of things like 'up to Michael's place, then turn left' and 'when you get to the place that used to be a smallholding, turn down there'. But she was worried and sleepless so I just nodded and smiled. Davin had killed his sunlight-rivalling smile and was drinking the coffee which must have been scalding from the steam rising off it and, when the last of it seemed to have gone down, I headed for the door.

'Right. We'd better go and look at this place then. Let's hope it's a goer; otherwise I'm going to be spending Christmas making little sorties into Devon and Somerset.' I hadn't really got any *other* plans for Christmas, admittedly. My mum and dad were usually on call, giving up their Christmases now that they had grown-up children so that those with younger families could enjoy the day. My sister went to her husband's family and I... well, I'd had Noah for the last three years. And we'd spent Christmas in exotic places, congratulating ourselves on being successful enough to take a whole month off to go to Australia or Bali.

This year it was a freezing camper van, sand, and a dog insisting on a three-course meal and petit fours. Oh bugger.

'Um, Tansy.' Rory jumped up and dropped the Nintendo into his pocket. 'Actually, Keenan gave me some cash today so I might stay here, if that's OK.' The lightning glance he threw in his mum's direction told me that he might have overheard at least a little bit of our conversation in the kitchen. I'd forgotten the bat-eared tendency of those who think others might be talking about them, and, given what had happened to me, I didn't know how I'd managed to forget. Some of the gossip I'd overheard about myself from the staff on their breaks, when I'd been in my office, had been one of the reasons I'd been persuaded to sell so easily. Rory gave an uncomfortable sort of grin. 'We could go over to Dorchester on the bus, Mum. I'll take you Christmas shopping! I haven't had a chance to get you a present yet; we could get Mags to mind the café.'

'All right, what have you done with the real Rory and can you make sure that I get to keep this one instead?' Karen said. 'You can drown the original; it's all right.' But she was clearly delighted. Maybe not so much at the actuality but that he'd got his pay packet and his first thought had been of his mum. 'And maybe not all the way up to Dorchester, but we could pop over to Lyme, maybe. Get a tree for the house, little one for here; make the place a bit seasonal. There's that games shop you like there, isn't there?'

Rory's eyes lit up and his thumbs twitched reflexively. My heart was sinking fast. I couldn't fault Rory and his altruistic motives, but they did mean I'd be stuck in a car with Davin with nobody to mitigate the sulk factor. And when you are relying on a teenager to take the sulk factor *down* a notch or two, things are bad. 'I suppose we'd better get on then,' I said in a tone that suggested the actual words I was saying were 'please don't make me do this.'

'See you tomorrow,' Rory said, cheerfully, and Karen waved. Her eyes were still red and I looked at the little café as we walked out to the car. She was right, there was nothing else around: just a lot of windswept beach, miles of country lanes and the small collection of houses around the all-purpose shop-cum-post office, where Karen, Rory and the rest of the village of Warram Bay lived. A lovely, and no doubt bustling, place in summer – with the car park full of windsurfers, kite flyers, families with their towels, beach umbrellas and sandwiches – but for eight months of the year effectively a wasteland.

Davin opened the passenger door and I gave an inward groan. I couldn't very well demand he sat in the back now Rory wasn't here, but the prospect of Mr Grumpy giving me side-eye every time I oversteered didn't fill me with joy. There was a thump as Brian jumped back down into the boot and a small circle of discarded hair showed that he'd had his paws up on the seat back since we went into the café. There was also a smell of doggy digestive processes that showed he'd been hoping I'd bring him out a sausage.

I followed the satnav out over the headland. Down lanes where the sun was held, corked back by high hedges and spilling over into gaps, throwing exaggerated shadows of overdrawn five-barred gates and small stone buildings across the road. Above us the sky curled like a blue trampoline and some gulls bounced about on its surface. If it hadn't been for Davin, arms folded and staring at his knees next to me, it would all have been rather lovely.

I made a couple of stabs at conversation, but he managed to kill them with one-word answers or sometimes just a grunt, and I stopped even trying, until we drove past a turning where a big sign said '*St Dabney's Pre-Preparatory School for Boys, 4–6 years*' and I stopped, momentarily confused.

'Straight on.' Davin gave a nod of his head, indicating the lane ahead, which crested the hill with the enthusiasm of a child on a plastic sledge, and headed down the far side. Between occasional hedge breaks I could see the metallic glint of the sea.

'Yes. I just –' Remembering Noah. An argument we'd had, early on, about children being sent away to boarding schools.

Something about the desolation of this clifftop, where the wind whipped the tendrils of bramble like tightly furled flags, made me remember his face. His uncompromising expression, telling me that any child of his would be sent away to school as young as possible and would be grateful for the opportunity to learn to be self-sufficient. I'd countered that no child of mine would learn self-sufficiency until they were ready. The sight of that sign had thrown me right back into that discussion, and I could almost hear his words 'never did me any harm' over the slight whine of the wind through the metalwork of the car.

'Well, go on then,' Davin said, sharply.

'What?' His voice, with the Irish intonation so unlike Noah's clipped Englishness, threw me into momentary cognitive dissonance before I realised what he'd said. 'Yes, all right. I'm just thinking.'

Noah. Who'd had such strong beliefs, held such high ideals. Who'd thrown everything I thought I knew into the air and made me doubt myself, to the extent that I'd trusted him. And he'd ended up with everything... whilst I lost everything.

'Well then.'

'Oh stop being so sanctimonious! I know which way to go and it's not like we're in a hurry, is it?' I could just see a building, the school itself I presumed, past the sign. I wondered how many small boys had begged their parents to take them home at this point, and then I wondered if Noah had ever begged *his* parents to take him home. He would never have admitted to that, though. Not to me, anyway. I had a brief pang for my home: the lovely flat in London, the walls painted sunshine colours, the balcony windows thrown open to let the day flap the curtains.

Not my home any more. Noah had bought me out of that too.

'Really, and I thought you couldn't wait to have me out of this car,' Davin practically drawled, picking what I was pretty sure was an imaginary thread from the knee of his jeans.

'I'm just looking.' He was bang on with his assumption, but I didn't want to stoop to his level of rudeness and confirm it. Actually, I wasn't sure I *could* stoop to his level, not without taking my shoes off.

'Why?' He looked around. At the sign, at the lane and then, finally, at the sky. 'It's not very exciting, is it?'

I waved a hand at the sign. 'It just – well, they're so young, aren't they? And this place isn't exactly Enid Blyton land; it's a bit bleak.'

Davin just shrugged. 'Dunno,' he said.

'Really? You have no opinion about boarding school for little boys? What, *none*? Not even a "shouldn't let them out until they're nineteen"?' I made a very bad attempt to impersonate his accent. 'Aren't actors allowed to have original thoughts or something?'

'Was that supposed to be me talking then? Were you doing an impression of me?' He scratched his cheek and stared at the sign again.

'Let's just get on down to the beach.' I started the car again. 'What's this place called, anyway – Karen said but I can't remember.'

'Steepleton. And I don't sound anything like that.'

'Like what?'

'Like you made me sound. All "harharhar" or something; we don't put it on for comedy effect, you know.' Davin actually sounded rather hurt.

'I was just…'

'You made it sound like I was an extra in fecking *Father Ted*.'

I felt slightly ashamed of myself. I should know better. I'd worked with people from all backgrounds and cultures setting up the business; I'd had employees from Poland, Ukraine, Serbia – and I'd never called their accents into question, had I? Damn it, bloody Davin was perfectly right to be insulted.

'I'm sorry.' I tried to sound properly contrite. 'I shouldn't make fun of your accent.'

He snorted. 'You are so easy to wind up.'

I stopped being sorry. The tyres protested at my lack of sorry and I heard a rattle from the boot as Brian's paws struggled for traction. The road led us over the hilltop and then began a steep descent. After a while we began to encounter houses, dotted at first sparsely along the roadside like a very dispersed bus queue, then clustering together, as though gaining some measure of reassurance from one another. Some were set back high above the road with gardens that stretched up the hillside; others sat with their front doors practically level with the car. There was nobody about.

I slowed down to allow for the gradient, which was precipitating us alarmingly towards the sea which heaved and bobbed at the bottom of the little street. We reached the end, where a turning circle and tiny car park allowed me to finally lose the feeling that the sea was sucking us in, and I stopped. Davin immediately got out, as though my driving had been offensive.

Brian put his paws up and shoved his nose through the guard again. 'All right, you can come, but you're not allowed to say why we're here, all right?' Talking to Brian was a lot nicer than talking to Davin. Although Davin didn't leap from the car and try to lick my ears, that was still nicer than the feeling that he was laughing at me, somehow, and without moving his mouth from the expression of permanent scowl which seemed to be his natural resting state.

I attached Brian to a bit of hairy string I'd found in the van. I'd cut the belt down to form a makeshift collar. He now looked like he should have been sitting on a street corner next to a man in a sleeping bag, but at least I could keep hold of him, although every instinct begged me to release him into the wild, not unlike the instincts I had about Davin.

Brian and I walked around the car to where Davin was standing leaning against some railings. The sea was split by a breakwater which ran out several hundred yards; on one side it tamed the water into a gentle lapping against a sandy beach, which curved gently to parenthesise the end of the village. A young couple were walking along it, hand in hand, flipping the occasional pebble into the water, and my heart hurt, so I turned the other way.

Here the sea was rising and falling with a lot more force. A few fishing boats rose and fell with it, ropes slapping like soggy BDSM against their sides. Another wall enclosed the far side, forming a small harbour; nets and pots were stacked up on the roadway and a couple of men in waterproof leggings and enormous jumpers were standing pointing at a boat. It looked like an 'establishing shot' – 'harbour, boats at mooring'.

'Here,' Davin said.

'Where? What?' I looked at him, in case he was showing me something, but, unless it was contempt, there was nothing to see.

'Here. We can film here.' He pointed to a grey building which stuck out into the sea. 'That's an old lifeboat station. It could be my house.'

'Ignoring the fact that the people of this village might not want a film crew crawling all over the place.' I shaded my eyes and looked out along the beach into the sun, which had started the speedy slide towards evening, laying a liquid gold trackway down across the waves. The couple had gone, but they'd left a shadow on my heart.

'Ha, yeah, they couldn't possibly want all the tourists coming to watch filming, staying in their hotels and shopping in their shops.' He straightened away from the railings and set off along the seafront, which was a little way up the road and consisted of a parallel street, facing over the beach, some more railings keeping the buildings from plopping down onto the sand. I followed. The residents of this place didn't know what was about to hit them and, if it was fronted by Davin O'Riordan, I owed it to them to try to mitigate the damage.

Past the old lifeboat station which, annoyingly, bore a sign saying 'Old Lifeboat Station' – because I'd kind of hoped it would turn out to have been a garage or something just to take Davin down a peg or two – was a run of shops. Little shops, of the kind you often seem to find in slightly downtrodden coastal towns, where there's more enthusiasm than footfall and it all turns into grim determination around October. There was a grimly determined Christmas tree that seemed to have been bolted into the concrete: lights swung and bobbed from its branches and someone had placed some wrapped parcels underneath. They contained breeze blocks, I could see, where some of the paper had tattered. It looked both optimistic and deeply sad, like a queue of people outside a Job Centre.

The first shop had lights on and a display of bunting in the window that would have shamed a WI Summer Fete. To my horror, Davin threw open the door. His hair blew back from the draught of burning scented candles inside, but it didn't put him off and he'd gone in before I could catch up with him and tie him down with Brian's bit of hairy string.

'Davin!'

My cry was lost in the jangle of the bell as the door bounced shut. I looked at Brian. 'Well, it doesn't *say* no dogs,' I muttered and followed him in, Brian trailing slightly reluctantly. He'd clearly worked out that this shop wasn't going to be knee deep in sardines and sausages and that this walk was distinctly lacking in the 'whippets in heat and/or rabbits' stakes.

Inside, in the Christmas-candle-scented air, the girl behind the counter had thrown down the crochet she'd been working on. As I went in she turned a star-struck face to me. 'Look, it's Davin O'Riordan!' she squeaked.

'Yes, I know.'

'I just wondered…' Davin leaned forwards a little bit. There were fairy lights dotted around the shop and I couldn't help but be impressed with the volume of stock they'd managed to get displayed in such a small metreage. Watercolour sketches mingled with models of lighthouses and freakishly large carved seagulls, there were hand-knitted cushions and hangings piled casually among artful driftwood and shelves beautifully illuminated by the said fairy lights held shells and small, knitted sea creatures. Back in London they would have been queueing out of the doors for this kind of stuff – of course, it would have to have been a bit more 'urban themed', not a lot of market for lighthouse ornaments when you were kept awake all night by the neon sign across the road flashing. 'Who's in charge of the town?'

The girl's eyes widened. She had multi-coloured dreadlocks and a name badge that said 'Thea', but for all her trendiness she seemed to be knocked sideways by the presence of Davin.

'You sound like the lone gunslinger riding in to sort out the warring ranchers. You're just lacking the horse and the rifle. Oh, and the diplomacy. Keenan can work out filming potential; he knows how to deal with that kind of thing,' I tried, but Davin just kept leaning and the girl just kept staring. It was like they were locked in some sort of a face-off, sponsored by Yankee Candle.

At last, in a breathy sort of voice, she said, 'Will you sign something for me? I *love Watch Tower*; my friends and me went over the hill to see it being filmed in the summer! I was the one wearing a pink coat and you looked at me and waved, do you remember? We weren't allowed to come too close, but we watched this scene where you and Mary Narramore were arguing…?'

Davin gave the same smile as he'd given Karen. The fairy lights were instantly eclipsed and the candle flames flickered in the shade. 'I remember,' he said. And he started to sign the paper she thrust at him.

'Is that a dog?' Thea asked, obviously catching sight of Brian, who was doing his best to look macho amid the crochet.

'Yes,' I said, wearily, and held up my hand to show the string. 'He's on a lead.'

'Are you sure it's a dog?' She peered cautiously and Davin's smile wilted a bit. It clearly didn't like playing second fiddle to a hairy blob.

'Yes. His name's Brian.'

'You can't call a dog—'

'Here.' Davin handed the paper back and Thea squeaked in delight.

'Thank you! Oh, gosh, nobody is going to believe this! Can I have a picture?' and she brandished a mobile.

'Come on, Brian, before we melt.' I tugged the dog back out of the shop and breathed the cold, unscented air as the bell jangled the door shut. Why should I care if Davin told her exactly why we were scouting the place out? It didn't matter to me if he razed the whole village, like a *Godzilla* out-take, upset the entire Board of Trade and ravished all the maidens. None of it was my problem. I was just being paid to drive around and look at places. He could estrange the whole of Dorset for all I cared…

I leaned on the railings and looked down at the sea eating its way into the narrow strip of sand below. A chilly wind slithered its way under my jacket and I shivered, staring out at the endless miles of heaving grey ocean. Was this my life now? What the hell was I going to do with the rest of it, years and years stretching ahead of me, just as grey and uncertain as the water in front of me? I'd thought I had it all sorted – marry Noah, grow my business until I could afford to get people in to run it for me and then sit back in my house in the country while my name went over more and more shops and Noah and I brought up our children in Boden and rural splendour.

How had I got it so wrong? I should have kept the business. I'd been diversifying since cupcakes stopped being the Next Big Thing and just became the Thing that made Everyone Bigger. We could have taken on more shops, spread the load, redone the business plan…

The realisation hit me as coldly as if a larger than usual wave had burst over the railings. Not even a new realisation, but the old one only with sharper edges. It was all gone. My so-sassy London friends – the ones who'd popped in to the shop for little boxes of frou-frou iced cakes had gone, my convertible car had gone. Noah. Had. Gone. This was it now. For the foreseeable future, and that future was mostly a camper van and – I looked down – a scruffy mongrel dog with ears of different sizes and a redolent smell of second-hand fish.

Behind me the bell jangled, but I didn't bother to turn around, so Davin appearing beside me at the railings was a bit of a surprise. He leaned his arms against the top rail and gazed out towards the horizon in the same way I was. I could see him out of the corner of my eye, the wind tousling his hair and playfully flicking the neck of his probably designer top. He was almost unfairly good-looking. I wondered if there were three guys out there going bald and gaining weight by looking at a pasty because Davin had their share of good genes as well as his own. Even Brian dribbling on his foot couldn't really lower the glamour.

We stood together and watched the tide inching its way in up the sand, as though the sea had heard about erosion but wanted to take things slowly, see how it went, not overinvest energy in something that wasn't going to work out for it.

After a few minutes silent staring and sloshing, Davin said, 'So. What are we going to do about the café?'

'What do you mean?' And then I mentally kicked myself because it was a fairly self-explanatory question.

'Seems like the place needs not to be a burger joint. Your fella and his mam need a job all year round. And the coffee isn't bad.' He gave me a sideways look. 'And that's me saying it, so.'

'Will you stop calling him my fella and my man? He's fourteen bloody years old; he's not my anything!'

'Ah. Thought he was your assistant.'

It was only when I caught the smile on his face that I realised he was, as he would say, winding me up again. And that he had, in fact, treated Rory as my assistant the whole time in the car. 'Well, he's not. As you well know, but thank you.'

Another moment's silence except for the sea sluicing at the sand and a few gulls doing their 'squeaky wheelbarrow' impressions into the air above our heads. Clouds had drawn across the sky like tattered silk sheets, and the light had a 'filmy' quality, as though it was thickening.

'What do we do about the café?' Davin said again, finally.

'Look, I don't know! I'm supposed to be here clearing my head and deciding what I want to do with my life, not getting involved in other people's futures. I will sympathise and I will give ideas, but I'm not staying here!'

'Long-winded way of saying it's nothing to do with you.' Davin rearranged his arms on the rail. 'I'd have thought, with your business expertise, you'd be the very person to be brought in on this one.' The way he said 'business expertise' made it sound as though he was saying something in Polish, pronouncing it very carefully. 'Keenan told me you'd had a load of shops and it all went south.'

'It did *not* go south! It... and what is Keenan doing discussing it with you? It's none of your business.' Brian looked up at my angry tone. 'And now you've upset the dog!' I peeled myself away from the railings and, tugging Brian by his hairy string, I marched back along the little street, back towards where the car was parked between the harbour and the beach. Another squally gust thrashed against me, this time bringing the prick of incipient rain and a smell of chips from somewhere further along the coast. Brian was dribbling.

And there was Davin again, joining me silently, head bent into the wind, hands in pockets. The wind had stopped being squally now and had settled in for the long haul, lifting the sand into interesting shapes to toss along the beach, rattling signs and scraping left over plastic along the concrete. 'So. Café?' Davin said again as we reached the car.

I popped open the boot and Brian jumped in with gratitude. The wind had begun to do things to his fur that nobody outside a qualified dog-groomer should even attempt. 'I don't know!'

'Try.' He stood by the passenger door and, as a petty kind of revenge, I didn't open it.

I shook my head. The wind was bringing splatters of water, maybe rain or maybe bits it had scooped off the surface of the sea. 'I really don't. We could try raising enough money to buy it, I suppose. If all the community donated, there might be enough. I can't see it being exactly a money-spinner except in the season; we might get a reasonable price for it.'

Davin stared out over the roof of the car, down towards the harbour. The rising gale was pushing the boats to and fro so they bobbed dramatically amid metallic pinging and rattling. Inside the car, Brian's breath was steaming up the windows. 'Backwards,' Davin said. 'That's backwards.'

A sharp shower of something like sleet, quick-fire delivered on a gust, splashed into my face and I gave up and unlocked the car. Davin didn't immediately get in like I did; he stayed leaning against the car, staring across the tiny bay, then up the narrow road where all the houses seemed to be arrested in the process of sliding towards the sea. I bet if you'd put a stop-frame camera on the village, there would have been movement. It looked as though he was doing a slow panning shot of Christmas Steepleton. 'Come on, it's getting dark.'

He looked in at me through the window. 'Dorset. Not Transylvania.'

'What?' It struck me that I seemed to say that a lot when Davin was about. I'd never had to say 'what' when I'd lived in London. The occasional 'pardon?' when I hadn't caught something, but not this constant questioning of a train of thought. Davin didn't really seem to *have* a train of thought; his brain seemed to be more like a rubber duck on a fast flowing river.

'No vampires after dark. We're safe enough.'

He changed his mind very quickly when a car pulled up alongside us and about fourteen women got out. 'It *is*! It bloody *is!* Thea was right; it's Davin O'Riordan!' I saw the brief look of panic cross his face and the car door moved slightly, but then he seemed to compose himself and that billion-watt smile illuminated the car park and the sea as far as Norway.

'Hello,' was as far as he got before the women, who must have been packed into the little car like clowns, were brandishing mobiles and pictures and chattering away at him, whilst flicking their hair and making duck faces. I sighed and rolled the window down a bit to stop Brian's attempts to make the car look as if I'd put net curtains up. A smell of frying food wafted in and made my stomach churn, but the fact it was overlaid with the cold, organic smell of seaweed made me feel slightly queasy. Another blustery squall hit the windscreen, peppering it with shards of ice and the smell intensified for a moment, borne on the wind along with the shrieking laughter from the women surrounding Davin. It was like pick-up time outside a pilchards' nightclub. And with added seagull – one was walking about on the wall by the car, tipping its head to one side and staring at me with an eye like a little marble that's been rinsed in acid. The seagull was huge, but it didn't scare me. I was from London, where the seagulls were raised on rubbish and dead rats and flew around like wartime bombers only with less humanity. People were scared to let their cats out when the gulls came strutting down the road like a bunch of yellow-legged bully boys, bumming cigarettes off passers-by, clicking their fingers and humming 'Mack the Knife'.

I beeped the horn for the pleasure of watching the seagull flounder into the air and the girls stopped squealing for a moment. One of them stuck her head against the passenger window. 'Are you famous?' she asked. 'Or are you his minder?'

'I'm the person who wants him to get his starry backside into this car so I can go home.' It wasn't exactly a witty riposte; not what I would have said if I'd been given ten minutes' warning and a thesaurus, but it kind of summed up how I was feeling right now. I don't think he would have taken any notice if it hadn't been for the rain intensifying into a grey shroud, which blew in off the sea. The water broke over the windscreen and a second later the door opened and Davin slithered in, looking as though his clothes had been chewed.

'Nice girls,' he said, laconically. 'Now drive.'

'*Please*,' I added, pointedly, but he didn't speak again.

Davin – 1989

'Dav!' He'd been asleep, dreaming, warm under the weight of coats and dogs, and snuggled up to Killian; even though he knew that Killian wet the bed most nights, it was worth it to be warm. Now Niall was sitting on his chest with the superiority that being eighteen months older gave him. 'Dav! Are you awake?'

Davin blinked. The little room was dark and dusty, a torn blind at the window was shredding the moonlight into the caravan and, with his four years' experience, Davin immediately knew something was wrong. Something was always wrong, but this felt like it was big. He looked over to the other mattress squeezed into the little room, where Niall, Teague and Patrick slept. It was empty and stripped bare. Had one of them wet the bed too? Was someone ill?

'Wha'?' He tried to sit up but his older brother's weight pinned him down.

'You need to get up. We've got to go. Da's fetching the car; the big boys are packing. Wake up Killi and tell him to piss before we leave; might be a long drive.'

'Where's Mam?' Davin was still blinking. It had been a nice dream, something about a new puppy and Da letting him choose its name...

'Getting stuff ready to put in the car. Come on!' And Niall gave him a short punch on the shoulder and was gone, leaving Davin to pull himself out of the warm cocoon that their little mattress on the van floor had become and try to wake his younger brother, without scaring him into pissing on the bed.

They slept in their clothes, it was too cold to strip off, but Mam had promised him *Bosco* pyjamas for Christmas this year. He loved *Bosco*, even though the big boys teased him about it, and always worried they wouldn't get reception on the old set, or that the battery would have gone flat and he wouldn't be able to watch. Davin pushed his feet into the old sandals he was wearing this year, now that Niall had grown out of them, worried that he'd got them on the wrong feet again and Da would shout, but then thought that, if Da was fetching the car, he probably wouldn't notice. And it was dark, so.

Even at four years old, this late night moving wasn't strange to him. Once Da had exhausted the patience at the local bar, with his never-ending 'slate', and Mam refused to go to the store any more without some pennies, they'd be packing up and moving on, leaving whichever farm Da had been working on without a backward glance. They would all jam in to the elderly Volvo: big boys in the seats and the youngest pair in the boot under the bedding, covered over in case of any *Gardaí* being about, with Da's working dogs sitting on top of them and sometimes nuzzling down under the blankets to lick their faces.

One day, Da always said, one day we'll live somewhere in a house. Somewhere there are other children to play with and a proper bedroom, like on *Bosco*. Somewhere you can go to school and do your lessons and learn your letters. But for now – ah, for now it was all squeezing into the car under the flickering light of the moon, stuffing everything in that would fit and leaving what wouldn't, and heading off out for another caravan on another farm. Or, if they were lucky, there would be a cottage with a proper cooker and where the TV reception stayed steady. Mam was having another baby, Davin was sure of it although nothing had been said; she was as round as a ewe at lambing, and they always tried for a job with a cottage when there was a new baby.

He shook Killi and waited until he was properly awake before he rolled up the covers, helped his two-and-a-half-year old brother into his boots and coat, and they headed out to help Mam and the big boys with the packing up.

Chapter Six

I woke up in the middle of the night, reaching out for Noah's comforting warmth and encountering something sticky and furry, which grunted at me and moved to the end of the bed, whereupon I woke up properly.

Something about the heartbeat of the sea and the blackness outside made me feel horribly lonely, which was ironic because back home I'd pined for quiet and a night that was proper night, without lights and sirens and car alarms. Then I'd thought I wanted rural quiet and a lack of streetlights; now I realised that the van had become a sensory deprivation tank and that the absence of anything to focus on was letting my brain freewheel around my business disasters. I longed for a flashing blue light to dash past, siren howling into the night, showing me that other people were out there too, having a worse time than me.

Here, in the iron-cold, there was just me, the sea and the thoughts.

I sat up in the thin-mattressed bed. I'd folded down the whole of the back seating which, in effect, should make a triple bed, but the mattress was really only the seat cushions, and Brian took up most of the single portion, so it wasn't as comfortable as I'd thought it would be. And when I woke in the night to nothing but a snoring dog and birds tap dancing on the roof, it no longer seemed like the perfect escape vehicle, more a different kind of prison.

And then, totally unwarranted, I found myself thinking about Davin. Well, maybe not *totally* unwarranted; he'd been my only adult contact for the last couple of days, apart from Karen, Kee shooing me off the film site and Rory, who wasn't an adult. Plus, if you discounted the inscrutable comments, the general rudeness and the loooooong silences, he wasn't such a bad companion. Well, he was good to look at and… no, that was pretty much it. But as the only other thing I'd had to distract me today had been Brian, and he was taciturn, smelly and didn't even have good looks to make up for it, thinking about Davin was practically natural. Besides, if I was thinking about Davin I wasn't on the 'where did we go wrong?' roundabout of thoughts about Noah, the business and everything I'd lost.

I got up and wrapped myself in a fleece blanket to keep away the chill of the night. I hunched my legs up, hugged myself into a cube, and pushed open a window. The sounds of the night that I'd thought weren't there flooded in. The sea was hushing the shore with the regularity of a mother soothing a baby to sleep, some early rising birds were clearing their throats and the wind in the dunes was being sliced to pieces by the razor-edged grasses which grew there. It made a noise like a crowd of fans waiting for a star to pick up his guitar and begin playing, an expectant, breath-holding sort of noise.

The only reason I was holding my breath was that it was too cold and the end of my nose hurt. And the knowledge that I should have had everything I'd ever wanted, but it was all gone, suddenly overwhelmed me again and I cried hard, deep-body sobs, with the fleece over my head and my arms wrapped around myself.

Something even colder than the air nudged under my throw and touched my ear. A warm, wet flannel-like article began to wash away the tears and, in my half-asleep state, I almost believed that Noah was here, soothing away the pain, holding me, making everything all right again. And then I smelled the smell and realised that Brian was in my misery-tent with me, huddled up against my body and licking at my face. I opened my eyes and met an expression of eyebrow-furrowed concern, a paw came over and rested on my leg and the licking increased to such a level that I worried about my outer layer of skin.

'Sorry, Brian.' I sniffed and went to push him away, but something in the button-eyed anxiety stopped me and instead I put my arm around the warm little body. Half his fur was prickly short, the other half silky and long – albeit with some lumps that seemed to be foreign matter tangled in it – so it was like hugging an ancient fireside rug, but it was comforting. In a strange, odiferous way. His tail wafted more smell as it wagged enthusiastically about this late-night outbreak of affection. 'I'm just being a bit daft.'

More dramatic wagging. Then, looking behind to check that I was getting the point, Brian jumped up onto the bed again. 'Yes, all right.' I followed him and curled up on the mattress, pulling the throw tighter around me and the covers back up to my chin. Brian curled, watchfully, next to me, close enough to take my body heat but not close enough to risk another hugging. He was clearly rationing his affection very carefully. But it worked and I fell asleep again, with a mixture of tears and Brian-dribble still on my cheeks.

When I woke up again, the beach was invisible behind the curtain of rain that had been drawn across it. The sea, closer now, had stopped hushing and was into a rock-and-roll soundtrack and the birds were dotted around the dunes outside the van, attempting to gain shelter from the big metal rock that was the camper.

I picked up Rory from the café, where today Karen wasn't even sweeping; she was just hunched at a corner table with a cup of coffee in front of her, muttering under her breath about wishing she hadn't given up smoking. She barely even looked up to growl at Rory when he stuffed a pastry into his mouth on the way out. Things must be bad.

Brian had raised his head and looked at me with such an eloquent expression of utter resignation to fate that I hadn't had the heart to drag him outside on his string. I'd warned him about what would happen if he ate any more of my socks and left him on guard, so it was only Rory and I that arrived in the next bay, carried in on a wind that felt as though it had been carved from a glacier somewhere.

The set was quiet, apart from the waves booming and scraping onto the sand further down the beach. Through the rain I could see a thin thread of birds passing through a needle eye of cloud, heading for somewhere drier, or with a less restless surface, and Rory and I sat in the car for a minute or two, watching the rain splatter the windscreen.

'We've found a possible site for filming now,' I said. 'So Kee probably won't need me any more.'

'And I've got to get Mum something for Christmas.' Rory looked glum. 'Didn't see anything she might like yesterday and I can't just get her another giant bar of Dairy Milk; she must be sick of that stuff by now. Stupid, I've actually got, like, real money, but nowhere to spend it 'cept the Post Office and I don't really think half a dozen first class stamps are gonna be her thing.' A moment of thought. 'But I did get Fallout Four, Special Edition. Spence and Ryder are gonna go *ape*. Hey look, there's Neil the sound guy!'

With a typical teenage disregard for the weather, or maybe an incipient 'bloke' fear of talking about what was really bothering him, he leaped out of the car and headed over to where Neil was piling some equipment up in the shelter of a portacabin. Neil handed him some headphones and a jacket and Rory happily started helping him do whatever it was he was doing. I stayed in the car and watched. All Rory's life was here: his home, his school, his friends – how on earth would he manage if Karen had to relocate him somewhere she could find a job and afford to rent a house? The big city might have cinemas and takeaways and all that, but there was a strong likelihood that a boy like Rory would get lost in the cracks between GCSE's and finding a job and I'd seen too many people ripped away from everything they knew and floundering to think it was going to be easy for him.

There was a rattling tap on the car window and I nearly fell under the steering wheel. 'Kee!'

'Hey Tan.' He opened the door and got in. 'Didn't know if I'd see you today. Davin says there's a possibility for filming up the coast there?' He went to point, realised he was holding a doughnut, tried to hide it and there was a certain amount of sugary fallout.

'Yes. I'm here to return the car and hand it all back over to you. With thanks for employing me and all.' I gave him an awkward cheek-kiss. 'I've got enough money to move on now; might move the van on somewhere a bit more populated. And warmer.'

'Ah.' Kee did another doughnut shuffle. 'Meaning to talk to you about that. Ah.'

'I can't stay here, Kee. There is literally *nothing* for me here: no work, no house, no… well. I need to get going.'

Out on the film site, Larch was walking slowly across the sand wearing a huge quilted coat and big padded boots, making her look as though she was being eaten by a duvet. She paced slowly up to where the froth of the surf was slumping ashore, leaving clumps of seaweed rolled and dangling, and poked one with a toe.

'Just for a wee while? You know I said it was all going to shit before? Well, it's all going shitter now. The catering people have gone down with flu so half the sound crew are running the food; Dav's agent's assistant, who was *supposed* to be coming down after her operation, has got complications and can't come until after Christmas; we're behind on schedule and I'd promised we'd be wrapped up by now, but it looks as though we're going to be here until the New Year and they're all rioting.' He stopped and looked close to tears. 'And Benoit's taken the Villeroy & Boch cutlery set!'

I patted his arm, whilst my thoughts ran off over the hills and hid. I couldn't leave Kee in the lurch and Davin obviously thought I could come up with some solution to Karen's problem, plus there was Brian – what would I do with Brian when I moved on? I'd been going to leave him with Rory but his precarious housing situation wouldn't be helped by the addition of a disgustingly hairy dog. And a tiny part of me wanted to see this thing through, find out what happened when they tried to make a new series in the unlikely, and somewhat fan-filled, location of Christmas Steepleton. I felt a tickle of proprietorial interest. *I'd* found that village; now what were they going to do with it?

'Oh bugger,' I said.

'We'll have a hiatus, obviously, over the actual Christmas period.' Keenan looked out across the beach. 'I can't keep them here over the holiday. Larch is, apparently, a practising pagan and I'm afraid she might come over a bit "Wicker Man" if I try to stop her going home. And most of the crew have families to get back to. But we can film right up to Christmas Eve, and then start again in the new year, and I *really* just need someone else sane and sensible on site, Tan. I can't do this on my own!'

'You aren't on your own,' I pointed out. 'There's Neil and Chloe and the lighting boys and props and costume and everyone. There's probably more people living here than in the next village.'

Kee turned desperate eyes to me, over the top of the doughnut. 'But you're not totally wrapped up in all this,' he said, slightly muffled. 'You're my breath of fresh air.'

'If you use the phrase "tell it like it is", I will personally kill you with this...' I brandished a cable that snaked away to a port somewhere in the dashboard, 'even if I have absolutely no idea what it is.'

'Sorry, sorry.' The doughnut lowered and I could see his bearded lower lip was trembling slightly. 'You've probably got family yourself to get back to.'

I took a deep breath. 'Well, not really. But, even so, Kee.'

'*Please*, Tansy. There's a lot to do yet with sussing out this whole new series, the writers are on it and there's this whole drive to turn Davin into a superstar – they've got him doing some kind of video casting for America who are, by the way, welcome to him – and I just want...' he stopped talking and turned to look out of the window. 'I want Benoit back,' he finished quietly. 'But I know that's not going to happen. I need a friend here, Tansy.'

I stared out over the rain-wracked beach and thought. Where *was* I going to go for Christmas? Probably one of my London friends, who'd get me drunk on designer gin on Christmas Eve and let me sleep in their soulless spare room... 'OK,' I said, watching a seagull peck tentatively at one of the cables Neil and Rory were moving, as though it thought the local worms had mutated into something both delicious and potentially aggressive. 'OK Kee. I'll stay around until after Christmas. By then you should be sorted, yes?'

'If not I shall be heading off to a retreat somewhere in Bhutan. Thanks, Tansy. Honestly.'

I just snorted and watched a couple of men in headsets come carefully down the catering van steps carrying steaming cups. 'Your catering crew are down with flu, you said?' An idea forming in the back of my mind.

'Yep. All but one, confined to their beds.'

'OK. Get out of the car. I think I can solve that one...'

Davin – 1995

'Come away, Rook!' Davin shouted across the field at the small collie, which was darting among the sheep like a small brindled shadow.

'She's a good one, that.' Da leaned on the gate. 'You've done a good job there, Dav.'

Davin glowed with pride. It wasn't often that Da had anything much to say to any of them these days, so his praise for the training of Rook was doubly unusual. He looked across the rocky field, where forty Blackface ewes were now grazing. Rook had brought them down off the high hill without turning a hair, and him only a year old. And he'd trained him to do it, and *him* only ten! The glow of pride intensified. Even Patrick hadn't been training dogs to work when he was ten. He'd probably been picking his nose and pooing his pants still, when he was ten. You had to be special to train a collie, Davin knew, and Patrick, Teague and Niall weren't special: they were just big and loud and smoked cheap cigarettes and thought of themselves as men.

Patrick and Teague were out on the tractor, bringing up some hay from the old barn for the ewes. Winter had been hard this year and had taken its toll on the beasts. Davin knew they needed to get condition on their backs before they brought the rams in; otherwise the lamb crop would be disappointing and Da might lose his job again.

He leaned against a wind-torn hawthorn tree and sighed. It wasn't a *bad* life, not really. It was fun sometimes, when Mam was in a good mood and the babbies were asleep and she'd baked griddle cakes and sang for them in the evenings. And Da stopped at the second bottle and told them stories of when he'd been young and the farms he'd worked at and the things he'd seen. There were the beasts and the dogs and his brothers to play with when they'd finished their jobs, although Patrick was too old now to play, at fifteen. Da took him to the sales now, and on strange night-time missions from which they'd return with a rabbit or two for Mam's pot, or sometimes other things which they'd hide in the back of the car and not talk about in front of the younger ones. Even Teague had been once or twice, out with the 'men'.

Davin knew one day it would be his turn. Out across the neighbouring lands with a dog and a gun and an eye open for an unlocked barn door… He gave a small shiver and rubbed a hand across his face, watching Rook, his job done now, collapse panting and grinning in the shelter of a boulder. Did he want this to be his life? He knew from *Echo Stream* on the TV that there were other ways to live; he'd seen it. Seen boys his age learning how to make sweets or what went into producing the clothes they wore; he'd seen the world was bigger than this circle of farms. Even though Da only let them watch TV for a couple of hours a day, sometimes Davin and Killi would sneak downstairs in the evening when Da was out with the drinking or the big boys, and Mam would let them watch *Prime Time* or one of her soaps.

Davin loved it. Loved the 'otherworldness' that the TV let him see. Families which weren't all boys, where there were only a couple of kids, who wore school uniforms and did home-work. Or glamorous ladies who sat in bars and drank and didn't have children at all, but waited for men with hair spun like the candyfloss at the fair to take them dancing. Those ladies weren't like Mam at all. He loved Mam, utterly: she stopped Da when he threatened to beat the boys for some indiscretion or other, or for a dog going bad, or when one of the ferrets got loose. She tucked them up in bed and kissed them; she'd even read them a story or two, if the babbies had gone to bed easily. But, unlike those ladies with the swish dresses and the make-up on TV, Mam wasn't happy. Davin had heard her cry sometimes at night, waiting for Da to come back. He'd found her once, when Lorcan was a tiny babby and Finbar was just a toddling wee thing; she was holding the two of them on her lap and sobbing into Lorcan's little swaddled body. She pretended she'd just got a headache when he asked, but he knew, even then, she was only pretending. It was something bigger than a headache that had upset Mam.

But for now there was Rook, there were mountains and snow and space. Nobody bothered him too much and the cottage was big enough that he only had to share a room with Killi and Niall.

And one day, one day, Davin promised, to the brindled col-lie, the wind and the mountainside, life would be like he saw on the TV.

Chapter Seven

Karen was somewhat confused about what I was asking of her, but got 'Mags' in to look after the café and came with me to the film site, where I delivered her to the catering van. 'She'll whip people into shape and get the catering up and running,' I told Kee. 'What's next?'

He looked shifty. 'Ah. Um.'

'Kee? Oh, this is going to be bad. I can feel it.'

He looked around the filming site. The rain had started to clear, far out to sea the faintest shimmer of distant sunlight was sparking off the ocean as the clouds fussed and bustled away over the cliffs behind us. People were unrolling cables, two minor characters were rehearsing a scene – their scripts tugged and flipped in their hands, bookmarked by the wind. Over near the foot of the cliff, Neil, still being assisted by Rory, was doing something electrical, whilst Seelie bounced like a blue ghost around their feet.

'You know I said Davin's agent's assistant can't get here…' Kee tailed off and looked expectantly at me.

A slow-dawning horror crept over the crown of my head as his words sank in and pulled my eyes open like a cheap facelift. 'What? Oh, no. No.'

'He's asked for you.'

'He's *what*?!' Somehow my mind couldn't get around an image of Davin actually requesting my presence; all I could envisage was him muttering something darkly into his duffel coat and being misheard. 'No. He can't have. Come on, Kee, admit it, it's just that nobody else will go near him and you're desperate.'

Keenan waved at someone trying to get his attention from one of the caravans. 'Look, I've got to go and do something, Tan. Just – I don't know, talk to him. Find out what he wants. He might just want someone to walk the dog for him.'

We both stared at where Seelie was, resolutely, walking herself along the sand. Little paw marks etched into the beach showed where she'd run, turned and sauntered. 'I think she's pretty much got that covered herself.'

'Well, look at it this way, she might be carrying your grand-puppies.' Kee gave me a sheepish grin. 'Yeah, Davin's been making the crew promise to take any pups that result. So you might want to keep Brian away, you know, not put them off. Everyone loves Seelie but if they see the potential father it might just sway them the other way; we don't all have a Dennis the Menace complex.'

'He's not my dog,' I said, reflexively. 'OK, Kee. For you I will go and find out what Davin wants. He's in his trailer? If I'm not back by lunchtime, come in, armed. Oh, and if you hear things breaking you might want to come and rescue him. I might have finally reached the end of my very long tether.'

Keenan gave me a brief kiss on the cheek. 'Thanks Tan. I now owe you several whatever it is that you really, really want.' Then, following the frantic beckoning, he headed off across the site towards whatever awaited him.

You can't give me back what I want. It's gone. I caught the intrusive thought before it brought me to reluctant tears again and distracted myself by walking off across the gritty sand towards where the Winnebago was parked up, just off the actual beach and angled across so that it looked out towards the open sea.

There was no sound from within. I lifted my hand to knock and a small, slippery wet body pressed against my leg. 'Hello Seelie. Are you wanting in?'

The door flew open without me needing to knock. I nearly fell over and the dog dashed inside, past Davin, who was wearing a hooded top and jogging trousers that made him look like a rap artist. His feet were bare on the carpeted floor and I wondered if he'd just got out of bed. 'Ho Seelie. Get to your basket,' he said, not looking at me at all, but following the progress of the wet whippet.

'How do you do that thing with the door?' I looked suspiciously at him. 'You're not psychically linked to the dog, are you?'

'There's a camera.' He turned away but didn't close the door, so I stepped over the threshold behind him. 'Shut the fecking door. Don't want her overdoing it out there.'

I thought back to the little dog romping over the sand. 'I think that ship might have sailed. Have you seen a vet? I mean, if she's in pup…'

Inside the van was lighter than I'd thought. It was as far removed from my camper as – well, as Seelie was from Brian. Both basically the same thing, but one elegant, spare, beautifully designed and purpose built, and the other – not. We were standing in a lounge area, where leather sofas faced a massive TV screen. On the other side, a kitchen stretched back into the depths of the van. It was nicer than the one I'd had in my flat.

'She's fine,' Davin said, shortly. But then shortly was practically his only method of communication. I wondered if he ran out of breath during long speeches in *Watch Tower* and had to be resuscitated between takes.

'OK, good.' I stared around at the conspicuous luxury again. Davin slumped down onto the sofa and pulled his feet up underneath him. It was an odd movement, a little bit childlike, as though he was trying to hide the bareness of his feet from me. Seelie tucked her nose under her tail in her basket in the corner, but her ears were cocked, listening to him. I had the distinct impression that it was more usual for her to be sitting up on the sofa next to him, but they were both trying to look conventional.

After I'd stood awkwardly just inside the living area for a bit, watching him lounge, I cleared my throat. 'Kee said you wanted to see me.' I felt bizarrely ill at ease in here, which was strange. Usually I had the measure of meetings, of conversations, ran a few steps ahead of everyone; it was one of the things that had made my business successful. I knew what was coming and anticipated it. Right now though, I was completely at a loss.

'Yeah.'

'Right, OK, well a clue might be nice, because I haven't got all day to just stand here admiring your profile.'

That elicited a small smile, which he dropped his chin to hide in the folds of the grey hoodie. In her basket, Seelie cocked her ear again so he must have moved or done something for her to pick up on. 'Ah there, you see, you like me really, so.'

'No. I really don't.'

'Well I'm after needing a bit of help, and it's either you, your man or Brian, and you're the only one who walks upright and doesn't have a paper round to get to.' Davin paused and sort of scrumpled his hands into the sleeves of the hoodie. 'I need an assistant.'

'You also need charm lessons but I'm not doing that either.' I half turned. 'You've got through this far without having someone to dance attendance on your glorious self. I'm sure you can cope until after filming is finished.'

'I'll pay you. Proper money now, not the loose change Keenan was after shoving you.'

I paused, torn between standing on my dignity and the knowledge that the van was going to need fuel, new tyres and an MOT before too much longer. 'Why?' And even to me I sounded suspicious.

Davin raised his head. 'And you're sure you signed that non-disclosure?'

'Of course I am. I live in a van in the middle of sand dunes; trust me, there's not that much paperwork involved in my day to day existence. I remember signing it.'

'Well. All right then.' And Davin looked away now, his eyes roaming around the inside of the Winnebago like a couple of opportunistic thieves looking for portable goods. 'I need reading glasses.'

'So? I'm not magnifying the world for you. It's not like there's a little button on the side.'

'Tch. For my script. But your dog here –' Davin waved a hand at Seelie, who sighed and stretched her elegance across the basket, 'now she's eaten the only pair I brought with me. So I can't see to read the updates on the script.'

'You want to employ me to read you the script?'

Davin looked directly at me now. I couldn't help noticing that his eyes were very much like Seelie's, large and dark, and that his cheekbones also bore a resemblance to the whippet's high-boned aristocracy. Although her face was ninety per cent nose and Davin's was more classically beautiful man, the sort of thing you expect to see on billboards advertising designer suits. 'I want you to read them and record it. So I can play it back and learn my lines that way.' He stood up, uncoiling himself like a long grey snake. 'Now. Is it a coffee you're wanting?'

There was a coffee machine set up on the work surface in the kitchen, which explained the pervasive smell that almost overcame the scent of very new carpet. There was a slight top note of cinnamon and I suspected some form of scented candle, which made me wonder if the mysterious agent's assistant was working on trying to domesticate Davin. He didn't look, even from his back view as he filled the coffee machine with water, like the sort of man who would be into scented candles, not even if you forced him at gunpoint.

'I'm fine. Thank you,' I added, to show that I wasn't going to sink to his rudeness level. The coffee smell increased as Davin opened a packet of something and poured it.

'Ah, go on. You might as well; it's nicer in here than out there standing in that wind. Oh, and here.' He turned round and handed me a paper script, which looked as though it had been much amended, and had his name highlighted on the front. 'And you'll be needing this.' A small digital voice recorder plopped on top of the sheets of paper. 'You press this one, here.'

'Yes, I know how recorders work, I used to…' I stopped. Used to run, in London, dictating notes to myself about new shops, new spaces, new designs for shop fronts, as I swept through Covent Garden and Soho. 'I know how they work,' I corrected myself.

'Well then, so.' He went back to the coffee machine and I stayed staring around the conspicuous luxury. I ought to leave. But, damn him, he was right; it was nice in here. The invisible heating system warmed the coffee-and-cinnamon air and Davin bustling around in the kitchen threw me back to old times. Better times. I didn't move.

Through the enormous windscreen of the Winnebago I could see that the sunlight had been peeled and scattered by the windswept clouds. The van faced away from the film site, towards the monobrow of cliff that frowned over the far end of the beach, giving a view of rolling grass and a crowd of wading birds, chattering and paddling where the surf quietened into smooth water at the base of the cliff.

Behind me Davin said something, and I spun around, knocking the cup of coffee he'd been holding out to me from his hand and spraying it over him, the seating and the carpet, like brown blood at a murder scene. Seelie leaped out of the way and went to hide behind a door.

'God, sorry! Sorry!' I stared aghast at him, dripping gently, the now empty cup still held out towards me. 'Sorry Davin! Give me a cloth. I'll get it mopped up; you don't want it to stain the carpet, and...' I looked around, panic-stricken, searching for anything I could use to start wiping up the spill.

'Ah now, you could have just said you didn't want the fecking thing,' Davin said mildly. 'No need to throw it everywhere.'

'No, I really am sorry. Are you all right? Did it burn you?' I watched aghast as the stain slowly spread over the front of his sweatshirt.

'Am I hopping in agony now? No, you're fine; it's only on the sweater.'

My face flamed with mortification. 'Give it to me, I'll – wash it out in the sink or something.'

He raised an eyebrow. 'D'you think I can't rinse out my own clothes now?'

I was flustered. I worked hard to try to keep what vestiges of control over my life I had left, there were few enough, but lately life had seemed to want to blow those last remnants into smithereens – what with Brian the uncontrollable dog and events that ran so far outside my ability to influence them that I might as well have been yelling instructions from Australia. 'No, but I ought to…'

'Tch.' And he put the mug down and pulled the sweatshirt off over his head by the hood. 'I'll take it over to costume. Sharon over there has a machine; she'll know what to do about the staining.'

He was wearing a white shirt underneath, collarless and open at the throat. Fortunately the coffee didn't seem to have gone through, because the open neck, with the tiniest curl of dark hair visible, was exactly the sort of sex-symbol-building costume that his character would be wearing in *Watch Tower*, and I didn't want to be accused of sabotaging filming.

'Would you like me to take it?' I carried on pushing the point and I wasn't sure why. Because Noah had always deferred to me in the household department? Maybe. Maybe I'd got used to doing the day to day tasks of living, smoothing daily life by sorting dinner, filling the fridge, tidying the flat while he – no, actually, what *had* Noah been doing whilst I'd been making sure we didn't starve or invite rats and cockroaches to a party?

Davin 'tch'd' at me again and dragged a big coat out from a cupboard cunningly concealed in the corner. 'Eight brothers. I know about stains.' And then he was gone out of the van, pulling the coat on against the wind that was buffeting the sides of the Winnebago and carrying the hoodie carefully spread out so the stain didn't transfer to any other part.

I watched him go and shook my head. Then I found a cloth hanging over the side of the sink in the kitchen area, and set myself to wiping the drips of coffee that were clinging to the side of the leather seating and mopping the carpet. Luckily the script he'd handed me had been outside the blast radius and, apart from some creases and what looked like additions made in crayon, was untouched.

I wiped the upholstery and the side of the cupboard and went to rinse the cloth in the sink but, however hard I tried, I couldn't turn the tap on. I knew it worked; Davin had filled the coffee machine from it, but it was a weird mixer-tap arrangement, with levers and buttons which didn't seem to do anything, and I couldn't encourage more than a dribble of chilly water from its shiny chrome. The cloth was soggy and coffee-stained and every part of my desire to keep things clean and tidy, which was already strained at the seams from contact with Brian on a daily basis, told me to rinse it out, so I went in search of the bathroom that must exist. A place this gloriously luxurious almost certainly didn't have a bucket in a corner and torn up newspaper on a peg.

I found it, eventually, behind a door I'd thought contained a cupboard. It couldn't be the only bathroom, because it only held a toilet and a small basin – no shower – and I doubted Davin was sponging himself down every morning; his sort of looks surely required hours of tweezing and spraying and checking in the mirror. No power on earth would convince me he got out of bed looking like that.

There was a contact lens case on the narrow glass shelf in the bathroom. I frowned at it for a moment – why did Davin need reading glasses if he wore contact lenses? – but then I realised that he either wore contacts for long range and needed glasses for close work, or – and I gave a little smile to myself – his eyes really *weren't* that ninety per cent pure chocolate brown at all and he wore coloured contacts to live up to his own image. I bet he wore just the merest touch of eyeliner too. He'd probably had work done as well, maybe just a trim of the nose or something to correct a massive overbite. He just *couldn't* have been born looking like that. Nobody was that good-looking in real life; even Noah had his otherwise exemplary looks slightly knocked off-kilter by eyes just a smidgeon too close together. Actually, that was being kind; he could have stared down an oboe with both eyes simultaneously.

I rinsed the cloth in the small sink, surprised by the instant hot water that came out and then annoyed with myself. A few weeks living in a camper van which had hot water that only came from putting a kettle over a camping stove and suddenly the niceties of modern living were catching me by surprise? When once I'd lived in an apartment block that had boasted its own gym and swimming pool?

Again the enormity of what I'd lost came over me. It was as though I could forget it, pretend none of it had ever existed for a finite amount of time, and then when that time had extended as far as it could, the memories would rebound, snapping back like an overstretched elastic band. Stinging me with the thoughts of what could have been, what *should* have been.

I wrung the cloth out until my hands were blotched red and white and my wrists ached. *Forget it. Forget all of it. That was then and this is now, and now is…* I looked around the Winnebago, took in the wafty smell of Christmas that was the cinnamon and the acrid smell that was new carpet. There was a vague top note of damp dog too, hanging above Seelie's basket, where she was curled up now, one ear draped high in the air as though alert for Davin's return. *Actually I have no idea what 'now' is. Now is just existing, day to day, earning enough to keep me from starving.*

I picked up the script and flicked the pages. There was less dialogue than I'd thought, and it all seemed a bit disjointed, so I assumed that these were 'insert' shots, to be cut in to the rest of the already filmed stuff. Either that or *Watch Tower* was some arty series, consisting of long, lingering shots of the beach and the waves with someone saying deep, meaningful things like 'I see,' and 'you won't want to wait around then' superimposed over the top.

There was a bang on the door and Rory erupted into the van. 'Wicked! C'mon, Tansy. Mum's worked out the oven and she's making something with squid in it! And Neil's telling me all the exams I need to take to do what he does, and there's BTECs and all and he says I could do those up to Exeter, maybe.' The light of hero-worship was bright in his eyes and his hair was standing on end. He'd got a pair of headphones round his neck, the end of the cable trailing somewhere around his waist and he looked like a boy that's just discovered that the world of work doesn't have to consist of wiping tables and frying chips. Possibilities were unspooling in front of him, as limitless as the ocean.

'That sounds good.' I draped the cloth over the tap and tucked the script and dictaphone into my bag.

'Yeah. Mum can do great squid. The crew are going to lunch now, come on! You can come and talk to Neil; maybe he can tell you some stuff you could do!' Rory dragged open the door and clattered down the steps. Seelie opened one eye.

'Are you coming?' I stood, holding the door open. 'There's squid, apparently.'

The whippet regarded me haughtily for a moment, made a slight gagging noise and tucked her head back down under her tail.

'Pregnancy is a pain, isn't it,' I said, sympathetically, and closed the door behind us.

* * *

Karen was in her element in the catering van. She'd co-opted a few members of the crew to help her and was holding court in the kitchen area, but I judged, from the amount of raucous laughter, that she wasn't a bad boss to work for. I helped myself to a portion of the 'something with squid in', which turned out to be hand-battered and fried calamari, and caught her eye over the counter.

'Well, this is a turn up.' She came bustling out of the kitchen. 'You know they're paying me to do this?'

'I'd hope so.'

'But they've got a kitchen that practically cooks the food itself! There's a fridge that does reorders over the internet and an oven that programmes itself – it's like working inside one of they *Star Trek* film things. I keep expecting a little robot to shake its head and tell me I used too much pepper.'

'That would be illogical.' But she'd clearly not watched much *Star Trek* because she just made a face at me and adjusted her lanyard.

'And I've got an identity card with my picture on! It's a rubbish picture, mind – makes me look about twenty years older – but it means I can come down on site whenever.' She lowered her voice. 'And Neil has offered to drive me and Rory home, so we don't need to wait for you.' She gave me a hefty wink and her identity card nearly took the cheese sauce off a lone plate of vegetable lasagne. 'Saw you going off into that Davin O Riordan's caravan. Nice in there, is it?'

'The van is lovely; him, not so much. Apparently I'm his new assistant, until the old one gets over her operation which, please the powers that be, won't be long.'

'Oh, "assistant" is it then?' Another wink. 'Won't be seeing much of you for a while then. As you'll be so busy "assisting".'

'Oh come on, Karen, he's a pillock!' And then, thinking of that dark curl of hair, those cheekbones and the almost black eyes, 'He's just a photogenic pillock, that's all.' And then again, to change the subject, because Karen's expression of 'yeah, riii-iight' covered her face as completely as the cheese sauce covered the lasagne, 'Have you thought any more about how we could raise the money to buy the café?'

Karen instantly lost the spark of humour and her eyes sank down to rest on the salad bowl. 'To be honest, Tansy, I haven't got any idea. I'm pretty much resigned to moving up to Exeter and trying to find a cheap rental up to there.' She gave a long, slow blink. 'I need to find somewhere I can afford once the bene-fit payments stop for Rore, and it's not going to be easy.' Then she was distracted by an argument breaking out over chips and went off to sort that out.

I ate my calamari alone at a table, staring out through the window to the wind-scoured beach, where Kee was repeatedly filming Davin and Larch walking along the sand. Cameramen, sound technicians and someone whose entire job seemed to consist of sweeping the sand free of footprints, were all bat-tling against the stiff onshore breeze, and it must have been the mysterious stain-expert Sharon who ran on and off with coats between takes.

Behind me, the catering van filled up with those not required on set, chatter and warmth. The crew were clearly a close-knit group who seemed to have taken Karen into their midst, because she was laughing and joking with them as though she'd been here from the beginning. I wondered how she managed, someone as obviously sociable as she was, confined to the wilds of Dorset and a café with no customers for months of the year. Maybe she secretly did want to move to Devon, to a big city? Shops and a social life and more job opportunities weighed against her son's entire life – his education and friends. *She must feel so torn.*

Once my plate was clear, I went back to the car park and drove home to the camper van. I'd left Brian alone for long enough and the noisy hubbub of the film set wasn't going to be the best place for me to record Davin's script.

Brian was sitting bolt upright on the bed and, as soon as I opened the door, he flew for it with the desperation of a saggy pelvic floor. 'Sorry Brian. I really shouldn't be leaving you in here, should I?' I let him outside and then stood in the lee of the van. Overhead, a flock of black and white birds, with trailing orange legs, whistled and swung in the wind. The air smelled of cold metal, wet rock and salt and, apart from the birds piping peevishly overhead, it was quiet. Even the sea had hit the mute button, and was whispering up and down the dark spread of sand, sending occasional pulses of spray my way, to splash quietly against the windows of the van. It was so quiet I could practically hear the corrosion happening.

And I realised I was relaxing. Only a little bit, but my shoulders definitely didn't have the ache they usually carried from being up around my ears, and the feeling that I'd overindulged in a meal of enormous, greasy proportions was less. Which, when I thought about it, was strange. I was living on a beach in a van with audible rust, with a dog that… actually, I preferred *not* to think about what Brian was up to right now, and was now, apparently, employed to be an assistant to a man who made Shrek look mild-mannered and reasonable. How the hell had this even happened?

I shivered. A cloud of night was already starting to pull across the headland and the wind was getting colder. 'Brian! Come on.'

The little dog raised his head and looked towards me, his whiskers covered in sand. Somehow, *somehow*, he knew I was calling him, but the not being shut in the van was clearly heady and he cocked his tail sideways and ran, heading up towards the café, where it stood lonely and slightly weather-beaten, like an old boat dragged high on the beach and left to over-winter. I sighed and followed. I couldn't leave Brian out alone whilst I sat in and recorded this script. He might make a bid for world domination or chase seagulls or something worse. I ignored the fact that he'd managed to live a solo life until he'd come begging sardines at the camper van door and hadn't got himself run over, buried in a landslide or picked up by evil people intent on turning him into a small fish-scented hearthrug.

The sand squeaked and slid under my feet as I trudged in his general direction, following the scraped paw prints up the beach. Brian was sniffing animatedly up the wall of the café; either another dog had passed by recently or he could smell panini through the brick. As I stood and watched him, my phone beeped in my pocket and made me jump. I'd barely even thought of it in these last few days. Anyone I wanted to talk to now was usually standing right in front of me.

Texts. Quite a few, all arriving at once, all sent recently other-wise they'd have been picked up on the car's Wi-Fi, coming in now I was getting the café's signal.

Hey Tan, did you check the FT article?

Tansy, it's Peter. Just wondering how you're feeling?

Wow, Noah's really gone to town now, hasn't he? Where are you? We need to drown our sorrows under a tonne of Prosecco bubbles!

Nothing from Noah. My heart settled down and my stomach stopped squeezing. Had I been hoping there would be? Or that there wouldn't? We were over; that was unequivocal. After the way he'd betrayed me – taken everything I'd ever wanted from me – how could I ever even look at him again without wanting to rip his face off and feed it to the seagulls that bobbed over my head now, craning their necks to check that Brian hadn't found something edible for them to swoop down and steal.

So, what had Noah done? Did I want to know? Did I really want to check up on my erstwhile business and find out how little of me there was left in it?

Hell, yeah. Maybe he'd made some monumental cock-up and was facing losing everything – I could hope, couldn't I? So I leaned my back against the rough wall, tucked myself under the overhanging eaves to try to keep the wind out, and, with half an eye on Brian's attempts to overturn the bin, I googled.

'Noah Peterson'.

Several pages of results. *Financial Times*, Companies House, some business magazines. I opened the *Financial Times* page, where a whole-page article from today's issue detailed his expansion and diversification of the business.

I slid down the wall and sat on the concrete. Skim read and then, eyes pricking, read the whole gory story of what he'd done to my lovely little London-based personalised cupcake business. How he'd sold up in London. Bought new premises: a canal boat in Norfolk, a medieval guard tower on a bridge in York, a shepherd's hut on an organic 'pick your own veg' farm in Shropshire. He'd turned them into bookshop/cafés, all cosy and welcoming, buying in the cupcakes from our old bakery.

Inside me, a curious war was breaking out. My business brain admired his thinking. Bookshops were popular, and teaming them with a café so people could choose a book over a coffee and cake was an excellent move. And putting them in iconic locations, with a high-tourist footfall? Yep. The sort of thing I might have done, in fact.

My heart, on the other hand, was screaming inside my chest. Throwing itself against my ribs in a tantrum of 'that should have been me! *We* should have been doing that together! Planning and designing and decorating and working on special recipes, recruiting the bakery staff, and… and… there should have been so much more.' I let the phone drop and tipped my head forward so it rested on my knees, the sense of loss wrapping itself around me again. Why had I looked? Why couldn't I just let it go? I'd done my best, trusted the wrong man and now, through no fault of my own, I was here. *Not your fault. It's not your fault. You couldn't have done anything...*

And to think, just a few minutes ago, I'd been feeling relaxed. Nothing relaxed about me now. Both hands were closed into fists filled with gritty sand, my back and shoulders were rigid and there was the beginning of a headache just knocking against the base of my skull. *It really is over.* All those late-night fantasies I'd had of Noah getting in touch to say how he couldn't manage the business without me, how he needed my input, my imagination, my skills, how he'd learned his lesson and it would all be different now – not ever going to happen. As, secretly, I'd known it wouldn't. But there's knowing and *knowing* and, picking up my phone again and looking at the picture of the shepherd's hut which the *FT* had chosen to print to illustrate the article, now I really *knew.*

All right, that was over. Time to give myself some of the advice that I had been more used to handing out. Let it go, move on. Towards a new initiative, a new goal. Only I didn't have one. I was aimless and drifting. OK, so choose a goal then. What did I have that I could put my time and effort into?

A quick glance across at the bins showed me that Brian was carrying a lump of seaweed around in his mouth, with the proud look of a dog that's found treasure. Yep, there wasn't a lot of time and effort I could put in to Brian; Crufts was out of the question and so, it seemed, was basic obedience and anyway *he wasn't my dog!* So. What *did* I have? My brain tiptoed around the question for a moment and then tentatively looked in the direction of my current 'employment', whereupon it whirled away like a skittish horse coming upon a plastic bag in a hedge. No. Not that either. That was just… temporary. Yes, temporary. The van? I could clean it, I supposed. Maybe wash off some of the salt that was settling in the nooks and crannies. Paint some 'feel good' slogans on the outside: 'Live, Laugh, Love' – well, one out of three wasn't bad, but I wasn't exactly an advert for aspirational mottoes, was I? And there wasn't enough room on the van for 'Survive, Argue, Scrape Dog Poo off the Steps'.

My mind freewheeled. I could almost hear the cogs coming loose and spinning, unregulated. *I can't do this.* Can't live this life with no future, no hope, no purpose. I'd been aiming myself towards my own business since I was about fifteen – drawing designs on bits of paper, shutting myself in and studying rather than staying up all night with pizza and cheap wine with All Saints in the background and friends with crazy-coloured hair.

I let my eyes unfocus and stare out across the darkening sea. I was drifting, that was the problem, and I didn't *do* drifting. I did purpose and spreadsheets and business plans, and my brain just didn't know what it was supposed to be doing with itself; it needed a spotlight to head towards. What could I put my energies into? Yep, still not Brian, whose energetic digging and nosing in the sand as he buried the clearly treasured piece of seaweed, was putting me to shame… I picked my phone up again. Might as well check out my current employer, keep my mind in the here and now and stop it dropping back into the hole that was the past.

So I googled 'Davin O Riordan'.

'Bloody hell.' There were a *lot* of pages. And a lot of images too. The thumbnails showed shots of Davin in costume, presumably for *Watch Tower*, some smiling that smile that lit up his eyes and most of the surrounding landmass. A couple of him looking serious in a suit. And then a load of headings. I picked one and clicked it, to be told by a site called 'StarWatch' about Davin signing to play second lead in *Watch Tower*, after a successful career in modelling.

Modelling. Well, that figured. Also chimed with the many, many images of him.

I went to Wiki, which seemed to be the only page to actually tell me anything about Davin other than his agent's name, and read his details. Born in Cork (parents not named), right in the middle of nine brothers, he'd been signed up to a modelling agency after being spotted in a Dublin street. Three years ago he'd moved into acting and, after the obligatory appearances in *Doctors* and *Midsomer Murders*, he'd had a supporting role in a murder drama and had been snapped up for *Watch Tower*, to play Matt Connor, one of the coastguards. Name linked with lots of eligible women, mostly models and actresses whose profiles were as high as their hemlines. And then more pictures. The internet really seemed to like pictures of Davin. There were obvious fan-pictures, taken from the top of the cliff, of filming on the shore, that must have been taken earlier in the season when the rest of the cast were there. Publicity shots for the series, of Davin and Larch and other cast members, scenes from *Watch Tower*, and then pictures that must be from his modelling career of Davin looking moody in various locations and, occasionally, sunglasses.

I was so engrossed that I had a horrible hallucinatory moment when I heard his voice and thought, somehow, that they'd managed to get sound on Wikipedia.

'Where did you go to?'

I pulled myself together and gathered all my sarcasm. 'Well, I've always loved Paris at this time of year, thought I'd pop over, have a bit of a holiday.'

Brian gave a bark of joy as he noticed Davin and tore over to greet him, shedding sand and bits of chewed seaweed as he came. 'No need to be like that now. I just wanted to be sure you were OK with taking the job. I realise I sprang it on you a bit there, so.'

He was standing in front of me, shadowed in the half light, so I couldn't really see his face. 'Did you walk around the headland?' I asked, sounding brittle, even to myself.

'Well I didn't fly now, did I?' To my astonishment he held out a hand. 'Come on.'

I stared at his hand as though it was made out of cheese. 'What?'

'I got the people to send through a contract for you. You can sign it now, then we're all legal, y'know?'

'You came all the way round the headland just to get me to sign a contract? I could have done that tomorrow.' Or never. I still hadn't made a decision; would it be better to be employed by Davin or to hit the road and take my chances? I mean, yes, employment would be good, but, well, Davin.

'I thought you needed money.' He still had his hand stuck out in front of him. I reluctantly took it and he pulled me to my feet so suddenly that I trod on Brian in my attempt not to crash into him. Brian yelped piteously. 'And your man here is fine. You only stepped on his seaweed, he's exaggerating.'

'Of course I need money, *everyone* needs money. I'm just not quite sure I want to earn mine by doing whatever it is you want me to do.' I realised that I was standing very close to him and took a step back. Brian yelped again. 'And take that horrible stuff somewhere else.'

Davin looked at the brown envelope in his non-pulling-me-up hand. 'OK, just asking! Thought it might be a good chance for us to get together and work out what to do with this place – thinking you don't want Karen of the divine calamari and your man out on the street. But you don't, that's fine.'

'I was talking to Brian just then.'

'Oh.'

We stood in a semi-embarrassed silence for a moment. Brian eventually stood on my foot and rubbed his sandy eyebrows against my jeans. 'Well, I'm not going to sign it without reading it first,' I said at last.

'What?'

'The contract. I need to read through it. For all I know you've put clauses in about scrubbing your back in the bath and only speaking to you through a third party.'

Davin dragged his eyes up from where he was watching Brian's attempts to redistribute the beach over my trousers. 'I don't... do they put things like that in contracts?'

'You might be a special case.'

Behind us the headlights of a car swept into the car park and stopped. There were voices and doors opening and closing and I made out the excited tones of Rory, barely pausing for breath as he regaled someone with tales from the cable-winding department. It must be Neil bringing Karen back to check over the café before she went home. 'Why don't you ask Neil for a lift back?'

An expression that I couldn't read crossed Davin's face. 'Ah, that's a good idea now.'

'I'll take a read of the contract tonight and get back to you tomorrow if I've got any questions. Or give me the number of your office and I'll go direct to them.'

'Ah, tomorrow's fine.'

Another silence. Lights went on in the café.

'Are you going to give it to me then?'

Davin did a huge double take 'What are we talking about now?'

I snorted. 'The contract. Only I don't expect Neil is going to hang about forever,' although the car headlights had gone out and there were no engine starting noises and I suspected that Neil was in the café stuffing his face with whatever pastries Mags had left, 'and the tide's turning so you can't walk back.'

'Ah. The contract. Yes.' His hand came up and the brown envelope was unceremoniously poked at me, then he turned and started to walk around the building towards the café doors. I came too and he stopped walking after a few strides. 'Why are you following me?'

'I'm not. I'm going in to the café to talk to Karen. We're both just walking in the same direction. Why *would* I be following you?'

He stood, tall and slender, shoulders filling out a black Barbour jacket nicely, long legs in jeans that looked ordinary but probably cost a couple of hundred pounds a leg, with his hair gently moving on his collar in the wind and his cheekbones slicing the night into hours. I mentally kicked myself. Davin was the sort of man who'd be followed by women if he went into the Gents toilet. They wouldn't need a reason. He *was* the reason.

'I've no idea,' he said, tersely. 'Maybe you want to knock me over the head and bury me under the dunes.'

'Mmmm, it's a thought.' And then I carried on walking, which meant *he* was following *me* as we trudged up the concrete approach and in through the café door.

The light and warmth made my eyes widen and I had to blink several times. Karen looked up from a critical appraisal of the counter. 'Hi Tansy. Mags wouldn't know the right end of a good clean down if the other end was biting her jacksie, but she's done a right proper job of those apricot pastries.' Then she saw Davin behind me. 'Oh, it's the Attraction. Saw you filming this afternoon, Davin, with that there Larch. Looked right romantic, you did. But that was a lot of toing and froing with Keenan reading you the script – you could have done with a hand.'

Davin inclined his head in acknowledgement and I was slightly appalled by the fact that a wave of proprietorial interest crested over me and crashed to the sandy floor in front of me. If anyone was going to be watching Davin being romantic, it should be me! And then I strangled the feeling, realising that it wasn't starry-eyed tendencies but a recognition that I'd walked off a potential job. He needed an assistant. I was going to have to be it. The brown envelope wobbled in my hand, probably under a weight of clauses, sub-clauses and punitive small print, and I had to fight with myself not to whip out a pen, sign it there and then and push it back into his hand. The urge was so strong that I had to stare at Rory, who was eating a French baton whilst talking to Neil and stroking Brian's sandy head, just to ground myself.

Neil, hair still on end so maybe it wasn't the headphones, was leaning against the counter with his hands in his pockets, listening to Rory. But his eyes were on Karen.

'So they want me over there to help with the catering for the next few weeks at least,' she was saying. 'And the money will be a help, I can put a bit away to help with…' she threw a glance at Rory, who was spraying crumbs as he used both hands to demonstrate how he'd done something, 'unexpected expenses. There's always bills in the New Year. And I can pimp up Christmas.'

'Can I get a lift back, Neil?' Davin asked. 'Tide's up.'

'Sure. I'll… errr… I'll be over in the morning to pick you up, Karen? And I'll have a think about talking to your school, Rory. You're right; there's not enough careers advice these days, and we always need more people coming into the industry.'

Rory beamed. Karen nodded, then grabbed a bag from under the counter. 'Here. Take a few of these – not as good as mine, of course, but you need building up a bit, out there on that beach in the cold wind. Share them with Davin.' She filled the bag with pastries and handed it over to Neil, who was the last man I would have said needed 'building up'. He looked like a python in chinos. 'And can you drop Rory at the house on the way? I'll be over later. I need to check the kitchen first.'

The three men, already with their hands in the pastry bag, headed out of the door. I don't think Rory had stopped talking the whole time. There were clearly new potentials in his future, ones that didn't have anything to do with a lifetime to be spent in the catering industry, and the sound of horizons being widened ran underneath all his words. Karen walked around dragging her finger across surfaces, until we heard the car drive out of the car park and away up the hill, when she collapsed into a chair.

'Well,' she said. 'D'you know, I've had two congratulations on my son, loads of compliments on my cooking and a kiss from that there Neil. They're a nice bunch, them London types, aren't they?'

I sat opposite her. 'I take it you haven't met Larch yet then.'

'She was eating sprouted wheatgrass or something in her trailer. Girl looks like she needs someone to force feed her a fruit cake if you ask me.' Then she sighed and looked around at the wood-lined walls. ''S only temporary though, isn't it. Just a little hole where something good happens in all the rest of the rubbish. Won't help with this place; just a bit of breathing space.'

'Could you not go into the catering business? Maybe join up with the actual caterers and get a job with them?'

Karen lifted an eyebrow at me. 'And they'll pay enough for a place in London, will they? And with Rory about to go into his last year at school... he doesn't want moving about; he's only just got the hang of fractions.' She leaned forward. 'Like I said, nice bit of breathing space. Nothing permanent.'

Yep, that's my life at the moment... nothing permanent.

'Rory's been on about going to Exeter to do an apprentice-ship,' I said. 'So maybe moving to Exeter wouldn't be so bad.'

'He's *fourteen*. He's got to finish school first, or at least be six-teen, and if the café's not there – what do I do for money in between times? Or do I move now, run the risk of Rore blowing off all the exams, not getting an apprenticeship and having to live with me till he's forty and we're both wearing those old-people shoes that lace up and go all over at the sides!' Karen put her face in her hands. 'Kids. I tell you, Tansy, they should give you a bloody manual when they hand you the baby.' She sighed and raised her head to look around the wood-panelled interior, dark now that the light had completely gone from the sky. She'd put a little silver tinsel tree on the counter, and there was something about its cheerful gleam in the overhead lights that made her pre-dicament feel all the sadder. Brian scratched himself energetically under the table with a noise like a blanket being shaken.

'It's just all going round in circles, isn't it? Stay, go, chance what future I might have for something else – it's not even me I'm worried about, I'm a survivor. But Rore, well, this here place doesn't exactly get you ready for a life on the street.'

'Neil's nice,' I said, to change the subject. She was right; we were just circling round, no nearer solving anything, but a little bit nearer the drain every time.

Karen brightened. 'He is, isn't he? But, you know, Rory's dad was nice first up. Got to be, I suppose: not many women as will go with a bloke that says "you know I beat up women and steal from their purses" as a chat up line.'

'Men. Can't live with them, can't kill them and throw them in the sea.'

She gave me a very direct look. I realised that Karen probably wasn't as old as my brain had pigeonholed her. For some reason, maybe her having a teenage son, I'd sort of put her in the 'mother' category and, as none of my friends had had children, I'd pushed her forward a generation, to hover somewhere in the limbo between my own parents and me. She'd practically got a flashing sign that said 'favourite aunt' over her head. And the creases of worry between her eyes and round her mouth gave her a few more years, although she could be within five years of my age, if she'd had Rory young. 'I'm realistic,' she said. 'You come to it, when you come up tough. Being a single mum, paying all the bills without help, makes you realise it's nice to have a man about the place. As long as he's the right man.'

And I wondered how she saw me. She knew I had no money – well, that was obvious to anyone who saw the camper van. Nobody but the most holiday-deprived would choose to spend any time in a metal bucket with windows, but there was a huge gulf between my 'no money' and hers. Mine was, hopefully, temporary. I was just killing time here, licking my wounds; for all my wallowing in needing to earn money I knew I had the skills, the qualifications and the contacts to get myself back into the world of business. It was only the confidence I was lacking right now. That and a huge dose of not wanting to ever be in the same pool as sharks like Noah. But there were other pools I could swim in, and I knew it. Karen didn't have that choice. She wasn't cosmetically hard up, this was her *forever*. I could go home to my parents or my sister. She had nobody but Rory and a desperate need to do what was right for him.

I said, slightly desperately, 'I'm thinking about ways to save this place. Even *Davin*, God help us, is thinking about it. We'll find something.'

And that was why I was going to work for Davin, I suddenly rationalised. Earning some money whilst staying put to help out Karen, who had helped me out when I most needed it. And to have somewhere to celebrate Christmas, people to celebrate it with… yes, that was it, of course it was.

Karen patted my arm and sighed. 'Thanks, Tansy.' Then her chair scraped back. 'Better get on back before Rore eats the cat food. I ought to check in that Mags is OK to do the café while I'm over that there Landle Bay. Think she'll be glad of the pay; her lad works up to Lyme in the brewery but there's always room for more money. She's got a grandchild on the way too.'

Karen had the slightly disconcerting habit of talking to me about people I'd never met as though I knew them. So I didn't know whether or not to be sympathetic to Mags' having a grandchild on the way or overjoyed. I just muttered, which she could take as anything.

'Right. I'll give the rest of these pastries to you then. Mags has been baking fit to bust and they won't keep.'

'Karen, I don't need any food. I ate with the crew earlier.'

Even through the darkness I could feel her expression as it measured the gulf between us. 'Never turn down good food, my girl. These'll be good for a couple of days and you can always give them to Brian. Now, off you pop and let me lock up.'

I walked back to the camper van, the brown envelope stuffed under my jacket against the splinters of wind that sprang off the sea and Brian gallivanting through the sand in front of me.

Inside, I lit the lamp and changed for bed before I started reading through the small print.

Chapter Eight

The next day I didn't go over to the site. I texted Keenan to say I was reading through Davin's contract – which wasn't altogether a lie, but I'd finished reading it whilst lying in bed with Brian on my feet. There was absolutely nothing in there that shouldn't be – apart from the fact that he'd left the name of his previous assistant in, so I knew she was called Ruby Williams, and I'd amended it in biro – and I took Brian for a walk.

A sea mist had come in overnight and rubbed out the view, so it was like looking at the world through tracing paper. Waves pottered up the sand and then scurried back to the safety of the rest of the water as Brian nosed along and the seagulls wheeled overhead, screaming. My mind had gone pretty much as blank as the view: anything immediate and close was in focus, so I was amused by Brian digging and distracted by the smell of salty spray and damp grass, but anything further away was invisible. So my thoughts skittered away from what Noah had made of my business and from having to assist Davin, whatever that meant. Nothing existed right now except the damp grey that pressed against my cheeks, and the little shades-of-brown-and-black dog with the tail like a hairy comma.

We walked along the dunes and up a muddy track that led to a narrow lane which, in turn, led to a footpath and, before

I knew it, I was climbing up a steep chalk rise over crew-cut grass. Brian bobbed about beside me, clearly anxious at leaving his natural habitat of rotting seaweed and seagull poo, but distracted occasionally by rabbit holes and dead things in hedges. We broke through the mist to meet a bright sun in a crystal sky. The air was glassy clear up here, cold and faceted, and whichever way I turned all I could see was a bowl of fog, with distant glimmers that told me that the sea was out there somewhere.

It was beautiful. I mean, I couldn't see much of it, but what I could see was green and blue and white, a Rothko painting, with the edges all blurred. The freezing air stung my nose and the tips of my fingers and I could feel the urge for a clotted cream tea welling up inside me. Forget cafés on the beach – up here would be the perfect place for a little tea hut: a few seats spread across the flat top to the hill, a choice of Earl Grey or Darjeeling and freshly baked scones scenting the air with hot flour and fresh jam...

Only that was then. I didn't do that now. And, besides – I turned a small circle, watching the way the mist rolled and broke against the sides of the hill like an invading monster that just couldn't quite gain entry – did this place really need crowds of people drinking tea? Wasn't there something to be said for this vast empty space?

Brian gave a joyful bark and vanished down the hill, swallowed by the fog monster, but his yaps echoed back up towards me and were joined by another series of barks. Oh, great. Brian had kidnapped himself a friend. And then, toiling upwards towards me, I saw the unmistakable duffel coat of Davin.

I toyed with the idea of ducking down, hiding in the fog, but the presence of Brian, who shot back out into the circle of sunlight followed by Seelie as a silver flash weaving in and out of the mist, would have given me away in an instant. So I tucked my hands into my pockets, ignored the droplets that were crystallising on my hair and cheeks, and waited for him to reach me.

He had his hood up against the damp, so it was like playing grandmother's footsteps with a monk, as I half turned my shoulders and pretended not to have noticed him struggling up the grass slope towards me. When he got close enough that I could speak to him without shouting, I said, 'Are you following me?'

He stopped, panted, and said, 'Following, no. Walking behind you.'

'That *is* following!'

'Are you always this paranoid?'

I opened my mouth to retort and then realised that he had something of a point. 'So, why are you here?'

Seelie ran over and laid her head against my leg. I fussed her ears, so Brian came and leaned against my other leg. I just smiled down at him. I didn't stroke him because I didn't want typhoid.

'Walking my dog, so.'

'Out of the millions of hectares of Dorset available to you, you choose the very square metre that I am standing on?'

He did the 'sideways nod' thing, acknowledging my words but not replying. Then he flung back his hood and you could have told the time by the shadow cast by his gnomon-like cheekbones. 'Keenan said you weren't coming on site today.'

'Yes. I wanted to go through the contract, and I need peace and quiet to record that script for you, so there didn't seem to be any point.'

'Not avoiding me then?'

I looked sarcastically at the metre and a half space between us. 'That is clearly an impossibility.' Seelie yipped off, nosing through the grass and back into the mist. Brian sat damply on my foot. 'Have you got your prescription?'

Davin widened his eyes. 'My *what*?'

'For your glasses. If you've got your prescription, I could take it to the nearest optician and get you a new pair made up.'

'Glasses?'

'Look, if you're just going to repeat everything I say, why don't you go away and leave me to have this conversation by myself? I came up here for a bit of space and now it's like having a mobile conversation via satellite and all I can hear is my own words bouncing back at me.'

He raised an eyebrow. 'Are you after signing the contract?'

'You mean, am I going to be your assistant? Well, seeing as I'd like to get paid to find a way to sort out Karen and the café, I suppose I am.'

'You signed the non-disclosure.'

'This non-disclosure is beginning to assume mythic proportions,' I said, darkly.

He gave me a smile. It looked genuine, a proper, friendly, approachable smile that drove the fog a few feet further back and fried the dew onto the grass blades. I was not fooled. 'And you can stop doing that. I don't know about all your other assistants, but I'm not going to swoon at your feet and let you step all over me just because you look good in a costume.'

'Now, no need to be prickly,' Davin said, comfortably.

'And why do you need an assistant anyway? There's people on set who dress you and do your washing and cook for you and tell you what to say and where to stand – there's not much that you do that I can assist you *with*, unless you need someone to help you pee and I am *not* doing that, unless it involves sticking a plastic tube somewhere painful.'

He raised his eyebrows. The comfortable look had dropped a few centimetres. 'If you must know, I want to buy a house, up at that village there. Where we're going to be filming. And I want someone to help me.'

'Don't you have people? Back in London I mean? Like your agent and financial people and accountants and things? People who would all be far more qualified to help you with property than I am?'

There was the merest hint of something behind those dark eyes. 'Maybe. But they aren't here now, are they?'

'So why don't you just email them for advice and take it from there.'

He stopped smiling altogether and there was an edginess about him. 'I don't want to. I need someone here.' He dropped his eyes. 'Seelie. Over here.'

The little blue dog materialised back out of the mist and came to his side, where he bent down and stroked her face. She preened, half closing her eyes in pleasure at his touch and I wondered how a dog so obedient could be so wilfully destructive, chewing his script and… his… glasses…

Oh my god.

The air was suddenly a solid thing around me as I looked at him. His head was averted. He'd given me all the pieces. Told me without telling me. And, from his body language, he was hoping I'd put it all together without him having to actually come out and say the words.

But I said them anyway. 'Davin, you can't read, can you?'

He didn't move an inch. Stayed bent over his dog, but his hands were immobile on her coat.

Beyond our bowl of mist, the world was silent, taking in the enormity of my words and what they implied.

'How the hell have you got away with it so far? Oh, you had Ruby from your agency. So, who knows then? Your agent, Kee – does Kee know? What happened? How did you get through school, exams?'

'I don't have any exams.' Davin spoke very quietly. He dropped to one knee and rested his face on Seelie's head. Somehow it didn't look posey any more; he looked strangely vulnerable, bent in front of me, cupping the little dog's face in his hands and hiding in her short fur. 'My agent knows. That's why they send Ruby along to help. No one else knows.' Then he raised his face and looked at me, gravely. 'You know now.'

'And you thought I'd use that? That's why I had to sign all those non-disclosure things? And this contract? All because, what, you thought I'd go straight to the papers?' There was a heat of pre-emptive embarrassment rising in my cheeks. Was that how he saw me?

'That's a lot of questions there, Tansy.'

'Because I am feeling massively insulted that you would even consider that I would do such a thing,' I said, indignantly.

'What with you being so nice and reasonable and pleasant towards me and all, it never crossed my mind.' There was a hint of a smile about him now. Almost a look of relief, a lightening of his shoulders. Seelie's tail was beginning to wag, side to side, sweeping the damp droplets from the grass in a spray of enthusiasm. 'But you're right. And.' He stopped talking. The tail stopped moving.

'And? Oh, listen to me, now I'm doing the echo thing, and it's bloody annoying from this side too.'

'And I need no one to know.' The vulnerability was in his voice now.

'Davin –' I started to speak but realised I hadn't really got any idea what I was going to say. I decided to copy him and use the dog to deflect attention, so I crouched down next to Brian, who raised his furry eyebrows at me and then licked my cheek. 'Urgh. That was unnecessary.'

'I'm not stupid, y'know.' Davin was back to stroking Seelie; when I glanced at him I could see him furiously concentrating on pulling some burrs from her chest fur, fingers working mechanically through her coat. 'I can't not read because I'm thick.'

'Of course not.' My fingers jammed in Brian's coat. It was a mixture of old hair, undergrowth and an industrial greasing agent by the feel of it. 'But it must make life hard for you.'

'Harder hiding it than it is living with it.' He pulled a few green balls and flicked them away. 'Had a lifetime to practise that. But Da moved us around; he worked the farms and we went where the work was so school was a bit – hit and miss and we were never anywhere for long enough for – ach, never mind. Doesn't matter.'

I stopped trying to pet Brian. It was like trying to befriend an enthusiastic oil slick. 'What about your mum?'

'She moved out to Dublin. By that time Teague and Patrick had left home, so Niall, Killian and I stayed with Da and she took the young ones with her. Got them all into a good school.' He threw me another one of those looks. 'So they can read and all, y'know.'

I thought of him sitting in the back of the car, arms folded. 'No wonder you were so shitty when I asked you to help with map reading.'

He twitched the last green ball from Seelie's thin fur. 'Ah, and there's more column inches for you if you're a bit of a likely lad an' all. Nice guys come on page eleven, no headshots. They can write whole articles on why you can't keep a relationship and why you're hard to work with; there's nothing in it for them if you're just nice to everyone.'

Then I remembered him freeing the sheep from the wire fence and his insistence on finding out what was wrong with Rory. 'So, the big secret with you is that you're really a nice guy? That the sulky pain-in-the-arse thing is all an act to get you more publicity?'

Davin sighed and raised his head. A few last beads of mist still hung on the carefully cultivated stubble that darkened his cheeks and chin as though he was created from the weather around us. Solid and brooding as the clouds that hung above the sea and as changeable as the air. 'Were you just listening back then? My big secret is that I can't read. Whether I'm nice or not doesn't fecking matter. I say words and walk up and down a bit and call it a job.'

He'd stopped being Davin O'Riordan, star of *Watch Tower*, scourge of the set and focus of the vision of a huge number of women who would all tear him to pieces at the first opportunity. Now he was just a bloke, forced to be honest and slightly humiliated in front of a woman he barely knew. It wouldn't be true to say I felt sorry for him – I mean, scourge of the set and women and everything – but I did have a hot rising of pity in my chest. 'How the hell have you got by this far?'

He shrugged and the beads of mist coruscated along the shoulders of his coat. 'It was all right when I was modelling. Didn't want to go into the acting yoke, but my agent – they think I need to move on. Getting older, y'know?' A snorted laugh. 'And now I'm just a shit so nobody dares ask me anything. Ruby reads me anything I need to know and records my script, so.'

Seelie, freed now from his touch, looked into his face and then leaped away, bounding through the grass with the sun making her fur a greyish smear. Brian gave my cheek another lick and joined her. 'What's the gestation for whippets?' I asked, more to swing the subject away and give him a chance to lose the expression on his face that made him look like a nine-year-old boy who expects his mother to send him to bed early for stealing sweets.

'Nine weeks.' His response was so prompt that I wondered if he'd already looked it up on Google, and then gave myself a mental slap. *He can't google anything. How much of a problem is that?* He must have caught my expression because he said, very matter-of-factly, 'We bred dogs. Collies and then later whippets too. Great rabbit dogs and you can't beat a decent lurcher around the place.' A glance to where Seelie was scrabbling in the chalky soil, with a dedicated Brian watching her. 'She's the last of the family line. Da went out of whippets; he's got sheepdogs again now.'

Overhead, the sunlight's acidic gleam was cut by a rolling cloud that sandwiched us between the lower fog bank and an encroaching grey sky. 'We ought to go down. They'll be missing you on set.'

'Nah. Kee's got Larch to deal with. Doing some pick-ups of her in her cottage, and it's over Bridport way so they don't want me.' A quick flick of a glance. 'That's why I brought Seelie up on the hill. Change of scenery and getting away from a set full of people who think I'm a pain in the arse.'

'You could try being nice. For a change.' I started to walk down the hill, hoping that Brian wouldn't show me up by refusing to follow.

'Ah, and they wouldn't know what to do if I was nice. They'd think I'd got a brain tumour or something.'

'You're being nice now.'

He gave me a grin. 'Maybe I have got a brain tumour.'

We walked down the hill with our dogs running ahead of us, back into the fog bank. I wondered, as we went, what it had cost him to tell me what he had. Wondered how much of his smile was real and how much was acting to cover up the embarrassment and pain. How much of Davin was shell, something to hide behind to keep himself, his secret, hidden?

I watched Davin out of the corner of my eye. He'd slipped back into his moody actor persona as easily as he had slipped back into the fog, hands in pockets and hood covering his head. The only spot of brightness about him now was his expression when he looked at Seelie; his mouth lifted a little and his dark eyes burned a track through the mist. It made me wonder about my own shell, the little carapace of protection I was keeping in my turn.

Davin – 1999

'Shit! Shitshitshitshit!' Teague came barrelling into the room he shared with Davin. Dav was lying on the bed, kicking the wall, in a dreamlike state. 'Get up, you feckin' bastard. It's all going to hell out here.'

'What?' Davin swung his legs down, taking his time. Teague was given to dramatic outbursts and catastrophising; he'd once run away when his dog had got lost bringing some cows down into the home pasture. 'Highly strung' Mam called him. The brothers had another word for it, but they kept it to themselves, because Teague was pretty handy with his fists, as well as his tongue.

'It's Mam. She's gone.'

And with those words Teague destroyed Davin's world. OK, it hadn't been a perfect world – it had eight brothers in for a start, the youngest only a matter of weeks old now. But it was a comfortable world, steady, the boys out on the farm with Da, or working other local farms, like Patrick, coming home to rabbit stew and fresh bread smells, and the noise and chatter and crying of the babbies and the dogs fighting over scraps. But now…

'How? How can she be gone?' Davin reached down and felt the soft fur of Rook under his hand. The dog was, as usual, sitting at his feet. 'Where? And what about Turlough; she can't have left him, so. He's still on milk.'

'She's taken the young ones. She left a note. I just found it down on the table. Shit, Dav, what do we do? What do I say to Da? He's still out in the top field, with the hay turner, he won't know… shitshitshit.' Teague turned terrified brown eyes to his younger brother. 'What are we going to do, Dav?'

I'm fourteen! Davin wanted to shout. *Don't ask me! I've only just discovered that I fancy Britney Spears and that I really hate cabbage! How the feck am I supposed to know what to do?* 'Can we not get Patrick?' Davin suggested cautiously. 'He might know what we do now. He's a grown man, he'll know about these things. But, are you sure she's gone, Teague? I mean, not just to the shops and all?'

Teague fumbled in the pocket of his worn overalls. 'Here. Read it.' He shoved a folded piece of paper, torn from one of the notebooks that Mam used to write shopping lists and other things she needed to remember, towards Dav. Davin just stared at him. 'Oh, yeah, feck, sorry man. Look, I'll read it to you.'

> 'My darlings.
> I am so, so sorry. I can't live like this any more. I'm taking Finn, Lor, Carrig and the baby, we're going to Dublin. I've found a house there, and the boys can go to school and I can have some kind of life. When I've got the house done properly you can come and stay and decide where you want to live. Ciaran, I still love you, but this is no kind of life.
> Remember, I love you all more than life itself.
> Mam'

Davin sat, feeling the world changing around him. That 'taken for granted' world, where Mam and Da argued, Da drank in the pub every evening and took tractors to pieces for fun, where the boys smoked and drank and swore when Mam wasn't around. Where evenings in front of the little TV, once the beasts were fed and bedded and the final round of the yard had been done, were the highlight of his life. Where he and Rook, up on the high hills, felt as though they could take on the world. That had all gone.

He felt the tears come into his eyes and didn't know how Teague would react if he let them fall.

'What do we do, Dav?' Teague's eyes were suspiciously red themselves. 'I mean… *what the feck do we do?*'

Davin's hand felt the reassuring warmth of the collie's head. They'd been supposed to be up checking the tups in the high pasture, but he'd dipped out to lie in the quiet of the house for a while. He'd been lying here, while Mam packed… his fingers tightened on the striped fur. 'Ah, we need to fetch Patrick down. He's up at *Coill na Sidhe* today, isn't he, planting potatoes? Take the car and go get him, he can talk to Da.'

Teague seemed grateful not to have to think. 'Sure, you're right, Dav. Patrick will know what to do. Will you tell Killian?'

Davin nodded and slowly got off the bed. 'He was down sorting out the pig arks. I'll go over there now, you go down the valley.' Being practical. Sorting things out. And all the while his brain was screaming at him, *She's left you. Mam has gone and left you…*

Chapter Nine

I might not have been in Dorset long, but living with nothing between me and the elements but a thin skin of metal and a fleecy blanket was giving me a crash course in weather forecasting. There was something about the slow, reluctant sunrise through a rag-rolled red sky the next morning that told me today was going to be uncomfortably precipitous and, feeling sorry for Brian even with his fur coat, I put him in the back of the car for the drive to Landle Bay. I'd got the dictaphone, with Davin's script additions recorded as clearly as I could – I'd sometimes had to re-record for being drowned out by seagulls, or Brian's sudden barks or, in one case, some fairly extreme swearing on my part when I'd dropped the script in my cup of tea. I might not *want* to be Davin's assistant, but, by God, I was going to be the best assistant I could be while I was not wanting to do it.

Why can't I just do a half-arsed job? I mean, money, yes, obviously, but it's a bit like I am physically incapable of being a bit 'meh'. I looked over at the café, one light shining across the car park from the back showed that Mags was already in and firing up the ovens for a probably deserted shift. Someone – Karen? Rory? – had strung some coloured lights up across the window, so the beaten sand was tattooed with lurid colours in the just breaking dawn light. *I'm a perfectionist. A perfectionist whose perfection has been ruined, so what does that make me now?*

The sea was a grey, flat disc of mercury behind us as I drove up the track and onto the little road that led to Landle over the top of the cliff, but I was hardly aware of any of it. My brain was firing me from my own personality type and I was suffering.

I'd *always* been driven to succeed. Having two high-achieving parents, it was always assumed that my sister and I would do well and she had. She'd gone into medical research, married another researcher and had a happy, orderly married life. They had a house, holidays and job satisfaction, all within the contained environment of the laboratory – well, they didn't actually *live* in the laboratory, or go on holiday there, although they were both so devoted to their work that a fortnight on the centrifuge was probably their idea of heaven – but their lives certainly centred on their work.

And so had mine. My own business. My name on the cupcake boxes. 'Tansycakes' was actually a *thing*! People asked for them for birthdays! I was a fucking *brand*! And now – with the car windscreen freezing up as we drove along because I didn't know which button was the heated window one and when I pressed the most likely square symbol with a line through it the back window had opened and Brian had let out a squeal of protest – what was I?

The unwilling owner of a hairy dog, the unwilling assistant of a grumpy Irishman, the unwilling occupant of a cold van on a beach. I felt a little bit as though my life was a skateboard, on which I'd been scooting along, all balanced and freewheeling, everything a smooth forward direction of travel. And suddenly I'd been knocked sideways, the skateboard was still going on but I was clinging to it with my arms flailing and hoping we didn't go under any low railings.

To add verisimilitude to my analogy, the car did a bit of a sideways slip as we hit some ice, then ABS kicked in, the four-wheel drive system did its thing and we continued on our way with nothing more than a slight alteration of course as the car righted itself. Why could my life not do that?

I caught Brian's eye in the mirror. He was sitting behind the fixed guard in the boot, watching me. 'Stop staring at me, it's not my fault the road is a bit icy.' His eyebrows lifted and rearranged themselves. 'I'm not going to crash, don't worry.'

Oh God. The shock was so great that I almost did crash the car. It slithered a bit but regained control by itself. *I'm responsible for Brian. I have another life dependent on me and I...*

I turned the radio on and lots of thundering beats and loud but inaudible lyrics managed to keep me concentrating on the road until we got to the bay.

It was more deserted than usual. In the day that I'd not been here, it seemed that some of the vehicles had left. There were fewer caravans parked up and at least two of the lorries had gone. The catering truck was still a well-lit homely hub though and someone had put tinsel around the windows, giving the effect of a really thick coat of mould. Davin's Winnebago was still there too, parked out on the sand, and, in front of it, Kee and Larch were clearly arguing.

I got out of the car and let Brian jump down into the wind-blown sand. There was an edge to the weather now and the sun had vanished behind an ominous bank of cloud coming at us over the sea.

'Hi Tansy.' Kee seemed distracted, pushing his glasses up his nose and shoving his hands through his already ruffled hair. 'I've not seen Davin yet. Do you want me to knock him up for you?'

'It's OK, I've just brought him…' I stopped. Kee didn't know about Davin and I wasn't about to blow that particular ship out of the water. 'Some things he asked for.'

'We're all going over to Steepleton!' Larch announced brightly. 'To look at the new location. It's over there.' She pointed. 'I went there yesterday; it's very pretty.'

I felt curiously proprietorial on the two counts of Davin and Steepleton. 'Yes, I've been there. And it's OK, Kee, I'll see Davin whenever he drags his personality out of bed. I can't think there's much assisting he can want me to do today.'

'Well, I need him up and out so we can get moving. I want to have a look around the place and make sure that Davin and Larch are happy about filming there.'

'I don't think the words "happy" and "Davin" can be used in the same sentence without the air catching fire,' I said.

There was a tinny sort of whistle and over an intercom an Irish voice said, 'I can hear you, you know.'

A moment's silence and then Larch said, 'It's a bit like if there was a God and he was Irish and a bit cross, isn't it?' which made me laugh and actually like her a little bit.

'Still listening,' came the voice.

'Well stop earwigging and come and open the door then. I've brought your… stuff.' I threw a quick glance at Kee and Larch, who were both showing absolutely no signs of curiosity at all, 'And Kee wants to head over to Steepleton.'

Another moment's silence. Then, 'Kee and Larch can go ahead. You can drive me over, can't you? I want to look at properties on the way anyway and I don't think Larch is up for poking her head into mouldy old houses.'

Keenan shrugged. 'Well, all right. But don't be meandering around the Dorset countryside for too long; we'll lose the light.' And then, to me in a much quieter voice, 'No really, please don't hang about. I can't entertain too much of Larch without distractions; she's trying to get me into homeopathy and I'm running out of excuses.'

I looked out over the little narrow beach. Brian had found Rory and Neil and was trying to get them to throw seaweed for him, but they were both engaged in rolling up cables. 'Why don't you take Rory with you?' I asked. 'He knows all the local landmarks; he can point out places you might like to film.' And then dropping my voice down to Kee's level again. 'Plus his unadulterated hero-worship should keep Larch happy for hours. He doesn't even seem to mind a little light patronising. Which can only be a bonus,' I added, with a sideways look at Larch.

'Good idea. This lot need diluting with some real people.' Kee ran his hands through his hair again.

I also had the idea that Karen might quite like having a chance to get to know Neil a bit better without her son hanging around watching her every move, but wild horses and an attack of plague would never make me admit to *that* ulterior motive.

'Right. So I'll leave Davin to you then.'

'Yes, if you could manage to sound a *bit* less thankful I'd probably be relieved.'

'Hey, this thing is permanently switched on you know.' Davin's voice echoed tinnily again. 'And you lot fighting over who *doesn't* get me is not doing my ego any good.'

'Your ego does not need any encouragement,' I said, tartly. 'You get on, Kee. I'll deal with Brian Boru in there.'

Kee, trailing Larch, headed off across the beach, where the wind was now whipping the sand into ghostly little shapes and the black cloud was obliterating most of the sky. The intercom had gone silent.

'Are you coming then, or what?'

'The need to organise is strong in this one,' came the reply, slightly muffled, so I presumed he was getting dressed.

'You want an assistant. If you want one that *doesn't* organise you, that's called a wife.' My tone was still tart.

'Are you proposing to me now?' The door opened and Seelie burst forth, closely followed by Davin in his duffel coat. 'Sure, and we hardly know each other yet.' While I was still opening and closing my mouth, my brain fumbling for the right words to put him down, he gave me a grin and said, 'Right. Are we away to this Steepleton, then?'

He gave a whistle and Seelie, who had been sniffing around the wheels of the Winnebago, trotted up obediently. I yelled to Brian and, after a few half-hearted attempts to gain entry to the catering van and hide behind Karen's continent-sized lasagne, he came over. It was more the lure of Seelie than any training. I didn't kid myself.

We got into the car, Brian and Seelie in the boot together. 'Worst has already happened,' Davin said, philosophically. 'They might as well get to know each other properly.' I drove us up the precipitous trackway and on to the only slightly bigger and less steep track that led along the clifftops.

A faint sleet began to fall, shrouding us in a stretched circle of grey that the wipers didn't do much about. 'Oh yes, your script recording is here.' I pointed to the glove compartment where I'd put the dictaphone. 'Don't forget it.'

'Now then. And that's you not organising me again, is it?'

I flashed him a quick look. He seemed to be very amused by something; although he wasn't actually smiling there was a light in his eyes that said he might very easily. 'Shut up.'

An acknowledgement with a nod of the head. Then, 'Don't think I didn't notice you shipping your man out. Setting up the lovely Karen with our Neil now, is it?'

'You're very observant,' I said, crisply. I was actually hiding my surprise that he'd seen through what I'd done, and realising that Davin clearly registered a lot more than I suspected. I hadn't even thought he'd noticed any kind of spark between Neil and Karen.

'Think about it for a moment,' Davin said, quietly.

I twisted the car through the bubble of grey that the outside world had become. 'What do you mean?'

He sighed and shoved his hands into the pockets of the duffel coat, half turning away to look out of the window at the slithery colourless world passing by. 'When you're like me, you have to pick up other clues, so.' He spoke with his eyes focused outside the car. 'When you can't do the words, you look to see what other people are doing. There's a sign, other people are avoiding walking on the grass, so *you* don't walk on the grass. It doesn't matter what the sign says, it's what everyone *does* that counts.'

I threw a quick look. 'You're a lot more sensitive than you come across, aren't you?'

'Well, I come across as a sullen arse; it's not so hard to be more sensitive than that. There's slime mould that's more sensitive than I pretend to be.' He sounded, not bitter, but a little bit sad.

'So you pretend not to be sensitive, so nobody realises how decent you really are? Good grief, man, what with that and actually being quite a thoughtful bloke underneath…' I stopped.

'Didn't think you'd noticed.' The almost-smile was back.

'Well, the sheep and you seem to really have a handle on Rory and his life.'

'I was fourteen once, y'know. Around that age when Mam and Da split up, so, yeah, I know a bit about how it feels to maybe lose everything. It's not a great age. You've got floppy hair and a stiff – well, it's just a rough time. Oh, and you turn left just here.'

I'd been about to go speeding past the narrow break in the hedge. 'Are you sure?'

Another sideways nod. 'Tell you, when you can't read you get a really good memory.'

We bumped down the narrow road, past the boys' school and into the spread out community that was Christmas Steepleton. Past the drawn-out beginning to the village and on down to where the houses seemed to huddle together for adhesion to the steep surface. Everything was grey in the sleety fog, but occasional bright windows cheered the gloom and overhead Christmas decorations, strung across the main street, swung in the breeze. I parked where I'd stopped before, right on the front, and we got out.

'Yes,' he said, faintly. 'I need to live here.'

'Why? What's so special about it?' I stared out across the grey, shifting sea.

Davin stood quietly for a second, eyes closed. His shoulders rose and fell and I could hear the rasp of the air as he drew it right down. 'Have you never had that feeling? Y'know, when you're in a place and you just think, "yep, this is it, I'm home"?'

I shook my head and let the sting of the wind from the sea burn my eyes. *Of course I know that feeling. It was the way I used to feel coming home at the end of the day to the flat. Noah sitting playing guitar on the balcony on a summer evening, that dusty smell of old baking and new paintwork that told me this was where I lived. My centre of gravity. Pulling on an old shirt and picking up the paint roller to make a start on the...*

'So why here?'

Davin looked around, at the sea, its surface ripped and boiling. At the boats clanking at anchor in the harbour. And then up across the cliff face and towards the little collection of houses clinging grimly to the road as though midway through an earthquake. 'It reminds me of Ireland,' he said, simply.

There was something about his expression, something almost hopeless, that made my heart squirm. 'Are you homesick?' I asked, quietly.

'Always. But there's nothing there for me now. Just the family, and the boys are all grown up and Mam has a little place in Dublin, so I get over to visit her when I can. Da... yeah, I see Da now and then too. But...' and he tailed off in a shrug that made the toggles on his duffel coat swing and bang on the metal railings.

'There's more to you than meets the eye, isn't there, Davin?' I said, and a strange sense of wistfulness crept over me that I didn't understand. 'Sounds like you don't get to talk about them much.'

'Not good for the image, coming from where I do. Think the publicity people would prefer me to come from aristocracy, some good old Irish family with seven thousand acres of bog and a title that died out in sixteen something.' He still sounded melancholy and his eyes were moving over the whole inland scene as though stroking it and trying to hold it close. 'So I keep it quiet.'

'Thank you for feeling that you can tell me.' My voice was so quiet now that it almost sank under the waves.

'Well, my assistant and all.' He threw his head back and let the wind blow through his hair, which ruffled out like a horse's tail. 'And you signed the non-disclosure, so.' Davin closed his eyes and greeted the wind as though it directly carried memories of Ireland, as though each fragment of the sleety rain was a postcard from Dublin.

Behind us, in the car, Brian gave a peremptory yap and I turned to see his shaggy head pressed next to Seelie's smooth one, both of them sighting on us like a pair of snipers. 'I think we'd better get the dogs out and go and find Kee,' I said, trying to shake off the feeling of despondency that was moving with the breeze by being forthright and active. There was nothing, absolutely nothing, to be gained from dwelling on the past.

Davin just opened the boot. Seelie shot out, curved round the parking spot and then moved to her customary place at his side, pushing her nose into his hand as though looking for reassurance. Or maybe close proximity to Brian had knocked her sense of smell out of kilter and she wanted it back.

Brian poddled out of the boot and I had to grab him to attach his bit of string before he either wandered off into town to bum chips off passers-by or fell into the harbour. 'Right then,' I said, brightly. 'Where first?'

Again Davin's eyes moved over the town. 'Shops.'

'Really? *Shopping*? I thought we'd come to look for houses; well, that and show Larch that the natives of Dorset walk upright and don't turn into anything at full moon.'

Davin had already set out for the little row of shops near the old lifeboat station. 'And who else'll know all the business in the town but someone in the local shop, now?' He spoke over his shoulder. 'And I need some Christmas shopping.'

I almost strangled Brian as I came to a dead stop. Christmas. It could only be a matter of days away now, but I'd lost track. Mum and Dad wouldn't expect a present; they always told me to spend money on enjoying myself, not on them, but Rue and her husband would at least want a card. How had I forgotten?

'Christmas shopping?'

'And now you're with the echo thing again.' Davin sounded amused; all trace of the hollow almost-loneliness that had been in his voice earlier was gone. 'Yes. Are you not after wanting to get Karen and your man a little knick-knack for the shelves, now?'

Oh God, he's right. I've been so absorbed in what I'm doing that I've taken my eye off the ball. Karen wouldn't get much for Christmas, and Rory... well, I had no doubt that Karen would do something for him but I should show my appreciation for what they'd done for me by at least getting some token. I shook my head slowly. *I've been an utter self-absorbed plonker. Here's me calling Davin every name under the sun but he's thought about Christmas presents for people, when I haven't.*

'Er,' I said and followed him up off the car park and along the little road to the shops.

Windows shone with fairy lights, and little lanterns were wound around the railings, unlit at the moment. A couple walked ahead of us and went into the first shop, the man holding the door open for Davin.

'Are you coming in?' he asked. 'I know it smells a bit of *Eau de Auntie Mary* but it's fine really. Are you visiting Christmas Steepleton or are you unfortunately trapped here by a freak weather event – trust me, I know all about those.'

'Shut up, Tobes' the woman said, swinging round just before she entered the shop. 'Honestly. Just hit him with a cushion or something; it normally resets him.'

Davin did his big, famous smile and the woman missed the step into the shop, stumbling across the threshold into a big pile of crocheted rugs. 'We're thinking of filming here. New series, starting in the spring.'

The woman picked herself up, squeaked, 'Thought I recognised you! You're Davin O'Riordan.'

'Steady, Matz,' said "Tobes". 'There was way too much hero-worship in the way you said that and if you're worshipping any heroes round here then one of them had better be me. Or Cthulhu, cos worshipping strange, tentacled sea beasts is probably wise when you live where we do.' He pulled at the woman's hand, she swung around into his embrace and her coat flapped open to show an enormous pregnant belly.

Suddenly the heat of the inside of the shop, combined with the smell from the candles, was too much for me. 'I'm just going to look in some of the other shops,' I said to Davin. 'Catch you up later.'

'Sure,' he said, comfortably. 'Just come by and check I haven't been hero-worshipped to death, will you?'

'You'll be fine.' I closed the door on him, the sickening smell of candles and the couple, and pulled Brian further along the row.

The mix of shops was probably what would be called 'eclectic'. The buildings themselves had a roofline that rose and dipped like a ship's prow in a gale, wind-worn wooden decoration mingled with the clean lines of new infill building, and your eyes could get seasick by ranging along the wobbly line of front doors. There was a general-store-type shop, which, combined with a Post Office, meant that I could send off a card and a jokey little book on Dorset customs for Rue. She'd put it in the downstairs toilet, where they had a bookshelf of 'humour' for anyone who wanted to spend their toilet time profitably, but at least it showed I'd thought of her at this time of year.

Further along the row was an electrical DIY shop, where I bought a massive pair of headphones that I thought Rory might like, and, at the end, a shop selling the sort of women's fashion that you usually only see in old films. An ancient mannequin modelled a brown suit circa 1965 and I was astonished they were still open, but inside proved more modern and I bought a soft, fluffy hooded top for Karen.

Brian accompanied me with fairly good grace, but when we reached the end of the row he refused to turn round and head back towards the car park. Instead he tugged on his hairy string lead and pulled me further along, to where the row of shops petered out into a narrow path, sandwiched between the ever-slumping cliffside and the greedy sea. I found out why fairly shortly; tucked against the cliff and hidden from view by the shops was a little kiosk. It looked as though it had been built in better days for serving ice cream to the strolling masses, but was now a little woodwork shop, with an elderly spaniel lying outside. Brian was very interested in the spaniel, who seemed to have given up on doing much more than guarding the doorway and dribbling.

Whilst the dogs compared dribble, I looked in through the kiosk flap to where an elderly man was scooping at a large piece of tree trunk with something like a long-handled spoon. He noticed me loom in his airspace and looked up. 'Hello,' he said, cheerfully. 'Looking for a Christmas present? It's the only sensible reason that anyone would be here on a day like this – desperation. Oh, calm down, Lily,' he added to the spaniel. 'It's only a… it is a dog, I suppose? It's got a collar on.'

'Yes, that's Brian.' I stuck my head further through the flap, appreciating the smell of sawdust and old wood. 'And yes, it's not really a dog's name.'

'From *Family Guy* I suppose,' said the man, which surprised me because he had the 'dessicated farmer' look of a man who thought that television hadn't been any good since they got rid of the Test Card. 'If you like dogs, you might like these.' He slid open a cabinet and revealed the most beautiful carved model dogs, all arranged on a shelf in various lifelike poses. 'Or is it for someone who hates dogs and should, therefore, not be allowed to live?'

I laughed. 'No, I'm really just browsing…' And then I saw it. Right at the back, behind a gorgeous golden retriever carved in some yellow wood, each and every hair perfectly rendered. 'But can I have a look at that?' I pointed.

The man shrugged. 'If you like. It's not my favourite, can't seem to get the ears right on these.' It was a carving of a sheepdog, in a kind of wood that made the coat look brindled and fine, caught in the act of running, all limbs bunched together conserving energy for the gallop and the face showing an expression of pure delight. Even the ears were perfectly good. I couldn't see his problem.

He fetched it over for me to have a look at and I ran my hands over the smooth wood. It felt warm and firm and somehow alive. Davin had said he used to have sheepdogs… and in the absence of any carved whippets, or a better idea, this would do.

'You wouldn't rather have something like this?' He fetched another model, a Border terrier, square-faced and serious, sitting intently. 'Bit more like your 'un there.'

We both looked down at Brian, who was trying to engage the spaniel's enthusiasm with a bit of dried seaweed. The spaniel had clearly run out of enthusiasm a decade ago and the only part of her moving was her eyebrows as she watched Brian's increasingly desperate attempts.

'I don't think you could make a model of him,' I said. 'There isn't a wood in existence that's that scruffy. But the sheepdog, yes. I'll take it.' I could hardly stop touching the little carving for long enough for the man to wrap it in tissue for me to take away. There was something hypnotic both in the swirls of colour that formed the brindle coat and in the firm smoothness of the wood. It sat against my hand with a velvety coolness, like the top of Seelie's knobbly head.

I paid, wincing slightly, but my card wasn't declined. Maybe Davin had got my payment details from Kee and had already started paying for my 'assistanting'. Or 'buying my silence'?

When Brian had been prised away from the spaniel, who got custody of the seaweed, we turned and went back the way we'd come, to the little row of shops. Davin was standing outside the 'Candle and Outsize Lighthouse Emporium' chatting to the couple and the colourfully dreadlocked girl. They were all laughing, and there was a degree of pointing going on too, all aimed up towards the middle of the town, by the look of it. Looked also as though the hero-worship had been replaced by something a bit more down-to-earth too; nobody was staring at Davin now.

'Toby and Mattie say there's a house for sale just up the road here,' Davin said, as we approached. 'Are you game for having a look?'

'It's not very big,' Thea, dreadlocked and as colourful as a manga character, frowned. 'But then, everywhere over three beds is a B and B out here.'

'Small is good, don't you reckon, Tansy?' Davin using my name made me jump a little bit. I wondered if he'd spun them some tale about us being a couple, although why on earth that would be of benefit to either of us I couldn't imagine. 'Small is what I'm looking for.'

They all gave us directions – not very complicated ones as the entire village seemed to consist of one street – and then with waves and grins and, in the case of Toby, two furtive selfies with Davin, they went on their way. Thea went back into her shop, from where the sound of whale-song was now beginning to echo. I hoped she wasn't putting out a call to Cthulhu.

Davin and I began walking up the hill. 'There's Larch's car.' He pointed to a Land Rover, parked at about as insolent an angle as was possible. If a big wave had come up, it would have taken the back end off. 'She must have driven them over.'

'Blimey, they let that girl have a driving licence?'

He raised his eyebrows at me. 'It's just us thickos that can't pass a driving test. Got to be able to read to get through the theory.'

'Davin, you are not thick. Actually you're –' I had been about to say that he was the most emotionally observant man I'd ever met, but his ego didn't need any encouragement. 'You're not as bad as Larch,' I said, instead.

He grinned at me, a proper grin. 'Ah, and she's not as bad as we all make out. She's a good actress.' And I wasn't sure if he was referring to her performance on-screen or something else. As I knew that he wasn't quite as straightforward as he seemed either, I didn't say anything. 'This is the place.' A 'For Sale' sign hung askew in the tiny, and somewhat weedy, front garden of the little house.

'Any closer to the sea and you'd get your windows washed for free every high tide.'

The cottage was turned through ninety degrees to the rest of the houses on the road, which all stood sideways on to the sea, facing one another across the narrow strip of tarmac. This one faced the sea down in a four-square, defiant kind of way. A small rectangle of garden was walled off at hip height and three steps led up to the gate, which contained the front garden. The place seemed to have been built out of wood, which the wind and spray had stripped of paint, so it stood bleached and bare, the colour of the winter sea.

'Hello you two.' Keenan, coming down the street, halted beside the wall. 'Looking for property?'

'Makes more sense than living in that metal box on wheels for another year if we're going to be filming over this side.'

'Oh, it's sweet!' Larch appeared beside Kee. 'But it's so small! Where will you keep your shoes?'

We all looked down at Davin's perfectly normal-sized feet. 'I suppose I could leave them sticking out the front door,' he said, mildly.

Larch rolled her eyes. 'I have a whole bedroom for my shoes,' she said. 'And a walk-in cupboard for my dresses.'

'Ah, well, my dresses can all bunk up together in the wardrobe, can't they, now,' Davin said, peering through the front window. We all watched him walk right around the little house, which was the approximate size and shape of a box of tissues, two windows upstairs and two downstairs, one either side of the front door. It looked like a house that a five-year-old with a steady hand and an artistic eye might draw, down to the chimney perched in the middle of the roof. 'It's empty,' he announced, completing the circuit. 'Toby said the old lady who lived here died and the estate just want the money.'

Larch gave a very dramatic shiver. 'It's probably haunted,' she said. 'I'm very sensitive to these things; I couldn't ever stay in a house that had spirits.'

'And I'd never invite you,' Davin said, cheerfully. 'Cos you're a fecking lunatic. So that's all right then.'

'Tansy!' It was Rory calling from across the road. 'Look at what I got for Mum!' He was waving a plastic bag which, on closer inspection, proved to hold a box which, in turn, held a silver necklace which said 'Mum' in swirly, italic lettering.

Rory looked at us anxiously. 'Do you think she'll like it?' He flashed the box to each of us. 'I usually just get her chocolate.'

'It's lovely,' I said, although there was a cold draught running down my back. I was sure Karen would love it, even though I couldn't see the point in wearing a necklace that reiterated your role in life. It seemed to me a bit like wearing a badge that said 'I'll be your waitress tonight'. 'Very pretty.'

'Aw, it's sweet.' Keenan turned the box so the silver glinted. 'Very flash.' Even Larch made approving noises and then, to Rory's embarrassment, patted his cheek. It seemed to be embarrassment anyway; his face went pink from his chin to his hair and he turned away to make a business of packing the little box back into the bag.

'So,' Davin said eventually, when it became evident we were all stuck in some kind of 'staring loop'. 'Let's get this place bought then.'

'I don't think it works quite like that,' I said. 'There are land registry searches and surveys and all kinds of things.'

'There's an estate agent up there.' Keenan pointed back up the road. 'I took a quick look. I must admit there's something about this bit of coast, plus I could do with getting out of London now Benoit's gone.'

I looked around suspiciously. 'Is there someone standing on the cliff hypnotising you two? Kee, you love London!'

'Yes, well, I loved Benoit and look how that ended.' Kee sighed. 'Maybe it's time for a change. A complete change. I might meet a lovely Dorset farmer and take to life on the land.'

I gave his casual loafers, skinny jeans and trendy sweatshirt a quick once over. 'Stranger things have happened. Just, not *much* stranger.'

'Living off the land is good for the soul,' put in Larch but, since she was obsessed with designer juices and clothes that obviously didn't keep the cold out, I took no notice. She was actually wearing Kee's coat.

The estate agency was also a teashop. Rory and Kee sat and ate scones with Larch watching them and wondering aloud repeatedly when someone would make kale biscuits. Davin and I made the year of the young man behind the desk by, basically, throwing money at him until he gave in and allowed Davin to rent the place until the proper paperwork was done to let him buy it. I gave all the agreements a quick read through, precised them to Dav very quickly whilst the agent was photocopying, and Davin signed the documents with a firm, steady hand, collected the key and we were done within half an hour. Since it had taken me four months to even be approved to buy my flat, I was impressed at what a famous name, an uncompromising stare and unlimited cash could achieve.

'I'll bring everything over tomorrow,' Davin said. 'You can help me move in.'

'I'm your assistant, not your indentured servant,' I said, waspishly. The fact that neither Kee nor Larch seemed to find anything unusual in Davin getting exactly what he wanted in the way of housing made me a little terse. 'And the place might not even be watertight. You need a surveyor to check the place out, although you'd probably just pay him loads of money to tell you everything was fine anyway. Plus, serve you right.'

Brian, tied up outside to some convenient railings, scratched on the pavement. Seelie was lying down, untethered, waiting for her master. Even my dog made me feel inferior. But then owning Brian would make Bill Gates feel inferior. 'And we should get back.'

Kee sighed and licked up the last crumbs of a date and walnut scone. Those estate agents knew a thing or two about baking, from the look of it. 'True. It's three days to Christmas and I'm going to close down the shoot, send everyone home. We'll reconvene in the New Year to finish and then we'll just have to wait for the scripts for your new series, Dav.'

'*Spindrift*,' Davin said, laconically. 'Apparently I'm giving up the coastguarding and becoming an amateur detective with a complicated home life. You in it, Larch?'

'Recurring character,' she said.

'Ah well. Maybe you'll be my first murder,' he said, mildly. She didn't seem to take offence. 'And I can spend Christmas in my new home. No point in going back to Ireland. I can take the chance to start learning my scripts for the inserts.' He looked at me. 'You going back to London?'

Was I? Should I? Brian made up my mind for me, staring through the window of the café-cum-estate agency. His brown eyes held a baleful expression, as though he'd forecast his future and me going to London did not turn out well for him. 'No point. I'll stay in the van with Brian and eat Pot Noodles. It will be fine. It's just one day.'

Funny that. It had been 'just one day' for those years spent with Noah, but we'd always made something of it. Flying away from damp, cold London, into the sun. Exchanging presents on the beach, eating an enormous meal in the best restaurant we could find, FaceTiming everyone back home in grey, wintery Britain as though to show off our success. And now it was just a day to get through, like any other.

'I forgot!' Rory jumped up. 'Mum said she's going to open the catering van for Christmas dinner for everyone who's staying on set! You *have* to come, my mum does the best Christmas dinner on the *planet*! She does these cool potato things with all, like, cheesy stuff on and carrots with this green stuff and all butter and it's *brilliant*! And, and we can all show each other our Christmas presents and go and walk on the beach and stuff!'

'Or we could all come over here; christen my new home with a Christmas party,' Davin said, as we went outside. 'As long as there's an oven that works. Might be fun.'

'Might also be hypothermia with a side dose of hospitalisation,' I said, looking at the little box of a house down the road. The relatives of the elderly lady had clearly stripped the place of anything moveable; there weren't even curtains at the windows. 'I don't even think there are any light bulbs.'

'Ah, sure, put them on the list for tomorrow.' Davin turned and began walking down towards the car, Seelie, as usual, glued to his side. 'And you can order furniture and stuff on that online yoke, can't you?'

Keenan and I exchanged a look and rolled our eyes at each other.

'Oh, yes, you can have a cute little Shaker kitchen!' Larch squeaked. 'Range cooker, oh, and Habitat do some really lovely fabric for cushions.'

'Cushions,' I said, darkly. 'You two do realise that nobody is going to deliver all the way out here this close to Christmas, don't you?'

They ignored me. 'Cushions,' Davin repeated, cheerfully. 'Sounds good. Can you sew, Tansy?'

'No I bloody can't.'

'Ah, well then.'

We headed back to the car and I had the horrible feeling that I was being wound up, but nothing in Davin's demeanour spoke of anything other than a snotty amount of privilege and the belief that money could do anything.

Davin – 2004

OK, he was lost. He should admit it and ask for help, but pride and confusion wouldn't let him. Dublin was busier and full of more people than he'd seen in his entire life – shopping and chatting and drinking coffee in takeaway cups – and it terrified him. Mam had said, if he set out along the road and kept walking, he'd come to the shops, but he wasn't sure if she'd meant *these* shops, with their windows crammed full of fancy things and tourist stuff with the Irish shamrock on and whole, inexplicable pages of letters stuck to windows and lampposts and bus stops. He couldn't see Mam and the boys in all this. Finbar had offered to cut school and come with him into town, show him around, but Mam had put her stern face on and neither of them had wanted to argue, so, here he was. Dublin. His first visit. And Mam was like a stranger – no, not a stranger. She still smelled the same, of baking and that perfume she used, and she still talked the same. But she had habits now that she'd never had in the old days: she plumped up cushions on the sofas in her tidy, tiny front room; she shouted at his brothers to do their chores – even little Turlough, who was only four, had to bring down the wash baskets every day.

But Davin did have to admit, her house was nice. Cosy. Cleaner than anything with four boys in should ever really be.

Cleaner and cosier than the van he and Killian lived in now, with Da; cleaner even than Patrick's place, although Sally, Patrick's girlfriend seemed to be forever scrubbing and dusting to a level that Davin couldn't understand. And, when he'd turned up on Mam's doorstep, with nothing but a change of clothes and a train ticket, she'd brought him in, hugged him until he got impatient, and then demanded he strip to his boxers so she could put all his things through the washing machine.

Davin worried that Mam had got a cleaning problem. And then, he thought, maybe she didn't, but maybe it was *him* with the problem, being as how they only took their things to the laundrette or over to Patrick and Sally's place when the clothes could practically walk there themselves. And Teague was a hell of a cook but he wasn't in Mam's league so they'd all lost a bit of weight, except Da, who'd drank it back on again.

Davin turned around. There were people *everywhere*. For a second he longed for Rook to come and sort them out, get them all pointing the right way, and then the pang in his chest reminded him that Da had sold Rook, one wet night when they needed the money. To the farmer they'd been lodging with, who needed a good dog to oversee and help train up the youngsters, and Davin had cried and begged, but when he came back from taking the big Ford down to the tractor yard, Rook had been gone.

It could have been worse, of course. Just after Mam left, when Davin refused to go out with Niall and Da to 'fetch' some sheep that were running loose. Davin knew that the sheep would be scooped up in the back of the car and taken to 'some men' that Da knew, never to be seen again, and Da would have a pocket full of pound notes for a while. Davin didn't want to be part of that, and he didn't want Rook to be part of it either, and Da had been really angry. He'd got his shotgun and threatened to shoot the dog unless Davin went out and got the sheep. Davin still had nightmares about that night. Out in the dark and the rain, Rook with his fur sleeked smooth by the wet, and him so sure that the *Gardaí* were going to come round the corner and catch them that he was practically sick.

Mam had cried when he'd told her this. The boys had her phone number now; she had a proper phone, in the house, and they could call whenever they wanted, so they'd stop at random phone boxes whenever they had a few coins, and ring to tell her what was going on. And sometimes she'd put one of the younger boys on and they'd talk about school and friends and weekend jobs and it was like talking to aliens who knew the same language as you but who lived on another planet.

And now, here he was. His first visit in the four years since she left. Lost.

'Excuse me?' It was a young man and a girl, both dressed so smartly that he immediately tried to hide the fact that he'd got holes in the bottoms of his trainers.

'Ah, I'm sorry,' Davin said. 'But I'm lost myself, so.'

The girl laughed and looked at Davin in a way that made him slightly uncomfortable about the new jeans Mam had bought him down the market. They were tighter than the gear he wore around the farm and he was just getting used to them. They were suddenly a lot tighter. 'We're from the Sara Mendell Agency?' She phrased it as a question, as though he was supposed to know the answer. 'We were just – look, this is Warwick, my name's Amelia – are you free for a coffee just now?'

Davin didn't know what to say. He was lost, he had time to kill, and these two might just know how to put him on the right road back to Mam's place, plus they were offering him coffee he didn't have to pay for. If it was some kind of scam, well, they were out of luck there; he'd got two Euros and a button in his new pockets.

The girl held out a card to him. 'Just so you can see we're legit. What's your name?'

Davin stared at the squiggles on the card. He could see cameras on the logo and make out some of the letters: a capital S and M and then another M and an A. The rest was just stuff. 'Davin O'Riordan,' he said.

'OK, Davin,' said Amelia. 'Only, we've been watching you for a little while; don't worry, nothing sinister, as you can probably tell from us being from Sara Mendell!' She laughed. Warwick, who was tall and lanky, had dreadlocks and was the first black person Davin had ever met properly, laughed too. Davin felt he ought to laugh, because they were. He didn't. Amelia ushered him through the doorway of a coffee shop. At least, he supposed it was a coffee shop; it smelled of coffee beans but the window held a display of books and animal skulls and he felt horribly out of place for a moment in his market jeans, holey trainers and Finbar's slightly-too-small denim jacket.

'Davin, had you ever considered modelling?'

Chapter Ten

The next afternoon Keenan called a Crew Meeting. There weren't many crew left; the last bits of filming were being picked up by a skeleton staff so only a handful of us assembled in the catering van. Outside the seagulls were fighting raucously over some bits of discarded fish, and the wind buffeted the windows, making the van rock.

'Right, I'm closing down the shoot now,' Kee announced. 'Davin has very kindly – at least, I think it was kind; he might be planning to obliterate us all – offered his new home as a Christmas Day venue for everyone who's thinking of staying, Karen will be cooking what I'm promised is a "slap-up dinner", and the removal and clean up crew will be shifting vehicles this afternoon. So it just remains to say "thank you" to everyone leaving and hope to see most of you back in spring when we start filming *Spindrift* over in Christmas Steepleton.'

Everyone stood up, there were handshakes and back slaps and an air of general relief. I gathered that not many people were choosing to stay: Neil, who apparently had only been planning to have Christmas dinner with his ex-wife and her new husband; Keenan, who wanted to spend the holidays scoping out possible places to base himself in Dorset; Karen, perfectly happy to cook for as many as wanted it in an as-yet-unseen kitchen which may or may not even have a cooker; Rory, Davin and me. Larch was apparently 'undecided'.

'If you're going, then get going soon.' Karen came round the counter, a ladle in one hand from which drops of a fragrant sauce were falling. 'Got the radio on out here and there's a severe weather warning going out for tonight and Christmas Eve. High tides and storm force winds and you want to be clear of the coast roads before that there sort of weather comes in.'

Most eyes were on the sauce and it was clear that a few people were having a rethink about going, although whether that was based on the weather prospects or the thought of having Karen's fabulous cooking for Christmas dinner I wasn't sure.

'If I stay, it will have to be vegan food.' Larch rested her chin in her hand, showing off her lovely cheekbones to best advantage.

'I'm sure I can fry you a bit of kale,' Karen said, but the ladle was swaying ominously. I half wondered if she was going to try to beat Larch into eating what she considered 'proper food'.

'Oh no, I can't have fried things.'

'Right. Let's go and move my things up to the house and have a proper look around.' Davin broke the rather stony silence that had descended by standing up. He was wearing a chunky knitted sweater and dark jeans, with his hair swept back, as though he was still in his coastguard persona. 'Before this weather comes in.'

He strolled out of the van as though he expected me to follow as obediently as Seelie, so I deliberately stayed back to say goodbye to Sharon from the costume department and Chloe, Neil's sound crew. By the time I went back down the metal steps to the beach, Davin was already piling boxes outside the Winnebago, with the help of Seelie and Brian, who were sniffing everything, and probably in Brian's case also weeing on it.

There was surprisingly little to move, when it came down to it. 'Is this all of it?' I asked, looking at the three large cardboard boxes. 'Or are we coming back for the rest?'

Davin looked startled. 'Is there supposed to be more?'

'I left London with three huge suitcases. If you open a cupboard in my van you get hit on the head by stuff, and that's equally true of the low-level cupboards. Brian's stopped trying to get under the bed because of an avalanche of crockery.' *Well, I wasn't going to leave it all to Noah, was I? That lovely breakfast set that we'd chosen so carefully, poring over catalogues and websites... and my pure linen sheets? He'd got my business – wasn't that enough?*

'We moved around a lot, growing up.' Davin picked up two of the boxes. I grabbed the third, which, to my surprise, wasn't as heavy as it looked. 'You learn to travel light. Or sometimes,' he said quietly, 'with nothing at all, when you're running from the landlord.'

'Davin...'

'Right, so these on the back seat?'

We piled the boxes into the car, on newspaper in case Brian had done his worst, put the dogs in the boot and drove over the clifftops. The wind was already increasing in strength and the car twitched alarmingly a couple of times when we passed gateways or open stretches of land where the gusts could get to us. Davin kept his eyes on the sea.

'Going to be a big blow, by the look of it,' he said, focusing on somewhere in France. 'See those clouds? We called them "mares' tails". Means there's a high wind up there, and it's coming.'

I took my eye off the road and looked up at the streaky, feathery clouds above. 'They're just clouds.'

'And there speaks a city dweller.' He sounded quite relaxed. 'When you live outdoors you keep one eye on the sky and one on the land. That bank of cloud out on the horizon – that's the weather that's coming on the edge of the wind. Rain or snow or suchlike.' He gave me a quick look. 'Where were you going to be, this Christmas? Before it all went wrong?'

I shrugged and the car twitched again, caught by a sudden opening in the hedge where the wind could reach us. 'We hadn't really made any plans. It all blew up over a year ago, last year I was – anyway, I suppose, I would have gone to my sister's.'

'Would you rather be there now?' His voice was very soft, accent very prominent. I could see him out of the corner of my eye, arms folded, slouching in his seat, much as he had the first time I'd driven him, when I'd taken it for sulking. It was really just the way he travelled.

And then I looked out at the huge sky, full of grey cloud, that stretched on down until it met the sea in an invisible horizon. There were no gulls to be seen now; the only birds were small brown ones that flew up from the hedges and dodged across in front of the car like little balls of wadded-up tissue. 'I'm getting used to Dorset,' I said. 'And Christmas with everyone will be fun. I've never really had a Christmas with lots of people before.'

Christmas as a child had been spent at home. Mum or Dad would usually be on call, so we couldn't go far, but Rue and I had had wonderful times. Once I left home I'd spent Christmas either alone and studying or driving between Mum and Dad's and Rue's homes. And then there had been Noah and the type of aspirational Christmases that you always suspect, in others, of being set up purely for Instagram and Facebook.

'OK.' Davin checked behind; Seelie's face had bobbed up in the boot.

'How about you? What were your Christmases like?'

A long pause. 'Official version? Chaos, all the boys home with whatever girlfriends they had, Mam cooking and Da telling stories: all of us packed into whatever farmhouse we were living in at the time. Presents and confusion and too much food and hospitality to all the neighbours.' It seemed to roll off his tongue easily, a story often told.

'And really?' We'd reached the top of the cliff, the long drop down into Steepleton. The fields were stretched and grey, the hedges dipping under the weight of the wind. Even through the thick bodywork of the car I could hear the high skrilling of the sound of it, forcing its way through hawthorn and singing in the grass.

'Ah, really. Everyone fighting, Da getting maudlin, Mam losing her temper with always being in the kitchen, girlfriends falling out and the older boys taking themselves off to the barn with some bottles. And then when Mam moved to Dublin, Da stopped bothering; we all drifted apart. There's still beasts to be fed and done, even at Christmas. Ewes had been scanned for lambs so we had to sort out the feeding and get the barns ready to bring them in.' A sigh. 'And after I left, well, it's all been media Christmas since then. They usually set me up with some model wanting to raise her profile and take pictures of us shopping and that.'

We arrived at the bottom of the hill and I pulled the car in at the side of the road next to the little house. Davin sat for a moment and I didn't know whether he was lost in thought, waiting for me to say something, or about to criticise the distance I'd parked from the steps, so I stayed quiet.

'So, if nobody punches anyone, Karen cooks an edible dinner without storming out and there's no fecking drinking games that end with somebody naked in the river, it's grand.' He opened his door and swung out, clearly not wanting me to add anything. Or, maybe, not wanting me to realise that he'd just let me in on a part of his past that he remembered with a sort of nostalgic horror.

I let him go up to the house and open up, whilst I got the dogs and boxes out of the car. Seelie ran straight into the house. Brian looked at the steps, looked at me, sighed, and began hauling his little furry body up the steep steps that led to the front garden, inching himself up on his elbows as though he was climbing Everest, not concrete steps.

'It's grand,' Davin announced, coming back out. 'Bit dusty, but she's fine inside.'

Davin's idea of 'fine' and mine clearly differed by a factor of furniture, carpets and curtains. The little rooms were bare to the woodwork. Plain floorboards creaked and sent up dust in the two downstairs rooms, the kitchen had an ancient gas cooker that also creaked when you walked in the door and a sink you could have washed a cow in. Cautiously venturing upstairs behind Davin, I noticed one stair with a missing tread; the two bedrooms both had fireplaces and there were no radiators anywhere which probably meant no central heating, and the bathroom had clearly been fitted when indoor bathing was a new thing.

'Well,' I said, peering past him at the enormous cast-iron bath, 'if they ever want to film a murder for your next series, this is the house for it. It looks like Stephen King just moved out.' I looked into the pitted metal bath, which had some odd streaking. 'Or dissolved.'

'It's grand,' he repeated, eyes tracing the cornicing around the room, stammering over a few rusty-coloured stains which were hopefully only water leaks. 'It feels – right, y'know?'

We went back down to the kitchen, which was clearly going to be the heart of the house. I texted Karen to tell her about the cooker and to tell her to bring all the equipment from the catering van, and some furniture from the café. We were all chipping in financially to cover the cost of dinner, and Neil had volunteered to drive her and Rory over to the Cash and Carry to stock up.

Davin stood at the big window over the sink and looked out. The view showed the steep little garden sloping down to a patch of scrub, then the little car park, and then the sea. I could see we would be about a hundred yards from the restlessly tossing surf when the tide was fully in, just about midway between the beach and the harbour.

'You're going to need blinds,' I said. 'Otherwise you'll have all the paparazzi sticking their lenses into your soup.'

'Put them on the list.'

'I'm not making a list! Am I supposed to be making a list? It's your house.'

'Yeah.' He put his elbows on the edge of the sink and carried on staring at the sea. 'But you're my assistant. And making a list of what I need for the house is assisting. So, go on, assist.'

'Davin, you need *everything*! Haven't you got another house you could just move stuff over from?'

'No.' He didn't look away from the sea. 'This is my first home. Been hotels up to now, couple of rented apartments. Oh, and one castle, but that was for the magazines – nothing to do with me.'

He looked a lot less 'starry' now, in his well-fitting jeans and sloppy thick jersey. His hair had lost the carefully combed back style as the wind had had a go at it and he looked like a normal man. A very attractive and well-built normal man, but normal nonetheless. It was slowly dawning on me that he was actually quite a decent bloke, once you got past the exterior.

'Right then.' I had to clear my throat to speak. 'You'd better start me off with a list of what you want me to order and I'll add to it as we discover…' I tailed off, looking at a large hole in the kickboard, 'and I think I'll start with "mousetraps".'

'No need.' He finally turned back to face me. 'Seelie's a demon for anything that runs. And I bet Brian is one hell of a hunter.'

'No. Brian is all for seaweed and things that are already dead.' We watched the dogs snuffle around the skirting boards and then all of us jumped when an enormous gust of wind rattled the windows so hard that I was surprised they were still in their frames.

'And here comes the weather,' Davin said, laconically. 'Hope you moved your van up above high tideline.'

'Well I didn't know this was coming, did I?' I felt a tickle of anxiety down my back. 'But it should be fine; it's right up in the dunes, the sea won't get to it.'

Davin gave me a look that spoke of the difference between those raised in cities and those raised amid real weather. 'If you say so. Ah, you're probably right, even a good blow shouldn't get that far up the beach. That sand has been there for centuries, so.'

I ignored the feeling. I wasn't relishing the idea of going outside again anyway. Handfuls of rain were starting to hit the windows now. I could see the water feathering as the wind blew it along the glass. 'What about the Winnebago?'

'Clearance team have taken it off the beach. It's probably on its way back to London now. Good job too, never liked the fecking thing. Done my time living in a caravan. I'm too old to enjoy it now.'

I opened my mouth to reply then realised I had nothing to contribute. It seemed that Davin was giving me little snippets about his life, apropos of nothing. It felt a bit odd. He clearly didn't want me to feel sorry for him; maybe his assistants all got this little drip-feed of background to help us organise him? Or maybe he felt he could only talk about himself, really *talk*, to someone who'd signed the non-disclosure agreement?

I shivered. The house was chilly; the dust-hung air felt as though it hadn't been properly heated for years.

'Here.'

'What?' I looked across at Davin, who had opened one of the boxes.

'Put this on.' He was holding out a sweater, very similar to the one he had on. Cream, chunky-knit and smelling of the fabric softener that Sharon used. 'You're wearing city clothes and it's going to get colder yet.'

I looked down at my perfectly serviceable jumper and jacket. 'What's wrong with what I've got on?'

He didn't say anything, just tipped his head to one side and shoved the knitwear into my arms. It was surprisingly heavy and dense and he was right – it was cold and the air had the blunt-edged feeling of damp. I put it on. 'Great. Now I look like I'm about to tackle K2.'

'But you're warm, yes? Grand.' He looked for a second as though he was about to say something else, then wheeled away and started reeling off a list of things he wanted to buy for the house. I had to type quite furiously on the iPad to keep up.

We went from room to room, Davin swinging his arms and muttering random things like 'grey, for in here but with those little white yokes, y'know, for the frames'. I hadn't got a clue what he was on about, but wrote everything down pretty much verbatim, figuring that he knew what he was talking about and we could figure it out later.

Outside, the day drew in against the house and, when we went to what would be the living room, we could hear the tide rising. The room ran the width of the house, so when I looked out of one of the back windows, I could see the lights had gone on through the village. When I looked out of the front, I could see the row of shops, where the lanterns on the railings were swinging in the wind and occasional flurries of sea spray dashed up over the pavement. There were booming noises, which I finally identified as waves hitting the sea wall, and the rain had got heavier, which accounted for the general greyness of the air.

'I ought to get back,' I said, slightly nervously. 'It's getting a bit wild out there.'

At that point, my mobile rang. Again, I'd nearly forgotten that I owned it; nobody from my past life had bothered to ring, and, apart from the occasional text, it felt a little as though they'd forgotten I existed. It was Karen.

'Just letting you know, Neil and Rory and a few of the lads on their way back to London came by and they've shoved your van up to the car park.'

A sudden crackle as the signal faded.

'Wow, thanks, Karen. I thought it would be fine where it was.'

There were male voices in the background, then 'yes, it's going to be a wild one tonight. Neil can't get back; tide's too high and the sea is coming up over the road, so we're going to sit it out at our place, with a good film and some left-over lasagne.' A muttering and then 'no, Rory, we are not watching *A Perfect* bloody *Storm.* We're going to watch ladies in nice dresses, wrap presents and try to pretend that the shipping forecast hasn't basically predicted the end of the world. You stay safe there, Tansy.'

If she'd been going to say anything else, it was cut off as the signal died completely. The wind howled down the chimney like a disappointed wolf, sending a smell of old fires and a shower of soot into the grate.

Davin switched on the light and the bulb we'd fitted lit up and swung. The shadows whirligigged around us. 'I think, maybe,' he said carefully, 'we should stay fast here until this has blown itself out.'

As if in answer the tide boomed below us. The newly illuminated kitchen made outside suddenly darker, and all I could see was our reflections in the black window. I looked startled and out of place in my borrowed sweater, while Davin's image made him look very calm and collected, as though this was a perfectly normal day for him. And I pulled myself up short. *You have no idea what* is *a normal day for him. You know almost nothing about him.* 'I should – ' I stopped. Should what? Go back to the van, now in the car park?

'Ah, go on now. It won't be like this forever and you can look on it as an adventure!' Davin nudged my arm.

'But we've got no food, and the dogs…' Brian was already sitting on my foot. Seelie had hunched herself against Davin, looking miserable and flinching every time the wind caught the windows or the waves 'wumphed' against the wall below.

'Don't be daft now.' He bent to one of the boxes and took out a tin of beans and half a loaf of bread, plus two little sachet-sized things of dog meat. 'Don't tell them on set, because I swear they think I eat nothing but vinegar and wasps, but you can't beat beans on toast of an evening when you've been dealing with Larch for sixteen hours.'

I stared at him again.

'There's even two bars of Dairy Milk tucked away somewhere. What? You don't think us stars sometimes just want to sit and eat rubbish and watch *Britain's Got Talent*? Tansy, I'm a bloke, just an ordinary bloke, who got lucky because I've got a face that fits inside a television screen. I'm nothing special. Just a bloke,' he repeated and turned away to light the gas cooker.

And my mind went back to Noah, trying, always trying *so hard*, to convince me that he was more than ordinary. From the fact that he had to have his hair cut in one particular way, by one particular stylist, to the endless searches both online and in person for the right clothes. Clothes to fit the image of the man he felt he should be. And now here was Davin, doing the exact opposite. It felt as though they were two different species.

Davin scraped the meat onto the stone flagging of the kitchen floor and the dogs homed in with minimum fuss. There were no saucepans, so he stood the can of beans over the gas flame, propping it on the ring, and we grilled two slices of bread, then tipped the warm beans onto them and ate them like open sandwiches.

'This isn't – ' I said, and then stopped. Davin was looking at me over his bean-laden toast.

'Isn't what you expected of a TV star in the making?' His gaze slid off me and back out through that dark window again. 'Ah, I imagine it isn't.' A shrug. 'But you shouldn't always believe the hype, Tansy, you know that? There's a feck-tonne of words written about me, and almost none of them are true, but most people don't get close enough to find that out so I go with it. What's the point of being a poor kid from Cork, who grew up moving more than staying still, with a da always out on the farm and a mam who had more babies than she had a sense of self-preservation, if you can be some mysterious loner from the Emerald Isle who looks pretty and has no real feelings? Wouldn't you go for that one, rather than the real life version?'

He sounded bitter. More like the Davin I had first met. Above us, the bulb swung again, elongating the shadows, so a pair of wolves ate at our feet and the doorway led to a dungeon of unimagined depths.

'I suppose people see what they want to.' I licked the last of the beans off my fingers. 'They want you to be a blank slate so they can put any personality on you that they feel you should have.'

Dark eyes flicked back to mine. 'Perceptive of you. It's best to be a blank slate in my business. Messy upbringing is for when you're on the Oscar platform and they want to psychoanalyse how you got famous.' Then that flash of humour again that he seemed to keep well hidden but which bubbled to the surface every so often, 'But it's hard to be mysterious and all, when you've got beans down your jumper.'

I surprised myself by laughing at that.

The dogs had licked the tiles clean and come back to huddle close to us, under the swinging light. The tide must still be on the rise, because the waves were heaving and beating like a heart against the sea wall and every so often a splatter of spray would reach the windows, harder than the rain that was competing for glass-time out there.

Davin lit the gas stove, pulled a couple of jumpers out of the seemingly bottomless box and wodged them up to form cushions in front of the oven. 'Come on, we might as well stay warm and get comfortable now,' he said, sitting down and holding a hand up. 'Sure, and we don't need to stand up all night.'

'All *night*!' Brian instantly occupied the other cushion, but Davin gently elbowed him aside.

'Well, it's not high tide until midnight. Can't go anywhere until it's dropped back enough to let the road be passable.'

'But, all *night*,' I wailed. 'It's cold, it's dusty and it's Christmas Eve tomorrow and I haven't even wrapped the presents yet!'

Davin half rose until he could grab my wrist, then pulled me carefully down. I had to sit on the jumper-cushion beside him or I would have ended up on his lap. 'Christmas will come, whatever.' He leaned back against the warmth of the oven. Seelie lay on his other side, thin face resting on his leg and her eyes filled with worry. Brian sat next to me, his whiskers full of meat. Around us, the old house creaked and rattled like an old car over cobbles with each gust of wind.

'D'you think you'll go back to the cake business, so?' Davin asked eventually, not looking at me but at Seelie, stroking her smooth coat with a rhythm that was soothing to watch. 'Or maybe start up something else?'

I thought back, remembering that last year. 'I don't know. I don't think so. The stress... it was...' and then I went quiet. My mind was too full of the images of all the things I'd lost; the way it had all gone. 'I might just have a complete change. Dog training, perhaps.' I flattened the fur on Brian's head, but it stuck straight back up again, glued with a mixture of agar and seagull faeces, like a small, scatological punk.

'You could help run Karen's place. They could do with a business brain behind that one.'

I sighed. 'I don't know. There's no point in a place that only makes money for five... oh.' And suddenly it slotted into place. 'You were right. I *did* have it backwards. There's no point in them buying the place because it won't make any money. We have to get it to make money regularly *first*, because it needs to be self-sustaining.'

My hand continued petting Brian while my brain ran around the outside of the problem, putting up roadblocks and diverting thought-traffic. 'You were right. *How* were you right?'

Davin smiled a sideways sort of smile. 'Not just a pretty face,' he said. 'But, y'know, not being able to read is a bit of a handicap in the business world, so I keep it on the down-low.'

I wriggled my back against the warm enamel of the oven. Davin's leg was just touching mine and I could feel the pull and snag of his fisherman's sweater against mine, as though the two jumpers were trying to re-weave themselves into one garment. 'Once we work out how to get it to make money, then Karen needs to raise the money to buy it before whoever it is that owns it now that Mr Beverley has died works out what it is that *he* needs to do to turn it around and sells it for big bucks.'

'Now you are thinking.' He sounded a bit proud. 'Keep going. I'm following.'

'So.' I wanted to get up and pace, to walk and think, but the oven was warm against my spine, the dog was snuggled against me with a heavy, reassuring weight and sitting next to Davin was – was – 'OK, OK, I've got this now. Can you persuade Kee to set any of your new series over on the dunes? I don't know what influence you've got but, as it's your series, you must be able to suggest things? I've seen the way they shoot these things, pretending that somewhere twenty miles away is next door and all that. Surely we can get them to convince viewers that the sand dunes are in the same place as Christmas Steepleton?'

In the stripped-back light from the oscillating bulb, Davin's eyes gleamed dark. 'There'll be a way. What are you thinking?'

'I've seen the *Poldark* effect. People wanting to go and visit places they've seen on TV. You know how they come and hang around the set when you're filming? Up on the cliff and all that? Well, if there's a café, ready made for them to sit *in*, and if Kee can be convinced to maybe shoot some scenes actually in the café, and it goes on TV, and people can come and visit it all year round, and maybe get some props and pictures and stuff all round the walls? It could be like the official tourist centre for – what's the series called again?'

'*Spindrift*. I'm liking this,' Davin rearranged his legs, stretching them out across the tiles, against mine.

'And if we put it into place beforehand but don't tell anyone who might let it leak out then, just *maybe*, Karen can get the place at a knockdown price before it all goes mega.' I finished, and ruffled Brian's head rather more energetically than was concomitant with fur that was ninety per cent engine oil. 'What do you think?

It won't be forever – you'll stop filming eventually – but it might last at least until Rory finishes school. Could it work?'

'You're asking *me*, Mr "can't read anything more complicated than D.O.G."? You're the business brain of the outfit.'

An extra-loud *wumph* echoed up from the front of the cottage, like the bark of a very big and very irritated dog. It made me jump. Above us the bulb rotated one more circle and then went out, sliding us into sudden darkness, peppered with the shrapnel-burst of seawater against the windowpanes. 'Feck,' said Davin, 'there goes the electricity.'

I hadn't realised how much light had been coming in through the other windows. The lights of the village had all gone out too, so there was nothing but dark out there now. The only gleam that showed was the presumably battery-operated lanterns that were wound around the railings outside the shops. And they were nearly underwater. I hoped that all the shop owners had locked their shutters down securely and sandbagged the doors, then mentally slapped myself. They'd been here before. Seasonal high tides would be a 'thing'. I needn't try to pigeonhole them as yokels trying to keep the water at bay with incantations and ritual sacrifice.

The wind hit the walls again and I could swear they moved inwards a touch. Davin patted my arm. 'Sure, this place has been standing for two hundred years; it's seen a storm or two. It's not going to fall into the sea tonight.' He was relaxed, eyes half closed in what I could see of his face in the vague gleam from the gas flame that warmed us.

'How are you not worrying? You just bought this place and it sounds as though the roof might come off any moment!' In contrast to his half-slouch, I was bolt upright, the handle of the oven door digging into my shoulders. Brian's eyes were fixed on my face, his furry eyebrows caterpillaring with concern.

'When you've lived in caravans or houses where half the windows were missing, you get to be able to enjoy a place that's not about to tip over or let the rain in,' he said, laconically. 'This is a dream, Tansy, believe me.'

He smelled of Sharon's fabric softener. Of coffee and dust, a friendly, doggy sort of smell. And he was so sure that the house would withstand the weather that the rigid fist of worry in my gut began to uncoil. Brian clearly picked up on this and lay down alongside me, backside as close to the cooker as it could get and his tail tucked in. His head went down on his front paws and he gave a fishy scented sigh.

'What are your brothers called?' For some reason I wanted to keep the conversation going. The soft Irish lilt was pleasant to listen to, when he wasn't being an arse.

Davin held up a hand. 'Patrick, Teague, Niall, Killian, Finbar, Lorcan, Carrig and Turlough.' He ticked them off on his fingers. 'Nine boys in all. Da was pleased but I think it damn near killed Mam that she never had a girl.'

'Where are they now? I mean, do you keep in touch?'

A raised eyebrow. 'An Irish family, a mammy with nine boys, and you wonder if we keep in touch? She'd skin us alive if we didn't. I try to see them right. Niall still works with Da, still going from farm to farm. Carrig just left university, Turlough is still there, third year of his engineering degree.' He began picking at the sweater, pulling at the pattern. 'Told you Mam took the young ones to Dublin. They're clever lads; they're all making something of themselves. Lor and Fin came over to London; they're in a band.' A note of pride in his voice. 'They did backing for Ed Sheeran, so I'm told. The others, well, they're still over in Ireland: farming a bit, labouring a bit. I'm the white sheep of the family, y'see.' A dark smile. 'And how about you now? There's more to you than meets the eye, Tansy

Merriwether. You've lost something. I can see it in the way you move; the way you keep the world out.'

I felt a deep tremor somewhere under my heart. He'd seen it, that thing that I kept hidden so far down that I'd almost convinced myself nobody would ever find it. The fact that there was a part of me missing.

'Yes, my whole company. My flat, my boyfriend.' The words fell flat under the weight of the wind and the thump and hiss of the tide.

'More than that,' Davin said, quietly. The hand that had been plucking at his jumper reached out and took my wrist. 'There are things you can't even bring yourself to think about. Places in your head that you daren't go.'

Thump. Crack. The heartbeat of the sea was getting closer. Beat by beat, driving up onto the land, climbing up the shingle and sand and inching its way towards us like a beast from a horror movie. Spray like pebbles rattled off the window.

And really? What did it matter now? There was nothing to be gained by keeping her memory close, not now. Never saying her name aloud again... 'Freya,' I said, softly. 'Her name was Freya.'

Tansy – August 2017

A hot August day, with the tarmac smell heavy in the air. Short showers kept blowing through, damping down the dust with weighty drops, then away to let the heat build again. My hair was sticking to my face.

'Let's go out,' I said.

'What? We're supposed to be having a meeting with the bank tomorrow; we need to get all the paperwork together.' Noah was in the newly painted spare room, on the laptop. He leaned over the computer, keeping his body between me and the screen as I put my head round the door. 'Anyway, I'm just doing this.'

'What *are* you doing?' I dodged, half playfully, around, trying to get a look. 'Are you ordering stuff again? Only I've told you, we've got loads. She really doesn't need…'

He closed the laptop. 'Yes. You said.' A sigh. 'All right. Look, why don't you go out? I'll stay and finish the paperwork. How about Hampton Court? Or you could go down by the river, where it's cooler?'

'Oh, think I'll go to the river. Pop in to the Southwark shop; see how things are doing.' I adjusted my waistband. 'I swear I'm getting bigger every minute. Give it another four months and you'll have to roll me down the hill to the office.'

There was something distracted about Noah today. As though his body was here but his head was somewhere else. Bloody typical: here I was feeling like a whale already – only twenty weeks gone and another million to go or so it felt – and he was more worried about bank meetings than getting out in the fresh air. 'Hmm, yeah.' He wasn't even listening. 'OK. Well, you go get ready and I'll just finish this…'

'I *am* ready.' I twanged my waistband again and felt that little bubble and pop that was our daughter just starting to exercise her limbs. 'I've been ready for the last hour. But I need to pee again now, so that's your fault.'

When I came back out, Noah was on the phone in the living room, talking quietly. I waved at him from the front door to show I was about to leave – wanting an acknowledgement, a farewell kiss – but he gave me a quick smile and then turned his back, carrying on his conversation. I leaned against the wall for a moment and then stuck my head into the spare room. The nursery, as it would be. Walls painted, a few boxes of equipment stacked up. Not the pram, not yet, but a cot, in pieces, its mattress leaning against a changing table. A few soft toys that I hadn't been able to resist. Jemima Puddle-Duck curtains. And I wondered what Noah had been ordering.

Whilst he chatted, I casually flicked the screen up. Clicked to open it.

Then there had been the pain, then the blood. Ambulances and hospital and then the doctors explaining to me that she was coming; they'd tried to stop it but there was nothing they could do. And a lovely, lovely nurse, in tears, helping to deliver my beautiful, perfect, tiny baby girl. My Freya. Born at just twenty weeks. Or, rather, not born, because she counted as a late miscarriage not a stillbirth – just one of those things, a doctor said. *Just one of those things.* A phrase that I couldn't hear now without remembering that day. And I still didn't know if the doctor had meant the whole event had been one of those things or that Freya wasn't even a real child, just a 'thing'. But nobody would be that cruel, would they?

Would they?

Noah had been. He'd taken my business, used my complete collapse to take everything from me. I'd signed papers, signed anything put in front of me to make it go away, make me stop having to think. Little by little I'd lost my company, but I didn't care. Couldn't care. There was nothing left to care about. And as I slowly surfaced from my grief a year or so later, it was all gone.

I'd spent last Christmas in hospital. Her due date. It had taken that long for the real pain to sink in and overwhelm me, and Noah had had me admitted 'for your own good'.

And by the time I came out, it was all over. He had the flat, the company, everything except a little money I'd had in a private savings account, and the old camper van I'd bought to do up so we could travel around Britain when Freya was old enough. I could have challenged him, of course. Could have lawyered up, sued him for taking advantage of me when I was at my lowest, getting me to sign things I should never have signed without legal advice. But I didn't. Couldn't. I'd just taken my van and driven out of Noah's life, out of everyone's lives, and I'd kept driving until I pitched up on the autumnal sands of Warram.

I was sobbing by now. Nearly eighteen months later, and I still couldn't think of those days without crying, however hard I tried. My perfect, perfect baby girl, who'd never drawn a breath and would never see a Christmas.

Davin had his arm around me, pulling me down against his shoulder and I let myself be pulled. Let the sobs gasp out and the pale wool scratch my cheek, both hands clenched into the fabric as though I was holding on to something that lay the other side of sanity. And Davin just sat and held me without speaking. No platitudes, no sympathy, just a kind of peaceful quietness that told me he couldn't be part of my suffering but that he understood it.

Eventually I had to stop or I would have desiccated. The sobs gradually lessened until I found I was listening to the sound of the wind and waves rather than my own crying. It must be nearly high tide, from the relentless throb of the sea and the spit of surf against the glass. My head ached and I didn't want to look up. Didn't want to see Davin's face.

'Well,' Davin said, and there was a shake to his voice, although that might have been occasioned by the heavy metal backdrop beat, 'at least the weather forecast was right.'

'Yes.' I waited a moment and then sort of slithered out from under his arm. He moved to let me go, but not so far away that I couldn't feel the warmth of his body still against the side of me. 'I hope everyone got away all right, those that were going back to London.'

'They'll be grand. Once they're away from the coast it will just be a bit of wind and rain.' He was keeping his face averted, looking towards the dark square where water smeared against the surface, blown and struck into rivulets. 'It's just here, where the land and the sea get together and there's nothing to stop it coming in at thirty miles an hour. It's like a big truck made of water and we're the first in line.'

'Very poetic.' I wiped my cheeks with the sleeve of the sweater. My throat felt raw and my nose hurt. I'd forgotten how much it hurt to cry like that. I shed tears every now and again, of course, but letting the pain out all in one go was too much to deal with these days.

'Well, I'm Irish. Goes with the territory, like Guinness and a way with horses. Only I don't much like Guinness.'

'Are you any good with horses?'

'Not so's you'd notice. Sheep now, great with sheep.' And he turned to face me, although the darkness made his expression not much more than an almost infernal shine of eye in the flame from the cooker that shone through the crack in the door. 'And I'm sorry. Sorry for making you talk about Freya. I should have known it was something really bad, the way you don't talk about what happened before you left London.'

Freya. The way he said her name, it made her feel real again.

'It's not really something you can casually bring up in conversation. People don't – they can't get it. And losing the company and everything – well, it's easier to let everyone assume that I made some stupid decisions and *had* to sell up, rather than explain that I –' I stopped. Thought for a moment. 'I suppose it was still just stupid decisions. I should never have signed the papers without reading them. So it's down to me, really, whichever way it happened.'

'No.' Davin reached up the arm that had been holding me and carefully disentangled the hair that was stuck to my face. 'No. It wasn't down to you. He took advantage of you.'

'Oh Noah was upset too. I don't want to make it sound like he just shrugged her off like she was nothing.' I let him. His fingers were so gentle and I was so tired. 'So he wasn't quite in his right mind either. But he –' I stopped again. Those things I'd seen on his laptop. Those messages, maybe even that phone call. Clearly I hadn't been quite the centre of his world as he had been mine. 'He wasn't what I thought, Davin. He wasn't honest with me.'

My eyes drifted closed. Davin was stroking my hair now and I was so, so weary. On my other side, Brian tucked himself in closer, my back was warm and I was drifting.

'I'm honest with you,' I heard Davin say. 'I'll always be honest with you.' But his voice was very quiet and very far away and I was falling now into a deeper darkness, with the rain and sea spray and the boom of the waves somehow moving together into an all-embracing background track.

Davin – 2015

'So, what's been going on in your life? Anything you particularly want to talk about today?'

Davin sat in the leather chair that squeaked like a piglet stuck in a fence whenever he moved and drank his latte. James, his counsellor, looked across the room at him and smiled and Davin knew there were things he ought to say, but he kept his mouth full of coffee instead.

'Did you talk to your brothers, like you said you were going to last time?'

Davin made a non-committal noise.

'And how did they take it? Are you still sure they resent your success?'

Davin put the cup down. 'They want me to be an actor.'

James raised his eyebrows. 'Your brothers want you to be an actor?'

'Ah, my agency. They want me to go into that acting yoke.'

James leaned forward. His white hair was on end, Davin noticed, and wondered whether James thought it made him look more approachable when he was scruffy. 'Acting? But you'll need to read scripts, learn parts… will you have to learn to read, Davin?'

Davin shook his head. His hair, recently cut for a job in Japan where he'd been modelling for the Irish Wool Board, felt oddly short around the nape of his neck. 'I'm not for learning to read. I've got this far now, without it. There'll be things I can do.'

James sighed and, Davin noticed, furtively looked at his watch. 'There's nothing to be afraid of in reading. You can learn, I've told you that. You're probably dyslexic; we could do a proper diagnosis, get you a teacher who's qualified to teach...'

Davin shook his head again. Not being able to read was part of who he *was*. He couldn't explain it, not to this man with the messy hair and the paint splashes up his jumper, not to his agent Amanda either. But it wasn't the fear of not being able to do it that kept him from going through with their suggestions; it was the feeling that they wanted to eradicate his past by making him read. Like the boy from Cork wasn't *quite* good enough for them as he was, they wanted him... glossier. Better.

'OK then. What about the rest of your life then, how's that looking?' James gave him a coy look over his own mug. 'Girlfriends?' Then a touch more hopefully. 'Boyfriends?'

Nobody real, Davin wanted to say. Nobody who actually cares who I am underneath the image. They're only girls who want to go out with the pretty guy with the great haircut, who's been on the billboards and in the magazines. They don't want to go out with the bloke from Cork, with the backwoods accent and the chaotic family. They don't want dragging back to the caravan to help Niall and Teague sort out Da's latest feud, to sit with Sally and talk about babies and knitting and the best way to cook chicken so it's not too fecking dry – 'No,' was what he, in fact, said. 'Nobody special.'

'Oh well.' James sat back. 'Don't worry, they'll soon be flocking round you.'

Davin stared into his coffee. He didn't want flocking. He didn't want what was being offered; although the lifestyle was great it was really just an extension of what he'd grown up with

– constant moving, no real home, a lot of mess and shouting and people telling him what to do and where to go next. And he wasn't even allowed to have a dog.

'I'm thinking I might just go into this acting thing,' he said, slowly. 'Y'never know, I might be some good at it.'

Chapter Eleven

It was light when I woke up. At least, the window had a kind of greyish sheen to it, which I presumed was daylight. Beside me, Davin was relaxed, his cheek pressed against the top of my head and his stubble pricking at my scalp, his arm was back around me again and I had my head on his chest. Brian was snoring and the gas hissed and popped behind us.

I moved, stretching out my legs, and Davin must have woken up because his head came up, bits of my hair trailing down as they caught against his unshaven cheek. There was a little bit of half-embarrassed disentanglement. 'Hey,' Davin said. 'Are you all right this morning?'

I did a mental audit. My eyes felt stiff and sore and my bum was completely numb, but the leaden sheet that lay over my heart had the smallest of holes in it. As though the memory of Freya had slipped a little and I wasn't sure I liked that feeling, because through that leaden sheet came the pinprick of guilt. 'My bottom hurts. And I'm hungry.' I lifted my head. 'But it sounds as though the storm is over.'

Davin laughed and I felt his body move against me, an interesting friction of his sweater and stubble on my neck. And for one instant it was Davin in a nutshell: a surface friction but warm and firm underneath. I packed this thought away with the memories of the night. This wasn't the place. And with my tears for Freya dried to a tautness on my face, definitely not the time to be thinking of Davin as a man.

'Ya townie.' His tone practically ruffled my hair and patted me on the head. 'It's not over; the tide's just gone out.'

The guilt was gnawing at me now. I'd talked about Freya, but I hadn't mentioned the one thing I *never* talked about. The one emotion I kept, held close against my heart like a photograph in a locket. *The guilt.* 'Don't patronise me.' I hadn't meant to snap quite so savagely but the words just fell out.

If I hadn't reacted. If I'd just stayed quiet about what was on Noah's laptop; if I'd pretended I hadn't seen, rather than yelling and screaming — would she be here, now, healthy and happy and nearly a year old?

These thoughts weren't new. The guilt wasn't new. It reared its head every time I thought about her, pushing its way into my mind like an intrusive visitor who didn't know when it was time to leave. It was one of the reasons I tried not to think about those days, because along with the memories came the self-reproach.

I struggled my body away from Davin's, getting to my feet with the help of the oven, in an undignified scramble. Brian sat up eagerly, clearly hoping that any cooker-related activities were going to end with bacon. 'I ought to go.'

'You think that was patronising?' Davin whipped his head round. 'Telling you that the only reason the noise has stopped is because the sea is currently about half a mile away?'

'No, it was patronising telling me that I was a townie.' Seelie was trying to burrow into Davin's jumper. I lowered my voice. 'It's not so bad being raised in the city, you know!'

'Sure, I didn't mean—'

I didn't let him finish. I knew I was being unreasonable. Knew he hadn't meant anything by it, but I needed something, *anything* to launch this guilt at. To stop me thinking. 'I might not be able to tell it's going to rain by some stupid cloud formation, but at least I learned to read a book!'

The silence was terrible. It wasn't even silence, because the wind was still gasping and wheezing around the house, but the stillness of Davin stopped the noise from getting through. Seelie burrowed deeper into his side.

'Davin…' I wasn't even sure how I was going to follow that up. I should apologise; I knew it. But him being angry with me was better than him feeling sorry for me, because sorrow brought the guilt. Anger I could deal with. Guilt was something that rode on my shoulder all the time; I could only ignore it – I couldn't handle it.

He didn't say anything. He didn't even look at me, instead his hand found the silken dome of the whippet's head and stroked, as though she was a comforter.

'I…' but there was still nothing coming to mind. There was a terrible blankness in his face. Then he got to his feet and clicked his fingers. 'Come on now, Seelie,' he said. 'You'll be after stretching your legs while the tide is still down.' And still without looking at me, but with a terrible jauntiness in his step, he opened the door and he and the dog went outside.

Brian looked at me. 'Yes, I know,' I said. Black and brown eyebrows moved and then he scratched himself vigorously. 'That was an awful, awful thing to say.' I put my face in my hands. 'I hate myself, Brian. Some days are just worse than others.'

A small nose poked at my leg and a paw rested on my foot. I wanted to take it as doggy understanding but in Brian's case it was more than likely just a full bladder. 'We need to go.' I couldn't stand there and wait for Davin to come back in, see that 'ah, I've heard worse, and it's not like you're pointing out something I don't know' expression that he would no doubt assume to cover the blank brokenness that I'd seen the very beginning of.

Brian and I went to the door. Outside the plants in the front garden had been beaten flat by the water. Splintered stems of bare rose bushes jutted up, what leaves had clung on through autumn had shredded and even the little square of grass looked as though a parade had been through. They didn't look any better after Brian had lifted his leg on them.

There was no sign of Davin or Seelie. Below the garden the tide was indeed out, a bare stretch of storm-scoured sand and a few boats lolling at anchor, just waiting for their cue to rise up and head out again. And far, far in the distance the sea was still prowling. The wind hit me as soon as I stepped over the threshold and even Brian's fur looked indignant. Davin was right; the storm hadn't gone, it had just backed off a bit.

I put Brian in the car and looked around again for Davin, but he must have gone up the street, through the village and maybe out onto the hill that loomed above the houses. I couldn't see him or the blue-grey flash of the whippet anywhere. Or maybe he was hiding, waiting for me to leave? My cheek felt the pressure of his shoulder, my back still bore the weight of his arm around me, that comforting closeness that had let me sleep through my tears. He'd seen the pain I carried, bearing it like I'd borne the weight of Freya for those months; he'd let me shed a little of it his way. And then I'd ruined everything.

Everything? I drove the somewhat salt-sprayed car up the hill slowly, keeping an eye open all the way, but there was still no man in a thick jumper or streak of blue dog. What, exactly, was there to ruin? Davin was – well, yes, Davin was a very attractive man. That whole well built, dark hair, photogenic face and Irish brogue thing he had going on was, yes, attractive. And, whilst he could be the most insufferable git, he had the self-awareness to know that being 'difficult' was more memorable than being just another nice guy; underneath the complaining and the high-maintenance lifestyle there was a genuine, down to earth man.

Shit. I didn't fancy Davin, did I? 'Oh bugger, no!' I slid my window down a few centimetres, to let the cold air slice the thought from my brain. 'No. I can't fancy Davin. There's a queue!' Besides which, I'd just behaved really, really badly towards him, bringing up the thing that made him feel inferior, stupid. The *only* thing. Instead of throwing a snowball at him, I'd thrown a nuclear weapon, and it was one he'd handed me in the first place. And why? Because of my own stupid guilt, to keep him at a distance before he saw that too.

Over the cliffs we went, swerving around mounds of debris, where soil had washed from the steep fields down over the road, and branches of trees lay snapped and bleak, half in hedges. Luckily nothing blocked the road completely, because in the mood I was in I would have just driven through it, shredded tyres, shattered sump and all. Down the track, until we arrived at Warram, now a bleak stretch of sea-scoured sand and the dunes slightly rearranged. Little sand devils rose to greet me as I parked outside the café; my van was still standing there, tucked into the flank of the building like a chick under its mother's feathers.

There was a light on inside. I let Brian out of the car and went to push the door open, surprising Karen, who was rolling tinsel at the counter.

'Bugger me! Oh, it's you, Tansy; got over all right then?' She turned her head. 'Davin not with you? Thought you'd both be here to help shift some of they chairs. I'm back over to the van in a bit, get ahead with some of the cooking. Neil and Rory went ahead to get the sprouts started.' Then she stopped, tipped her head on one side and her mouth went sideways. 'Oh. You look like the greenfly on the roses. Not a good evening, then, I take it?'

I slumped. 'No.'

'House still upright? Roof still on?'

'Well, yes.'

'Then it's nothing that can't be got over. Here.' Ever pragmatic, Karen thrust some bags into my hand. 'You can give us a hand getting that lot to the kitchen. I'm going to part-roast the turkey today and finish it off over at Davin's. What sort of a cooker is it?'

I thought about the atmosphere in that kitchen. Of Davin's clear hurt. 'It goes cold quite quickly,' I said, quietly. 'It's gas. Quite big.'

'Ah, that'll do. There's only six to cook for; that there Larch only eats raw things that have never had a face so we'll be good as long as she doesn't decide that sprouts are thinking beings between now and tomorrow lunchtime.'

I couldn't meet her eye so I just clasped the bag of whatever it was. 'I'll take this over to the catering van then.'

I had to look up eventually, because she was so quiet. 'Been hearing about your Davin,' Karen said, and her voice was very even. 'Surprising what you pick up when you're behind the scenes up to your elbows in tartare sauce and custard.'

'Oh yes?' I tried not to sound too interested. Karen was shoving the rolls of tinsel into another bag. 'Nothing good, I shouldn't think.'

'Ah, you'd be surprised.' The little fake Christmas tree went in on top. 'He's a bit of a bugger, they reckons, but his heart's in the right place. You know he makes sure that the crew gives a donation to the coastguard station up to Lyme Regis every series?'

I thought of Davin's keen interest in keeping the café open. His excitement when I seemed to have a plan. 'I think he has a bit of a thing about championing the underdog.' Then I looked down. 'Unless the underdog is Brian.' And then I thought again about his interest in Seelie's forthcoming pups and his hope that they'd be decent working lurchers. 'Although, come to think of it – '

'He's a good bloke, underneath, that's what they says. That's why he's getting his own series. That and he looks like Chris Hemsworth and Aidan Turner had a baby.' There was a moment's silence again as we jointly contemplated this pairing, compared it to Davin, and nodded. 'Just thought you should know.' She gave me a shrewd look. 'In case it influences anything. Now, you going to drive me over to Landle Bay then?'

So, with Brian in the boot and dribbling, I took Karen and her supplies over the cliff to the catering van, which now looked lonely and neglected on the beach. All the vans and lorries had gone, and the sand had been scoured clear by last night's storm. The sea was still thrashing and roaring further down the bay; occasional gobbets of spray were thrown into the air when it butted up against one of the big rocks. It almost felt as though the tide was eager to get at us but was being held back by an invisible force field.

Karen got out of the car and gazed out to sea, the wind whipping at her hair and clothes. 'Going to be another rough one when the tide turns,' she said, knowledgeably. 'High tide's at lunchtime; you might want to be indoors by then.'

I rubbed my eyes. 'I'm going back to the camper van to get some sleep.'

'Oh aye?' She gave me a grin. '*That* sort of night, was it? Mind you, I can't talk. Neil stayed over last night.'

I snatched my head around from its contemplation of the wide sands. 'Karen!'

She chuckled. 'Oh, love you, not much can happen in a two-bedroom cottage with spit and plasterboard walls and Rory in the next room! But we got on; he's, well, he's not like Rory's dad and he's going to be back working on *Spindrift* in the spring so we'll see what happens, shall we?'

My face spread into a big smile. Yes. Karen and Neil. They'd make a great couple and Rory had already practically assured Neil of sainthood. 'That's wonderful.'

'Well.' Karen had got all pragmatic again. 'We'll see. Anyway. So, you'll be over at Davin's new place for Christmas dinner then?'

His closed-down face. A splintered ego behind those eyes. 'I don't know. It might not be a good idea.'

'Oh. But Rore's got you a present! I think he's got one for Brian too, but I won't swear to it. There's something making strange noises in his room and I just hope it's a dog toy because otherwise I don't want to think about what he's got going on in there.'

'But Davin – '

'If Davin's having issues with you, well, he'll just have to man up, won't he? It's Christmas for all of us, not just him,' Karen said, very firmly. 'And I'd like Rore to have a decent Christmas with people about that he likes and all. He's fourteen, Tansy, and the best Christmas he's ever had was when my gran was still alive and she used to bring her friends over for a bit of a knees-up Christmas afternoon. Otherwise it's just been him and me, and your mum isn't really what you need when you're fourteen, is it? It's all hip-hop rap music and them computer game things.' She looked over at the catering van, big and re-assuringly bulky at the end of the track. 'Still, he was talking about that Fortnite thing, and Neil seemed to know what the hell he was on about, so that bodes well.' A sigh. 'Right. I'm up to the van; get tomorrow under control and I'll see you Christmas Day!'

Karen gathered her bags and, clutching her coat closed against the intrusive gale, headed off to the van, where lights were on and, when she opened the door, a burst of loud indie rock was snatched towards me on the wind. Neil and Rory were clearly having a great time, whatever they were putting the sprouts through.

I turned the car and headed back up the track. It was bleak at the top of the hill, so close to the starlings' wing dark of the sky. The wind was roaring across the clifftops, yanking the car between my hands, so it felt more like riding a shying horse, and I turned down the alley formed by the overgrowing hawthorns with relief. Here the wind came sieved through the branches and, while it still flung old leaves and road shrap-nel at the car, it was less boisterous contained in this tunnel. It had become automatic now – this drive up and over the hill between Warram Bay and Landle Bay. I could almost do it without thinking and thinking wasn't something I really wanted to do right now.

Didn't want to think about Christmas, not really. Freya had been due on 30th December. Last year, on the day she should have been born, I was attending a group therapy session, med-icated for depression and anxiety, talking about grieving and loss. But not guilt. *That* was a horror too far.

Down, past the little row of cottages that formed the village, where windows gleamed warmly backlit with decoration-hung trees or lanterns and the window of the Post Office was a mass of cotton wool snowballs and a self-satisfied looking snow-man. It looked like a Christmas card, except for the lack of snow and carol singers, but the low-thatched roofs and leaded windows letting light spill out onto the grassy verge were practically a jigsaw puzzle in the making. On I drove until I turned into the car park to the café, which now stood splendidly isolated, like a boat washed ashore on the rapidly rising tide. I parked the car back beside the now-dark café, and clambered into the camper, Brian leaping after me with the wind attacking him all the way. Once inside, I realised how insulated from the weather I'd been in Davin's house. It had sounded as though we'd been Ground Zero, but at least the walls hadn't been moving.

I wrapped a fleecy blanket around myself and put the gas ring on for a mug of tea and warmth. The café building was bearing the brunt of the wind, but ghost-gusts occasionally made it round and broke over the van, shaking the bodywork and making Brian whine piteously and hide his face under the edge of my blanket.

'It's fine,' I said, against all evidence. 'We just have to sit it out here.'

And then the rain returned.

'Right,' I said aloud, although I didn't know why because Brian was giving every indication that he didn't much care for any of this and was going to pretend that he was lying on a beach in the South of France in front of a lifetime's worth of sardines, 'so. It's Christmas Eve and I'm in a tin can while the weather – '

I glanced out of the window. Through the windscreen of the van I could see the white lacy ruff of the incoming surf gradually gnawing its way up the sand and meeting the downcoming sheets of water from the sky. It looked as though Dorset was auditioning for a remake of *Waterworld*. Although it was only ten in the morning, grey light crowded in at the windows making it feel more like evening, and the air was so cold that I could see my breath.

The kettle boiled and tea restored my spirits a little. I wrapped the presents I'd bought in Christmas Steepleton in left-over sheets of newspaper, since I hadn't thought to buy any wrapping paper, and hoped that they looked trendily retro and hygge, rather than slightly odd. Then I made more tea and huddled in the blanket, dozing on the bed with Brian stretched out alongside me and snoring.

* * *

I must have fallen into a deeper sleep, because I was woken suddenly by Brian's cacophonous barking. Blearily I sat up. My fleecy blanket had become bundled underneath me and I was wrapped too tightly for a swift exit so, in order to find out what he was barking at, I had to shuffle to open the door, all swathed in purple fleece, like a giant angry maggot.

The water was slashing at the dunes, dark and enraged, knifing at the sand with bladed waves. Running along the edge of the beach was a familiar blue shape, hurtling towards the van and dripping with water. When she saw me at the open door she stopped and let out a sharp bark.

'Seelie? What on earth are you doing here?' I looked around but couldn't see Davin. 'Did you escape?' I held the door wide, but the dog wouldn't come in; she just stayed at the foot of the steps and looked anxious, but then she always looked slightly anxious with those swept-back ears and worried big eyes. Her coat was soaked and her ribs very prominent. I dropped the blanket, hoping that she would try to get under it. She ignored me.

Brian leaped out to join her, but the pair didn't frolic off down the beach like they usually did; instead they stood side by side, sheltered by the van from the wind and the rain which was singing off the metalwork. 'What is it?' I asked again, realising how futile it was. 'Sorry. You're a whippet, not Lassie.'

Seelie looked at me, then down the beach to the narrowing strip of sand that led to the cliff and up which the rising tide was creeping. She barked, ran a couple of steps, stopped and barked again. I took a step forward, intending to catch hold of her collar, but she moved away from my hand and a gigantic gust of wind nearly knocked me off my feet. It rattled my ear-drums and pawed its way into my thick sweater. 'Hang on.' I unhooked my big coat and pulled it on, but by the time I came back out of the van, Seelie was half way down the beach, tail tucked between her legs, and Brian was haring after her, his fur being blown the wrong way so he seemed to have doubled in size.

'What? Wait!' I zipped the coat and set off after the dogs, who were skirting the very edge of the water, running the band of beach that was narrowing as I watched, each wave crashing that bit further up, huge curls of water that came down on the land as though they bore it a personal grudge. The rain blew into my eyes and attacked my cheeks, so I could only look through narrow slits, scanning the beach as though through a letterbox.

And then I saw where Seelie was running. A shape, huddled at the point where the cliff met the sand, water already starting to creep around it. A dark shape. My eyes tried to make sense of it, telling me at first it was a rock, then some kind of animal tumbled from the cliff. It was only when Seelie got right up to it and started licking it that my brain cut in properly and made out the form of Davin's black duffel coat with, presumably, Davin inside it.

My run got faster.

'Davin!' I yelled, trying to outdo the breaking surf and screeching wind, but there was no movement, other than that occasioned by the tugging gusts. The air was very cold out here and I shoved my hands into pockets as I ran, my nose numbing but still capable of taking on board the smell of iced salt that the waves were driving in. 'Davin!'

I reached him. He was huddled forwards, surrounded by detritus from the cliff; small rocks peppered the ever-decreasing sand around his body. It looked as though he had fallen whilst trying to scramble down. The first really threatening wave broke, sending spray over him, making Seelie skitter back in alarm.

'OK. OK,' I said trying to talk myself out of panic. I snatched at my phone, an automatic response, because of course there was no signal. In fact the battery was dead. I hadn't charged it all night or today, so I was surprised it switched on at all but there was not enough power to call for help. 'OK.'

I bent down to check he was still breathing as another wave crashed in. The noise, in this elbow of beach, was tremendous. The sea was relentless; waves that were higher than me were breaking against the cliff, sending spray and the odd forerunner up the beach. Davin was already wet and if I left him here he'd drown.

My cursory investigation showed a bump and a cut in the middle of his mass of black hair, but nothing else obvious. It looked as though he'd slipped half way down, knocked himself out and slithered the rest of the way in an unconscious slide, but that had saved him from bracing and injuring himself further. As long as the head wound wasn't worse than it looked...

'Davin! Come on!' A wave broke over my foot and I looked up to see that the sea had been creeping closer, improbably quietly given that it was bellowing and attacking the foot of the cliff. We were now on an apron of sand in the corner of the beach; the only way out was up the cliff face, or through still-shallow water that was being driven ever deeper by the rising tide that cut us off from the main beach. Seelie was running around and around Davin, letting out little yips of encouragement, darting in and out and licking at his chin or his nose as though trying to get him to jump up and play with her, but her seal-dark eyes turned to me full of pleading as she skipped in front of the crisp white of the surf.

Brian was standing up to his belly in water behind me, where the tide had already reached the edge of the land, as if he was showing me that it was still shallow enough to get through. The current pulled at him and he dug his little doggy legs further into the sand, braced. I made an executive decision.

'All right. We can do this.' I grabbed Davin's arm and pulled. He groaned, which was encouraging, and his body moved, slithering along the sand until he was just clear of the water which was lapping around both of us now, icy cold around my ankles. Using brute force, I levered him up so that his head was well above water and dragged him around the shoulders. Luckily the sand made it easier to move him, although his heels ploughed two little furrows all the way along. We hit the trench behind us where Brian stood in the deepening water, and the dogs suddenly shot ahead. Seelie leaped clear over the rivulet and Brian waded out, then both of them took off along the sand which was now only a metre or so wide along the bottom of the rising cliff face all the way to the dunes.

'Thanks, guys,' I puffed. The water was freezing as I splashed through, towing Davin like a tugboat towing a liner, only with more effort and a lot more toggle. Got him through and onto the ribbon of sand and then, with the spray in my hair, rain in streams down my face and the surf threatening to take my feet out from under me, I hauled and dragged Davin's recumbent form along, and then up and off the beach into the car park, where I had to drop him on the tarmac and get my breath back.

The car park itself was beginning to form one huge puddle. Between the rain and the surf, which was landing with increasing regularity, the water was collecting and I wondered how much it would take to float the van. The dogs and I stood for a moment under the shelter of the overhanging eaves of the café, where the wind was reduced to sporadic buffets and the rain couldn't get to us, although it was trying, via the medium of the tarmac. Davin, lying at our feet, was starting to make little whimpering sounds and one hand twitched under the cuff of the duffel coat. 'Don't move, lie still,' I said, although I really had to shout over the sound of the wind. 'You've got a head injury and we need to get a doctor.'

'Feck the doctor, I need to get out of this wind,' came a rather annoyed reply. 'I can't feel my ears and my balls have gone home to mammy.'

'What a quaint Irish expression.'

'Where are we?'

'Outside the café. Can you remember what happened?' There came a moment of quiet. I gathered he remembered only too well what had led him to be roaming the cliffs in a storm and the memory made me hot and pink and ashamed to the roots of my hair. 'Look, Davin—'

'Any chance we can get inside? Before me and my quaint Irishness die of hypothermia?' Davin struggled his way into a sitting position. 'Cork is where I'm from, not what I'm made of, y'know.'

I rattled the door of the café, but Karen had locked it firmly against marauders. I suppose Dorset had had more than its fair share of pirates. Or possibly the wind. Either way, the doors were firm. 'We'll have to get in the camper. Can you stand?'

Holding his head cautiously, as though slightly afraid it might fall off, and accompanied by Seelie who had applied herself to his leg as firmly as a bandage, Davin unfolded himself inside the duffel coat and I braved the force of the wind again to open the van door. Both dogs dashed inside and shook themselves, applying liberal amounts of sea and rain to the inside of the van, pretty much as the elements were doing to the outside.

By giving him something to lean against, I assisted Davin up the steps and into the van, which instantly looked much smaller with the application of a six-foot Irishman. With one foot I kicked yesterday's knickers underneath the bed, and shoved at it until it folded back into a seat, leaving enough floor space for both of us and the dogs – although I did note that Brian and Seelie had gone into the front section and were curling up together on the driver's seat.

'Well,' said Davin eventually. 'This is nice. It's a tin bucket with seats. Lovely.'

He sat down cautiously. The van was rocking under the force of the wind and the rapidly rising tide was smacking against the dunes and breaking over the café with a noise like lots of paper bags being popped at once. The effect of the weather outside and a large man inside was a bit claustrophobic but it was better once he was sitting.

I shook myself out of my soaked coat and took off my wet boots as another splatter of water hit the windscreen, and I shivered. The air had that horrible chill damp feel, like being inside old bones. 'Give me your coat, I'll hang it up.' I held a hand out to Davin.

'What as, curtains?'

'Just get it off. You must be soaked.'

Davin gave me a look. 'This is Italian wool. Might be wet, but it's warm.'

A silence descended. Well, it wasn't really a silence; more the sound of wind-assisted rain deluging onto glass and the noise of an ignored elephant trumpeting around the room. I stood in the tiny kitchen section, staring at the gas ring and trying not to look at Davin. Eventually he spoke.

'Thanks for coming, by the way. Dragging me off that beach before I drowned. How did you know I was there? Or were you out strolling in the wind and rain looking all moody and back lit?'

'Seelie. Davin –' I stopped and did manage to look at him.

'Don't.'

'I just want to ap—'

He stood up. 'Don't. Please. I know how it's going to go; you're going to say sorry and I'm going to say it's fine, but it's not.' Now he turned around, staring out of the window of the van, over the billows of spume that were blowing across the dunes, battering the sand out of shape. 'I liked you, Tansy. I never thought you'd be that way.'

For some reason the past tense made the back of my neck go cold. 'You did?'

Another turn, so he was facing me. His hair was hanging around his face in damp rats' tails but he still managed to look totally gorgeous. His cheekbones were dark under the stubble he cultivated and which never seemed to turn into an actual beard, and his eyes were even darker above it. 'I thought I could trust you.'

And I so wanted to tell him that my guilt and self-loathing had made me do it. Had armed me up with the only weapon I had against him and made me pull the trigger. But I couldn't. I still couldn't actually come out and say it, because it might make it real. People might agree with me that, yes, I'd caused the death of my daughter. I couldn't face that. While it was just a thought inside my head I could handle it, balance it, but if it came out into the open and became a real thing – no.

'Anyway, so.' Davin sounded more conversational now. 'You're my assistant and that's as far as it goes; we're grand.'

But the look in his eyes. That dark, guarded look that told me I was barricaded out by his hurt, and the worst of it was that I bloody well deserved it. I'd said something I should never have said, whatever the provocation. I opened my mouth to justify, to apologise, and then closed it. There was nothing I could say.

'You should see a doctor about your bump on the head,' I tried to swerve the conversation back on to a steadier path. 'It knocked you out cold so you should have it checked.'

'We've got a captive doctor up in the town. I'll go get Keenan to give him a callout.'

This was horrible. I wanted so much to reach out and touch him. To try to erase that awful splinter of hurt in his eyes and take us back to where we had been, leaning against that warm oven in the dark room, exchanging secrets and laying those first tentative foundations for something else. Although I could no more imagine a relationship with Davin than I could imagine dating Brian, I could at least admit to myself that I really liked the way he looked and had, maybe, hoped that we could have had – well – just something. The actual nature of that something I couldn't quite decide.

'I should go.'

'I'll drive you back to your place. You need to be careful; head injuries can be nasty.'

He shrugged. 'It's fine. Keenan is over at catering, giving Larch some notes for the next series. I'll go back up over the cliff.' We sat again for a moment, listening to the *crump* sound of the waves breaking up the beach. 'Or you could drive me. Either way, I'm good.'

I'd have to drive him. I couldn't take the risk of having to face Kee and tell him that his new rising star had fallen down dead with a suspected head injury. At least this way I could deliver him directly. Plus the waves were sweeping up and over the roof of the café and I didn't feel altogether safe sitting here in the van with the way it was rocking and the noise of the water on the roof. I could drive it up over the track and kill two birds with one stone, get my living accommodation out of the way of the worst of the storm and get Davin somewhere he could get medical attention.

Unfortunately, being parked in the dunes without starting up hadn't done the battery any good. Whilst Davin sat, arms folded and with an air of 'I told you so' even though he hadn't said anything of the sort, I tried to encourage some kind of life out of the engine. Nothing doing. The first turn elicited a dull kind of whirr and after that there was nothing but a click.

'Battery's flat.'

'You think so?' I sounded more sarcastic than I felt. It hadn't occurred to me that I should at least have turned the engine over now and again. The van had felt so permanent, so enduring, that I was having trouble rationalising that it was just a vehicle like any other. 'We'll have to take the car. Oh bugger! I wanted to move the van further back from the sea!'

'Pack everything you want.' Davin looked around at the overcrowded interior. 'OK, maybe not *everything*, but the stuff you need.'

The van rocked as a wave, breaking further onshore than others, sent powerful spray our way. There was a rising high pitch of the wind caught in the rubber sealing around the windscreen and one of the wipers began to wobble. 'I think it might be a good idea to head up to higher ground.'

I found a holdall and stuffed things inside. The Christmas presents, wrapped in their newspaper, went in first, then some clothes and paperwork. I opened various cupboards and looked inside at all the things I'd thought merited saving when I'd left the flat. At the crockery and linen sheets and my lovely wardrobe of work clothes which, now I came to think of it, I hadn't even pulled out let alone worn. Out here on the edge of the world, if it didn't stop rain, wind, Brian's dribble or all three, I didn't wear it.

'We're just getting out of the cold and damp, not fleeing a forest fire,' Davin said, impatiently. 'It will all be fine to leave. You only take what you need.' Another wave broke over us. The crump and splash made us both duck. 'Well, OK then, maybe some of the more breakable items,' he added. 'And hurry up.'

I pulled on my coat and a dry pair of boots. When I opened the door to leave, we realised the van was standing in six inches of water. Tide and rain were conspiring to turn the car park into an extension of the sea; the air smelled wild, like the deepest ocean.

'You take Brian,' Davin had to call to me over the sound of waves and wind. 'I'll carry the stuff.' With a wince and a squint that told me his head was still hurting, he lifted the holdall and clicked his fingers to Seelie and the two of them were gone, leaving only wading sounds and me looking at Brian.

'Come on.' I tried the clicky fingers thing but Brian was having none of it. He looked out of the door into the maelstrom and hid under the blanket. 'Come *on*. You're a dog, you're waterproof; what's the matter with you?'

A nose appeared and told me, quite clearly, that dogs had not evolved to live underwater and Brian was, therefore, quite happy to stay in the dry, even if the dry was floating. So I hauled him out, tail first and clutched him in my arms. He lay still, after a brief moment's face-saving wriggling, a warm heaviness against my chest, and I felt a horrible jolt in my heart that this was what it should have been like. That I should have been carrying, not an ugly dog of indeterminate breed and variously textured coat, but my daughter's warm weight snuggled in to me. Her head under my neck and her plump body warming my side. As though my life had turned around an angle and I was performing the actions but without the right people here. It should have been Noah and I and Freya living in this van, using my things: happy, smiling, sunny.

Then Davin shouted, 'It's raining out here, and I'm not too certain of this car!' and I was jerked back into reality. Back to the knowledge that Noah wasn't the man I really wanted any more, my daughter was mourned but gone, and I was left with a bad-tempered Irishman and an ugly terrier-derivative. But, I thought as Brian leaned up and licked me on the chin, maybe it wasn't the life I'd planned, but, OK, maybe planning wasn't everything it was cracked up to be. I had a new job, a new purpose in life; it was all an improvement on the awful lack of gravity that had left me floating for a year. Sometimes life surprised you.

It further surprised me by finding that the car was practically underwater. I'd parked it alongside the café and underestimated the amount the tide would rise, storm driven onto the coast. Davin was standing between the van and the car, looking incredulous. 'It's a fecking submarine,' he said.

'It might be all right.' My voice sounded weak.

'If it was built by people from Atlantis.'

Another wave broke and the spray came over the top of the café. We both moved back. Water landed on what remained of the tarmac with a slap and splashed into the deepening pools around the car. Surf was driving into the dunes, edges of waves eating further into the sand with each breaker; the tide was coming at us furtively around the sides.

'We're going to have to walk.' Davin didn't sound happy about it.

'But you've got a head injury.'

'And you've got enough in this bag to start a new life.' He weighed the holdall at the end of an arm. 'But you can put the dog down now, so.'

I looked down at Brian, who had snuggled into my coat and was using me as a windbreak. The rain was lashing down at us, managing to come both vertically and horizontally, like a set of really badly designed window blinds, while the gale was, from the feel of it, coming up from the ground. Add to this the regular inhale and exhale sounds that were the sea breaking and sucking against the beach, and the word 'inclement' wasn't quite enough.

Without another word we set off up the track. I put Brian down and took my bag from Davin and we put our heads down and headed into the wind. Within seconds we were blinded by the rain. All I could see was my feet. I couldn't look up or the rain hit my eyeballs in a freezing deluge and when I looked sideways I could see that Davin had flipped his hood up and was hiding inside it, like a monk trying to avoid vespers.

'This is trudging.' He had to half shout over the wind. 'Just for the record. Trudging.'

'There are probably people on retreat somewhere who would pay good money for this.' I was panting a bit. Beside me Brian looked wet through and utterly fed up. Seelie was dancing along in the rain like a fairy beast, her coat sleeked close to her bones, an ethereal being. Brian could only be called 'ethereal' by someone who thought it meant 'drenched and miserable'.

'Feckin' idiots.'

We lapsed into silence again. The wind was shrieking too loudly to speak over in any case. The track that led to the top of the cliff was only bordered by a bleakly utilitarian hedge, which delineated the track without doing anything to protect it from the elements, so it didn't shelter us so much as rip the wind to shreds so it could more effectively get at us in bits. From behind came the booming and graded crashing sounds of the sea assaulting the cliffs and I couldn't tell if the water was rain or spray or even, at this stage, gravy.

The wind was an actual force. It was like walking into a special effect, some kind of field that had been set up to repel us. I felt the skin on my face straining not to be re-sited somewhere round the back of my head and my clothes filled with the wind's energy as though someone else was in here with me. It was exhausting. Breathing was difficult enough with the gradient of the trackway taking its toll, but the strength of the gusts made taking the air in even harder, and walking against the wind was like pushing a boulder up the hill. Plus the rain, making its way into every nook, driven in on the storm force so that the drops felt solid enough to do damage and I had to keep wiping my arm over my face to keep my eyes clear enough to see and also to reassure myself that it was just rain, not blood, in my eyes.

We reached the top of the track and turned to cross the clifftop towards Landle Bay, the warmth of the catering van and relative civilisation. There was a footpath that tracked along the edge of the cliff but there was no chance of us taking that in a wind that seemed to want us dead. We turned on to the road, not as direct but offering a limited shelter behind some nastily whippy hawthorns.

'How's the head?' I managed to get alongside Davin as the wind tried to pull me back and fling me off the planet.

'Grand,' he replied shortly.

'Are you sure? Maybe you should sit down. Have a bit of a rest after climbing that hill.'

Davin gave me a look. 'Are you patronising me?'

I sighed but his snippiness was entirely my own fault, after all. If I hadn't, essentially, called him stupid… 'Look, you've just been knocked unconscious and your dog is pregnant. This is really not the time to be chasing around Dorset in a hurricane, is it? Let's slow down a bit.'

A pause and then he sort of slumped. 'Fair play. I feel all right but, like you say, head injury and all. Is there anywhere to sit down? Without being vertically drowned?'

A quick look up and down the lane, shielding my eyes with my hand, told me that the only shelter available was a small open-fronted stone-built barn across a field beside the road. The gate was open and the field was empty, but the barn was stacked with bales of straw, between which we crawled, happy to be out of the wind for a while. After a momentary rearrangement of bales, during which Brian and Seelie happily moused without notable success, we had a tiny square shelter, with bales to sit on and more bales between us and the elements. It smelled warmer than it was, of dust and feed and just a little bit as though animals had recently been corralled in there.

I flopped thankfully and peeled off my coat to try to give it chance to dry out. Davin looked at me thoughtfully and then followed suit. We were both still wearing the fisherman's sweaters of the night before, which we both noticed at the same time, and a strange silence fell. Inside the barn only, of course;

outside the Four Horsemen were not just riding in but taking part in a gymkhana.

'Let me have a look at your head,' I said. 'Just to check your brains haven't fallen out.'

'I hope that wasn't sarcasm there.'

'It was concern, you numpty.' I stood up again. 'Does it hurt?' I went round and stood on the bale he was sitting on.

'Ah, y'know.' He shrugged. 'Only when I think about it. And I try not to, cos, well, it's only words, isn't it.'

I went quiet. Gently parted his hair and ran my fingers over his scalp, where the dark hair was knotted by the wind and a little bit of blood. There was still a little bit of a lump, but the bleeding had stopped and he didn't yell when I gently pressed around the wound. 'I'm sorry.' He couldn't see my face, which made it easier. 'I should never have said it. It was cruel, and I only said it because – OK, never mind, that's none of your business. But I was wrong.'

'Yes, you were.'

Another silence. Somewhere in the roof a corner of corrugated iron was flapping up and down; I could hear the rusty, tinny squeak. It sounded as though it was punctuating our staccato conversation, trying to hurry us up to make a point with its clattering beckoning sound. But into that gusted clean air with the smell of harvest and the sound of words staying unsaid there was nothing I could add.

'There's a distance in you,' Davin said, slowly. 'I can see it, but it's like I can't reach through. Like you're holding out your hands and drowning but you don't really want to be rescued.'

'And there you go with the poetry again.' I jumped down off the bale and made sure I had my back to him so he couldn't see my face.

'Irish. Poetry, Guinness and horses, remember?'

'Or sheep, whippets and arseyness in your case.'

He sighed. 'Yeah. Sorry about that. I think it's my default now.' He surprised me then by standing up. 'Look, Tansy, I really like you. You're the first person I've met who doesn't seem to think I'm some kind of sex god.'

My snort would have rivalled all the mounts of the Apocalypse riders.

'Ah, you know what I mean. You're not bothered with the whole "image" thing. You're actually nice to me because I'm me, not because I'm this superhuman coastguard yoke, rescuing people more than is humanly possible. D'you know what it's like when people want to be with you because they think you're your job?'

'To be fair I've not really seen you acting. Just being a pain in the backside.'

'I can be nice too, sometimes.'

I thought back to that kitchen. A residual warmth slid down my back and I remembered the feel of his arm around me, his shoulder under my face when I'd cried. 'Yes. You can.'

'But it's not just about the baby, is it?' Davin paused. I half turned to see him watching me with his head tilted. It looked as though he was listening to the wind outside, rocketing towards us from the sea, catching briefly on the edge of the cliff and then hurtling the few yards across the flat clifftop fields to search for us amid the straw. 'I mean, yes, it's a bad thing, but you didn't make it happen, did you?'

I went very still. The desire to throw something hurtful at him again was enormous. Huge. Overwhelming me with a force like the force outside that was battering the walls of this barn and hunting underneath that metal, a giant monster trying to get to us by burrowing through stone. 'Didn't I?' I asked softly and it was a statement not a question, where my tone said the opposite to my words.

There must have been something there behind my words because Brian came crawling out from behind the bales, his coat covered in wheat husks, looking anxious. He sat on my foot and looked into my face with his eyebrows and beard nearly meeting.

'Is that what it's really about?' Davin sat now on the nearest bale and surprised me by taking one of my hands. 'You think you made it happen? Darlin', it doesn't work like that; if it did there'd never be an unwanted baby born anywhere in the world. You might be practically superhuman, but even you can't bring on something like that just by getting a bit worked up.'

I wanted to snatch my hand back. Couldn't cope with his brand of 'inside the head' thinking. Wanted to run away, get as far from someone who thought they knew how I felt as possible. Logically I knew he was right, of course he was. But –

On my foot Brian shifted his weight and his eyebrows. Outside the rain still thundered on the roof and the waves still thundered at the cliff edge. 'It's Christmas Eve,' I said, apropos of absolutely nothing. 'It should be snowing.'

'You need to talk to someone,' Davin went on, clearly refusing to be diverted. 'I know someone; he's grand, just lets you talk it out – would you fancy that, now?' He gave my hand a shake. 'And I can say from experience, he's been good for me.' In one of those leaps he could take, where he seemed to be able to read a situation, understand what lay behind it all, he lowered his voice and carried on. 'I told you it wasn't all the pretty picture Ireland when I was growing up. Eight brothers, no money, a da who drank and Mam trying to hold it all together. I don't blame her for going, but I did, for a long time; d'you hear what I'm saying?'

Slowly my eyes came up from the straw-lined floor, where they had dwelt for far longer than was good for them on the sight of Brian. Davin looked earnest. Seelie had her head against his leg. 'Davin, I...'

His hand was warm. 'Come here.' He pulled at my wrist until I sat next to him on the bale, Seelie moving to his other side to give me room. 'Y'know something, I have *never*, in my long life, had to work this hard to get a woman to talk to me?'

My mouth smiled, reluctantly it's true, but there was just something about him. 'Well, what with you being a sex god and all, it's hardly surprising.'

'Good woman, time you saw it.' His other arm went around me, but not in a seductive 'I am about to take your clothes off' way, which was good because I needed comfort right now. It was a gentle pressure around me that held me to the ground, stopped me flying in the pieces that my memories wanted to send me into. 'Anything that's said in here, stays in here.' He looked around the unprepossessing shed, where water was trickling down the back wall through a slipped tile in the roof, at the untidily stacked yellow bales and the skein of baler twine looped over a nail near the missing door. 'You can deny you said anything. And so can I. Head injury, y'know? Not in my right mind and my memory is broken.'

'You just said I need therapy.' I couldn't help myself but lean against him. It was that or slide off the end of the bale, and he was warm and bulky and reassuring, with the weather giving it End Of The World outside.

'You think you don't?'

'I got it. Sort of. Last year. Noah had me admitted. I wasn't coping.'

'And how did you feel about that?'

210

How had I felt about it? Nothing. A numb acceptance. Couldn't think, couldn't reason. Knew Noah wanted me out of the way, I'd picked up that much; our relationship was only hanging by a thread by then anyway, even though he'd tried talking his way out of what I'd seen on that screen. It had been 'a mistake', he was 'never going to go through with meeting them', he'd been 'curious, that was all. Just looking'. 'I didn't feel anything.'

'And now the feeling is starting to come back, so.'

I mentally probed. The memory of Noah and his careful coaxing me into the car, paying the clinic – out of money which was probably, actually *mine*. The anger swelled. 'Yes, I think it is.'

'So you're starting to feel a bit more about losing Freya, I suppose.'

Was I? I felt it, every day, the loss of something I'd so much wanted. I didn't think I *could* feel it any more and stay sane. And then more memories, of that day, the thoughts I'd had, the overarching feeling of *being responsible*. My eyes stung. 'Stop it, Davin.'

He gave my shoulders a small shake. 'Told you. Anything said in here, stays in here. And things need to be said, Tansy. I want – well, I want us to have more than a working relationship, if you see what I mean, but that's never going to happen until you can look me in the eye and tell me what you really think.'

I moved slightly until I was looking him full in the face. Dark, dark eyes that, I realised, always held a half-smile, even when he was being a grumpy git. Mischief held in check. A kind of Loki, stirring things up, turning things like compost to get to the good stuff underneath. 'I think you are a pain in the arse who likes making trouble,' I said.

The smile broke over his whole face. 'Got it in one,' he said. 'And that's why I like you; you don't fall for the image.' Then the smile was gone; his eyes were instantly serious and holding a cold depth like the universe. 'I'm all image, Tansy. The real Davin O'Riordan isn't what most people think; it's who I am underneath. And that's the person that you see, when you don't fall for the shitty behaviour and the arguments. It's me, in here.' He let go of my hand and slapped his chest. 'I play act for a living and sometimes it's hard to stop, y'know? Hard even for me to know what's underneath. Because I've buried a lot of who I am, who I was, back in the old country: not enough to eat and always fighting, Da giving us the end of his belt and Mam crying in the kitchen and threatening to leave us all. Life like that, it marks you, even if you don't let it show.' A quick, mercurial grin. 'And I only say this to my man who knows what to say. And to you.'

'Your assistant.'

A quick flick of the head. 'Could be more.' And now another grin. 'If you want. But first you have to be honest with me. No secrets, not now, not in here.'

'And what if I don't want any more? What if assistant is all I will ever be?' And I didn't want to investigate that. To look inside myself and find out how I really felt about Davin would be to have to look at too many things that were painful.

The grin intensified. 'Then friends is fine. It's not just partners, Tansy; friends are something I don't get much of either. Oh, I can get a shag whenever I want, that's fine, that's not what it's about; it's having something that's deeper, something that goes underneath that surface layer, if y'see what I mean.'

'I think you just humble-bragged there, Davin.'

'Maybe.' Another moment, in which the rain continued to sluice the world outside and the wind wailed through the torn bushes that hedged the field. 'I was coming to find you, you know. When I fell. I wanted to tell you that, yes, I know why you said it. I know why you brought up my not being able to read.'

'I wanted to keep you away. I wanted you angry with me, because it's easier to deal with anger than pity. Especially when – ' and I stopped. Too close. I'd nearly gone over the edge and said the words that kept me pinned to my guilt.

Davin very carefully wiped my wet hair away from my face. 'That's right. Like it's easier to deal with me being an arse?'

I could feel the edge now. Like a razor blade under my feet. But he might as well know. If I did – if there really *could* ever be anything between Davin and I, if we ever could have anything more than this – then he should know. And if I changed my mind, well, he'd said anything said in here would stay in here. I'd just claim that the bang on the head had affected his hearing. And his memory.

'It all got so blurred. I saw that stuff on his computer and in that second I realised. It was like everything, everything I'd ever thought about Noah, all that love and all the things we'd said; it was like it was all a lie. Everything. And I wanted him to hurt. For that one second I wanted him to feel his world fall apart like mine just had, even though he was trying to talk it away, pretend it was all nothing and I was overreacting. So I was thinking how could I hurt him most, what would make him really suffer – and I thought, if this baby dies, or there's something wrong, he'll have to face up to what he's done and it will all…' I stopped.

'You ill-willed your baby.' Davin's voice was very soft. I couldn't tell what he felt; there was no tone to it.

'And almost as soon as I thought it, the pains started, and then I was bleeding.' My throat had closed to a tube that would barely let the air in. 'I did it, Davin. Somehow, I made it happen.' And then something was rising up from my chest, my lungs, my heart. A solid mass of tears that had been waiting eighteen months to be shed. 'I made it happen.'

And I didn't know if it made it worse or better that he didn't try to deny it or pretend it didn't mean anything. Maybe any residual magic that his island of birth had, had seeped into him, made him understand in a way that someone else wouldn't, how deep that belief had gone. Rationally I knew, *knew* it was co-incidence, that you couldn't kill a child simply by thinking harm, but the idea that it just might have happened that way was incredibly hard to lose.

So I sobbed. Sobbed in a way I hadn't before. Not at the time, not in the hospital, not during those leaden months afterwards when I finally realised that it was all gone. Not even as I'd sobbed last night. These tears came from another place. The place where I'd kept all my secrets, the loss and the fear and the guilt. Davin was right, the feeling was coming back; all those feelings that I'd managed to put in a place where they couldn't hurt me, they were seeping back through. I thought I'd dealt with them, that they couldn't touch me because I'd processed them – I didn't realise that I'd just shoved them into a mental room and locked the door. Now that lock had given way and I was having to face them. And it hurt.

Davin sat quietly, letting me cry. Every so often he would rub a hand up and down my back in a comforting way, or tighten the hug to a squeeze, but there was an acceptance in his quiet that made me feel better. When the tears eventually slowed to the occasional hiccup and a snaily smear across my face, he sighed. 'You should really talk to my man. He's great at all the letting go and leaving stuff behind chat.' He looked down at Seelie, who was pressing herself against his leg and trembling, as though all this emotion was too much for her, in her condition.

'I don't know if I want to let go, though.' I rubbed my sleeve over my face. The rough patterned wool of the sweater was scratchy and my eyes were sore. 'If I let go, it means forgetting Freya. Just, sort of, casting her off as if she never was, and that's not right.'

'You could plant a tree.' Davin tipped my face towards him. I tried to resist because I didn't think the snot made me an appealing sight, but he didn't seem to notice. 'Put your memories into the tree? Then watch it grow for her?'

I wiped and smeared a bit more. 'Just shove a tree in a random hole? I'm not sure I could cope if rabbits ate it or someone cut it down because it was in the way of a road or something.'

He spoke slowly. 'I've got some land. Clonakilty way, near the Long Strand. Some acres I bought when they came up, when I was modelling and thought this whole yoke would be over in five years. Thought I might build a house down there one day. Anyway, there's a wood, and a little stream that flows out down into the bay, and these big white beaches with the lighthouse on the rocks and – never mind. One day. We could put a tree in for Freya, out there, in the wood. Keep it safe.' He gave my shoulders a little shake. 'Course, that means you'd have to come over with me. Check it out.'

'As your assistant, I'd probably have to. Make sure you didn't wander off and never come back.'

A slow moment. The wind lashed, the rain dropped cobbles on the roof.

'Sure. If that's what you want.'

I looked into his eyes. Deep and calm, despite what I'd told him, despite the lunatic weather outside that was leaving me unsure whether we'd actually make it out of this place alive. 'I'm not sure what I want, Davin,' I said and even my voice had slowed.

A careful thumb wiped the corners of my eyes. 'No,' he said, and his voice was very quiet under the weight of the wind. 'No, I don't suppose you are.' He leaned in and his kiss was so natural that it felt like the next step on an escalator, a step that dissolved smoothly into a surface that felt firm and confident. His mouth was warm, his hand fell from my face and lingered on the back of my neck, strong fingered but so careful that it was more of a shadow than an actuality. 'Does that help?' he asked, when he moved back.

Brian barked, one stern bark, that sounded as though he wanted an answer too.

'I'm – not sure.' I was breathless. I'd started holding my breath when he'd touched my face and the kiss had sent all the air underground, from where it now bubbled out in a gasp. 'Can you try again? Just to check?'

Davin O'Riordan. Scourge of the set, arsey, scowling Irishman, desired by women everywhere was kissing me. But not kissing me as that actor with something to prove, he was kissing me as a man who cared. The real man behind the persona, who'd let me in to his life a little at a time without me realising. He'd let down his barriers, told me about his bleak upbringing, the hole in his life that not being able to read made. So tired of being wanted for who he was, and wanting me to want him for what he was. Just a man. A flawed, if beautiful, man.

'I think I might have a bit of a clue now,' I said finally, when his lips had covered my face, and now rested on the top of my head. 'Wow, Davin.'

'I meant it. I know I'm an actor and I say a lot of stuff, but this is me. I'm just a man, Tansy, underneath it all, and I'm a man who likes this woman here.'

'But all those gorgeous actresses…'

'There's a reason that most of the showbiz relationships that last are when an actor gets with the backroom people, y'know?

Two actors together is like putting two prize bulls in a green field; starts off all pretty but by the end it's just blood and mud and fighting.'

'And that's an image that will stay with me,' I said, tartly. On my foot, Brian whined. At least, I think it was whining; he might just have had a bit of mouse stuck in his throat.

'Well, you're not much to look at, so. Must be your personality I'm after,' Davin said, and grinned. It was a proper, real grin; not one of the ones he used for the cameras, where he looked as though he was smiling but the giveaway was the lack of depth in his eyes. This grin came from his soul. Which was a shame, because I wanted to hit it.

'All right, sunshine, don't get cocky. A couple of hot kisses isn't getting you any promises, you know.' I said.

And at that moment, the barn fell into the sea.

Chapter Twelve

It started with the noise. A huge 'whumph' as a wave hit the cliff edge, then a slow slithering sound punctuated with a noise like an earthquake, and then the walls were dissolving around us like an artist was rubbing them out from below, bales disappearing, the water coming at us from every angle. Then it was a sliding fall, descent down a mud chute with bits of masonry, beams and bales falling past us, tumbling and hurtling. Instinct made me grab out, but all I got was a handful of Brian, who tucked himself in against my chest as we went down. Seelie bowled past us in a tangle of legs, but I couldn't see Davin anywhere, just straw and rock and lumps of soil and it was like being in a blender with extra water, all just falling and sliding and being hit by things. My holdall came behind me, clouting me on the head, ending up with me practically sitting on it, amid the rubble of tiles and stonework and straw, with the waves splashing up to reach us. Brian was still sitting on my chest and I still couldn't see Davin.

When I stopped being dizzy and audited my limbs, I found that I was largely intact, apart from a huge hole in the shoulder of my sweater and a distinctly bruised and wobbly feeling in my legs. We'd come to rest nearly at the bottom of a new crag, formed where the old cliff had collapsed. It was sheer to the top, but ended in a sort of muddy slope where everything had settled, but now the sea was doing its best to erode. The tide seemed to be on the retreat now, but waves were still climbing their way up the cliff, beating me with their edges, so I was soaked and freezing and lying stretched on a ledge that had all the stability of the mud it was made of and dropped underneath me another twenty feet or so to a narrow strip of shingle and the highly strung sea.

'Davin!' I yelled, but there was no answer. He'd been right next to me; he couldn't have gone far, surely! But the ledge ended practically where I did: there was room for me, Brian and the holdall of Christmas presents, with which I had become unreasonably obsessed, clutching on to it as though it was a combined lifebuoy and inflatable raft. 'Davin!'

Still no reply. I sat up slowly, very conscious of the unstable surface below me, bag behind me and Brian balanced on my lap. Brian's fur was soaked through and plastered to him so he looked black and bedraggled and there was mud on the tip of his nose. Waves continued to rise up and hit the cliff, but the landslip meant that the worst of their power was deflected around us, and the falling tide was taking the sheer volume of water back out to sea. Which meant anyone who'd gone into it was being dragged offshore.

'Davin!' I tried again, screaming this time, but I doubt I would have heard him, or he me, over the sound of the wind, the waves and the rain which was still sluicing down. I would never have believed that nature could have so much wet in it. A straw bale, which must have stuck further up the cliff, came sweeping down, dislodged by wind or weight of water, swept past my ledge and tumbled over the drop into the water beneath, which tore it apart into so many fragments and two floating bits of bailer twine in a very illustrative way.

And then I saw her. Seelie, who'd passed me in that complicated tangle of legs during the fall. She was floating beneath my ledge, head up out of the water but looking horribly still, her little body tossed about on the surf like a blue-grey extension of the wave. 'Seelie!' I called out but she didn't react, just washed up and down with the movement of the sea.

I looked down at the drop. From my ledge it looked sheer, but the sheerness tailed off about two metres down into a mud slope into the water. 'Brian, stay,' I instructed firmly, and put him against the holdall on the ledge. 'Wait here for me.'

Quite what I planned, I wasn't sure. I could get down into the water – that wasn't a problem, gravity would sort that out for me – but getting back up would be impossible. I'd never reach the ledge again. All I knew was that I couldn't leave the little whippet there, to be washed out to sea, whether she was dead or alive. 'Stay!' I reiterated. Brian huddled into the holdall, ducking his head under the weight of the rain and looked as miserable as it is possible for a wet terrier to look, which is very. I dropped a quick kiss on his matted head. 'See you later,' I whispered, touched his nose, and crawled to where my bit of the cliff ended.

I lowered myself over the edge, tried to dig my toes in to give me some grip but the ledge crumbled under my hands and I found myself plunging down, feet first, with my face pressed against the mud as I went. I hit the sea, went under, and fought my way to the surface, fighting not just the tide strength and the water, but the sheer weight of my fisherman's sweater. The cold was horrific but I'd been cold already, stuck to that ledge, so it didn't take my breath away as it might otherwise have done.

School swimming lessons came back to me. They'd been very keen on 'what to do if you found yourself swept into deep water' for a school based in Croydon, and I found that

I was automatically treading water and taking the waterlogged sweater off over my head. It sank into the depths below me and I felt the swirl as it was swept past my legs and dragged somewhere. There was a current pulling at me, tugging me out to sea with each pulsing wave that swept me onshore, in a kind of watery stasis, and I'd lost a shoe in the slide. My jeans were unreasonably tight and gave me little manoeuvrability, but I swam a small circle with the surface of the water beating against me. I had to screw my eyes up to be able to see as the waves bobbed me about and the cold ate its way into my soul.

Something passed across my vision. A small leg. I reached out, which made me sink further beneath the surface, and my reaching turned into a grab. Something solid, something warm, like living bone, and I was pulling it towards me, eyes closed against the onslaught of surf, as I was thrown from wave crest to wave crest. A limp little body was thrown into my arms by the movement of the surf; so light it was almost not there at all, with fur sleeked so tight to skin that it felt non-existent. The slackness was alarming, a lifelessness that made the body feel like a piece of driftwood and a million scenarios cascaded through me as the weightless little shape lay against my shoulder. Then something else warm touched my face and I caught sight of a little pink tongue. I'd got hold of Seelie and she was alive.

I tried to hold her head up against the waves while her paws scrabbled at me, trying to get above the surface and we were pitching about like a small boat, one minute high above the surface of the sea and the next minute dragged down into a trough, with my chest squeezed free of breath by the cold and the movement. All I could do was keep the pair of us afloat, heads above the iron-chill of the water, while the current shook us like Brian with a bit of seaweed. I couldn't swim and hold her up, so I draped her over my shoulder, her head up against my ear as I struggled against the tide. My strength was going; I could feel it, a slow-dawning weakness that gradually took the air from my lungs and turned the muscles of my arms to jelly. Seelie and I went under the waves, my head bubbled and my ears rang and I wasn't sure there was anything more I could do. I let her go; she'd stand a better chance of surviving if I wasn't dragging her down, but as soon as I released her she swam straight back and pulled herself up onto my shoulder again, shoving my head under the surface as she stood on it.

Another huge wave tossed us and this time – was I hallucinating? – there was something firm under my feet. We'd washed up against a section of the cliff fall, and I could touch the bottom. At first just the tiniest of tiptoe touches against something solid, and then I was swept back again, feet trailing in the water, but the next wave was slightly bigger and I managed to get both feet flat to the surface, which gave me enough purchase and strength to drag us up onto the shallow bottom. By crawling my knees along until the water was shallow enough to let me dig in my hands, little by little we gained on the outgoing tide, which stopped trying to suck me away from the cliff and became a wash that spat me out, until I flopped onto the newly emerging beach at the base of the cliff. It wasn't really a beach, it was mostly what had previously been the clifftop; wreckage from the barn was strewn around like the aftermath of an explosion amid mud and clumps of turf but it was solid. It wasn't underwater. It was safe.

Seelie and I fell down. My legs had no strength left and she looked as exhausted as I felt, so we lay there, breathing heavily and shivering. Waves flopped in and out around us as we lay, collapsing like inadequately set jellies over our bodies. Seelie could do no more than tuck herself against me, and I could barely lift my head to check we were safe. We were out of the water but no nearer not dying.

A yelp and a momentary sensation that I was wearing a very bad hat, and I realised that it was Brian, now covered in mud from where he had, presumably, abseiled down the cliff face after me. A cold nose nuzzled under my cheek and pushed, as though trying to get me to stand up, and when I failed to react, he ran around and tried the same tactic with Seelie, where he got a somewhat better result. The whippet tottered to her feet, staggering like a newborn lamb, and sneezed, whereupon Brian ran several circles on the newly emergent sand.

I stayed down. I couldn't have got up if you'd paid me, or if Brian had started licking my face. Neither ends of the contingency spectrum would have raised me. I was too cold, too exhausted. My legs and arms had lost all feeling, they were just wet bits of string hanging out of my clothes, the wind was laying planks of freezing air across me and my lungs hurt. Lying down, even if my feet were still half in the water and spray from the crashing breakers was lashing me with water mixed with small pebbles, sand, straw and dissolved sandstone from the eroded cliff, was all I could manage.

'Sorry, guys,' I said to the dogs, without moving my head. 'You just... stay.' My head buzzed and a grey film came over my eyes. I realised I was going to faint, knew I should stay conscious to make sure the dogs didn't get swept out to sea again, but felt too sick and dizzy to do anything to prevent it. Didn't know what had happened to Davin and I couldn't even muster the energy to keep his dog safe...

* * *

Sensation gradually returned. The noise of the wind and waves had gone, there was warmth around me and the hum and buzz of electricity and people. I was lying now on something softer than shingle and someone was manipulating my limbs.

'She should be fine,' a confident voice I didn't recognise asserted. 'Just warm her up gradually and keep an eye on her. And – is that a dog?'

'Oh, that's Brian.' That was Karen's voice. My brain, doing a kind of mental jigsaw, put a couple more pieces down and got an image of the catering van. The smell of cooking and sprouts was the real giveaway. 'He's her dog.'

'Not. My. Dog.' My voice was rusty and my throat hurt. When I opened my eyes to the glare of a light bulb swinging above me, they hurt too.

'Bollocks he's not,' Karen said, robustly. 'He was lying on you to keep you warm when you were found.'

Probably wondering when I'd be dead enough to start eating. But the thought had too many words in to say.

'Thank you so much for coming out, doctor.' That was Keenan. 'It's been a bit of a dramatic day, as you can tell.'

'Yes.' The doctor's voice went a bit tense. 'Most of the roads are blocked by fallen trees. Good job you all got to Steepleton when you did; I hear your catering van is half underwater.'

Not in the catering van then. 'Where. Am. I?' I said, feeling it was somewhat expected of me, and besides I wanted to know.

'Davin's place.' Keenan loomed across my line of vision. 'We had to abandon the van when the tide got underneath it. We all piled in Larch's Land Rover and made a run for it. You should have seen us, Tansy; it was like an exodus, with Karen trying to get all the food and Rory and Neil shouting at her to leave the pudding and run…' He tailed off for a moment. 'There were phrases said that will probably never be repeated,' he said, mistily.

The horror of what had happened to us was slowly coming back to me along with the movement in my arms and legs and my voice. 'Is Davin…?'

'Right here.' His voice was reassuringly grumpy. 'So don't say anything you might later regret.'

'Wouldn't dream of it.' More memory returned. 'And Seelie?'

'Vet was here a minute ago and checked her over. She's fine. Ridiculously so, in fact. Karen's been feeding her on turkey legs all afternoon.'

'Got to keep her strength up, she's expecting,' Karen said, perkily. There was a clattering noise. 'Rore! Can you get that gravy?'

More and more sensation returning. The realisation that my clothes were nearly dry, that I was rolled in a sleeping bag on floorboards and that I could smell the combination of old fish and deceased doormat that meant Brian was somewhere close to my nose. 'What the hell happened?'

'You can explain,' Karen said. 'I'm off to rescue the gravy. Rore wants to learn to manage his cornflour before he starts going anywhere near sound equipment, if you ask me.' There were retreating footsteps and a door closed. Keenan cleared his throat.

'I'm going to make sure Larch is all right,' he said. 'She drove like Lewis Hamilton to get us over here, through the storm. And entirely fuelled by wheatgrass and pak choi, which is even more impressive.' More footsteps. Door opened and closed.

'Can you sit up?' Davin asked. 'Only it's like talking to a chrysalis.'

I wriggled a bit. My limbs, what I could feel of them, were wobbly and pathetic but moved and I managed to prop myself up against the wall to see I was lying on the floor in Davin's living room. It was dark, but not so dark I couldn't see that rain was still pelting the windows. There was a cup of something brown and warm beside me, so I forced my fingers into a shape whereby I could hook the handle and drew it up to my mouth. There was spillage, but it was warm.

'So, what happened? We were in the barn and then…' I stopped talking. Emotions were coming back with the physical sensations. 'I thought I'd lost you,' I said, quietly. Drinking the tea stopped the tears from coming.

'I got washed down and further along the coast. I was half way to Landle Bay.' He looked rough, I noticed. He'd changed his clothes, but the white, open-necked shirt and grey jeans looked as though they came from the wardrobe department. His dark hair was half on end, which was a good trick for hair as long as his – he looked like he'd been electrocuted – and his eyes had shadows underneath them that all the make-up in the world couldn't have covered. 'Feck, Tansy, it was horrific. I didn't know where I was.'

A movement beside me, which at first made me worry about mice, but turned out to be Brian, snuggling against the sleeping bag. His eyebrows were full of mud and his coat was matted in a number of interesting ways which made him twice his real size in some parts, and half of it in others. He looked like a dog built by a committee. 'Hi, Brian.' I stroked him. It was tough, but I managed it.

'I've spent a load of time talking to the coastguard boys; we have them on secondment for consulting when we're filming.' Davin sounded as though he was trying to stop his voice from breaking up. 'The right way to go into the water, how to keep afloat, stop from freezing – all that. They're grand lads.' Another brief moment of choke. 'So, I was holding on to a beam from the barn to stay afloat. I could see you in the water, saw you grab Seelie – I hadn't even seen her go in. Then I got dragged further along, got myself ashore at Landle Bay only to find that every-one had gone already. So I broke the door into Keenan's van up on the shore there, took his keys and drove his car down over the sand to where we'd gone in the water, where I found you.'

'I didn't know you could drive,' I said, weakly.

'Can't pass a test without reading, but I grew up on farms. I can drive anything with an engine, just not on the roads. Ah, you should see me behind the wheel of a Massey Ferguson 35. I can make the old girl sit up and dance!'

'Shut up,' I said, but didn't mean it. 'So you drove Kee's car all the way along the beach?'

'Tide had gone out far enough by then. That car will never be the same, mind, but I found you. Lying there on the sand like some creature from the sea, with Seelie sitting next to you and Brian lying there trying to keep you warm.'

'Seelie got swept out. I had to go in after her.' I drank a bit more tea. My hand was shaking and I slopped a bit more. 'I thought we were both going to drown.'

'You saved my dog.'

'I got hold of her and pulled her out with me.'

'Tansy...' and now the break was complete. He coughed to try and hide it, but he was crying. He crouched down beside me and gathered me, sleeping bag and all, against his chest and I could feel it moving as he tried to breathe quietly and without sobbing.

'It's OK, Davin.' I wanted to touch him to reassure him, but both hands were holding the tea mug, trying to keep it steady. 'It's OK.'

'I know.' The words were breathed carefully. 'But it might not have been. I could have lost both of you in that feckin' water.'

To hell with the tea. I put the mug down and then wrapped my arms around Davin. We held on to one another as though we were still drowning. He smelled clean, but still of the sea, as though he'd been swept into my life on a storm and I drew him in with the air, so conscious that it could all have been different, still feeling that weakness that would have let me drown if I hadn't touched solid ground when I did.

Eventually the tears stopped and we just sat. I had my head on his shoulder and he had me pulled in tightly against him, the wall solid at my back and him solid in front of me. 'Tell you one thing,' he said quietly, 'you're not getting me up on that fecking cliff again. *Spindrift* gets filmed on the beach or in some nice solid city where the nearest we get to drowning is a large gin and tonic.'

'I'm sure Kee will take all this into consideration.' I moved a little way back. 'Are you sure Seelie is all right?'

'She's grand. I got the vet to her as soon as they could get one over here. She did a hormone test; everything's looking stable. We'll have to wait, of course, to make sure that the shock of it all isn't too much, but we're still looking at a good litter of lurchers in a few weeks. She even took a look at Brian and, yep, he's still a dog, just about. And a very healthy one too.'

I gave a shaky little laugh. 'That's hybrid vigour. He's part dog, part coconut matting.' And then a thought struck me. 'My bag! It's got all the Christmas presents in!' There was something about the thought of losing the holdall, after everything I'd gone through to try to keep it safe, that made me want to cry again.

Davin gave me a very straight look. His eyes were slightly reddened but still held that dark light of mischief that made him look as though he was about to burst into either laughter or profanities. 'You can't keep everything safe, y'know.'

'I know.' My record for protecting the things I cared about was pretty grim. 'Yes, I know, Davin. But it mattered. And I lost it.'

'It wasn't your fault.'

Were we still talking about the bag? Or something else?

'I should have been able to. If I'd just taken more care...'

Davin clicked his fingers. 'Seelie, here.'

A moment. Then the door nudged open, a small black nose appeared, followed by a narrow muzzle and calm yellow-brown eyes. The little dog slid through the smallest of gaps and trotted to his side, pushing her head under his hand. 'Whippets now, they're not the easiest dogs to breed, so. But look at her, Tansy.' I looked. Seelie looked back. 'She fell off a cliff and got all but drowned.'

'I know. I was there, drowning right beside her.'

'She hasn't lost the pups. Vet says her hormones are still strong. It's too early to scan yet; we'll do that in a few more weeks, but every test the vet could do says that she's still pregnant.' Davin gave me that dark-eyed look again. 'And she also said that if Seelie loses the pups, it won't be anything to do with what happened today; it'll be more like bad luck.'

'Are you trying to tell me something?' I picked up my mug again. The tea was pretty cold now and there was a bit of a scum on the surface, but drinking it meant I could hide my face.

'Maybe this is just the world's way of showing you that what happened to Freya wasn't anything to do with you. Of course, I'd be more than happy if the world wouldn't choose to use my poor old dog as an example, but there y'go. Look at her, Tansy. She's been through all that but her body still thinks being pregnant is important. You, Freya – it was always going to happen. Happening when it did was co-incidence and there was nothing you could have done, nothing you could have *thought* that would have made it any different.'

'That's what the doctors said.'

'Ah, Tansy.' Davin reached out a finger and pushed back my hair. 'Maybe it's time you started believing them.'

I looked at the beautiful dog. There was no sign of her pregnancy yet; she was as sleek as ever, her blue coat tight to her bones. She raised her head and looked back at me, her ears slightly raised in the way of the whippet, with the corners turned down like well-made beds.

I dug my fingers into Brian's fur. 'I don't know if I can,' I half-whispered the words. 'Because if I do, then I have to acknowledge that the world is just randomly cruel.'

There was a moment of quiet between us. In the kitchen I could hear Karen and Neil laughing and Rory's voice complaining. 'The world let me find you,' Davin said, eventually. 'It can't be so bad now, can it?'

I couldn't help myself and smiled. 'We hardly know each other,' I said.

'Reckon?' He was smiling now too, a slow and, it had to be said, really attractive smile. 'You know more about me than anyone else, apart from maybe my mam. I think that makes us friends, if nothing else.'

'Well, I *am* your assistant.' I tried to stroke Brian's fur flat. It was pointless.

'You are, so. Friend, assistant, you never know. There could be more to come.' A momentary pause and then, with more hesitancy. 'Can there? Earlier, up in that shed, it felt like you were saying you felt something.'

'And you said that what happened in the shed, stayed in the shed. How's the head, by the way?'

'Doc says I'm fine. Might have knocked some sense into me, that's all.' He looked away, and I watched him out of the corner of my eye. He was looking down at Seelie, gently caressing her knobbly head and smiling a soft smile. He looked a million miles away from the bad-tempered man who'd sat in my car and complained while we looked for a film site.

'I—' I began, but was interrupted when the door flew open.

'Tansy, mum says you nearly *drowned*!' Rory burst in, an incongruous ladle in one hand. 'Is it true? Did you nearly die? Did your life flash in front of you? Ryder once got stung by a bee and he swelled all up and he said that his whole life flashed in front of him. He was only four, mind, so it can't have been much of a flash, more of a flicker really, but did it?'

'No lives, no flashing,' Davin said, steadily.

'Oh, tunnel of light? Did you have to stay away from the light?' Rory was practically bouncing.

'Yes. And, do you know, it looked almost *exactly* like an Arcade Fire album cover?'

'Sick!' A cautious look. 'Are you taking the piss?'

'Rory! You get your arse back to this gravy otherwise any presents you might have been going to get tomorrow are going up the chimney and Father Christmas can kiss my aspic.' Karen arrived in the doorway. 'Sorry, you two. Rore, you've got all the subtleties of that there Brian.'

'Aw, Mum, I was just asking Tansy what it's like to nearly die.'

Beside me, Davin was silently shaking with laughter.

'You hang around here much longer, my lad, and you'll find out.' Karen grabbed her son by the back of his T-shirt and hauled until he was forced to step back out through the door, or be garrotted by a Rammstein graphic. 'They're talking. Leave 'em be. And you are cooking, so get back to that stove.'

I heard Neil's voice say something and everyone in the kitchen started to laugh, including Rory. Quietly, I reached over and took Davin's hand. He looked down in surprise and then smiled. 'You, me and a pair of dogs. It's going to be a fun ride, isn't it?'

'Three dogs. We have to keep one of the puppies, if only to remind us never ever to let Brian and Seelie be alone together again when she's in heat.'

His arm came around me again. 'Early days, so. Just be prepared for the paparazzi to find you incredibly interesting. And every woman in Great Britain to hate you.'

'Shut up,' I said, comfortably. 'Anyway. There are other things we need to talk about…'

Chapter Thirteen

A church in the village rang the bells at midnight, into a clearing, frosty sky. The storm had died, leaving streets scoured clean and huge piles of everything that had been scoured from them dumped at the bottom of the hill. The car park looked like a rock festival had passed through and a dumper truck of grit had followed, when we went out, cautiously, fetching things in from the Land Rover, as Christmas Eve turned into Christmas Day.

Other villagers were out too, coming back from church or just examining the damage the storm had done, so there were equal numbers of 'Happy Christmas!' and 'We're going to need a new front door!' called out, as they met in the street. The string of lanterns had been torn from the railings, and many of the overhead decorations had been so tattered and torn by wind and water that it looked more as though we were undergoing some kind of zombie festival, rather than Christmas.

Karen put the little plastic tree from the café on the kitchen worktop and plugged it in, then draped tinsel everywhere she could reach before we all trooped off to find somewhere to sleep. Larch slept alone in the downstairs room – at least, I assumed she slept; maybe she roamed around all night in search of alfalfa. Neil, Karen and Rory shared the little bedroom and

Davin, Keenan and I all got what sleep we could in the bigger room, on cushions rescued from the catering van and whatever blankets, sleeping bags and covers we could assemble.

Davin and I slept together, rolled up in the one sleeping bag. It wasn't quite how I'd envisaged our first night together, fully clothed and with a heavily snoring Keenan on the other side of the room, but maybe we weren't ready for anything else yet.

I lay curled under the weight of Davin's arm, huddled into his warmth, and smiled to myself. He was nothing like Noah, that much was true; he was famous and dazzlingly attractive for a start off, but he was also the most emotionally aware man I'd ever met. He knew I felt guilt over what happened to Freya, even though he would never know how soul-consuming that guilt was. Maybe he was right, maybe I did need to talk to 'his man'; another perspective on things might just help me to sort it all out in my own head. I'd never be over that sense of loss, that emptiness, but – well, planting a tree would be a good thing, environmentally, and memorially. And if we needed to spend some time together in a wood in Ireland, well, increasingly time spent with Davin was looking less like a punishment and more like something I looked forward to. *Could it work? Could it really?* I made a mental list of things for and things against, and when the only real thing I could find to put on the 'against' list was that he was ridiculously famous and on his way to becoming a national sex symbol, I had to give myself a stern talking to about the whole list-making thing.

I opened my eyes and looked at Davin's face. It had become so familiar, yet I had never really properly looked at him. Now I could see that lovely shaped mouth, the dark stubble that gave him a rugged, outdoors appearance without making him look like an unshaven thug. Those high cheekbones with his dark hair as a backdrop. Something inside me gave a little shiver and fizzle, like a spoonful of hot batter dropped onto a griddle. Yep, he was definitely attractive.

Just as the full 'Davin effect' hit me, I saw his eyes open, as though he could sense me looking at him. A moment passed, while his gaze travelled slowly over my face and then a slow smile broke out. 'Happy Christmas, Tansy, my love,' he whispered, cupping a hand around my cheek.

'Happy Christmas,' I whispered back. And, snuggling myself against his warmth, I fell asleep again.

* * *

Christmas morning was – well, it was unlike any Christmas morning I'd ever had before. For a start, it was spent in a house with no furniture, so there was a lot of standing, until we pulled the catering van chairs in from Larch's Land Rover, whereupon we sat dotted randomly around the little kitchen like a set of interviewees for a particularly onerous position. Rory dashed about from room to room; he had barely waited for dawn to open his presents from Karen, who'd given him some new games for his Xbox and some graphic novels. Neil had, apparently, pulled some strings with some sound guys he knew and got Rory a signed CD from a band he loved, and Rory was rocketing around the house telling everyone every detail about the band, whether they wanted to know or not.

Larch had given him a Christmas kiss which had turned him beetroot and let him take selfies with her. I had the feeling that his stock with his mates would be through the roof when they all went back to school and that would be a better present than almost anyone else could give him.

'I've got a confession to make,' Davin said as we stood outside watching Brian and Seelie sniff around the wind-scoured front garden of the bare little house.

'Is this a real thing? Or are you quoting song lyrics at me? Only I've had enough of that from Rory this morning.'

'Real thing.' He kept his eyes on the dogs, well, on Seelie really; nobody wanted to keep their eye on Brian for more than a few seconds after they found out what he was doing. In the background, the sea was providing the kind of soundtrack you get in expensive spas; gentle waves broke over sand and occasional gulls made little mewing cries in the distance. Yesterday's storm was barely even a memory for everyone except those with damaged doors and some of the boat owners who were staring out over the harbour this morning wondering where their dinghy went. Nature was pretending perfect manners.

'OK then, confess.'

I had my own little confession to make right now – his words had made my heart thunder and my palms go sweaty as I worried what he might be going to say. Right up to that moment I *still* hadn't been entirely sure how I felt about Davin – other than pure, visceral desire – but the way my system reacted to the thought that he might be about to confess to something really bad, and that I'd have to deal with that, told me that I really, *really* liked him.

'Come with me. It's something I need to show you.'

I raised my eyebrows. 'I am very much hoping that this isn't an "I'll show you mine if you show me yours" scenario. We are both at least twenty-five years too old for that one.'

Davin gave me a very old-fashioned look that made him look as though he was straight off the Victorian boat. 'Tansy, my love, I very much want to show you everything I've got – including fifteen acres of Western Ireland coastline, and a mother who's going to be so grateful I've found myself some-one who won't dump me for Tom Hiddleston first time around she'll probably give you a fish supper and offer to marry you herself. But none of those things are here, are they?'

'I suppose not.'

He led me down the steps to the road. I went down care-fully; my legs were still wobbly, and I needed the assistance of his hand to reach the bottom. It was horrible, feeling so vulnerable and shaky, but Davin didn't make a big thing of it, for which I was grateful. We walked a little way up the road and found Kee's car, slewed in at an angle which left half the back end out in the road. 'What? I said I can drive. I didn't say I could park,' Davin said. 'I just had to get over here when I realised everyone was gone from Landle Bay so I picked you up and drove over.'

I could only imagine that drive, in those weather conditions, by a man who'd never passed a test. I guessed the local police had had other things to worry about last night. 'It's less the parking,' I said, carefully. 'It's more – well, the car.'

One side had a huge scratch down it and half the door panel was dented as though by a giant fist. There was what looked like salt spray up to the windows, one tyre had collapsed and the alloy wheel was bent and cracked. 'Ah, it got us here, so.' Davin sounded very nonchalant for someone who had, essen-tially, written off his boss's car. He opened the boot.

'You left it *unlocked*?' I squeaked.

He looked up and down the road, dramatically. 'There was a great lack of opportunistic car thieves last night, what with the falling trees, the howling gale and the waves the size of tower blocks. Besides, I'm not sure it'll go again, the last mile was a bit – bumpy.'

'Oh Davin.'

We both went quiet for a moment as a vision in a floaty white dress, completely unsuited to December, wafted by us, heading up the hill. 'I'm just going to do my stretches and my vocal work,' Larch explained. 'I can't be around people. I need to free my body so I thought I'd go up to the clifftop and be one with the wind.'

'Just be careful. The cliffs might not be too sound right now,' Davin said, surprising me with his concern.

'I will.' She gave a wafty hand motion. 'Karen's promised me grilled tofu with a roast-vegetable salad and I wouldn't want to miss that!'

We watched her continue her walk up the hill, looking like a windblown bit of litter, all random movements and occasional spins. Davin winked at me. 'She's gone off to fart,' he said. 'Poor Larch; she's a martyr to her IBS. That's why she has such a nailed-down diet; she's not really being a fussy mare – anything else makes her sick.' Another wink. 'But you never heard that from me. She doesn't like people to know.'

'Oh, and I thought she was just being all "actorly" and highly strung.' I felt bad for some of the thoughts I'd had about Larch and her fussy eating and decided to be nicer to her from now on.

'But look. Here's my confession.' He reached into the car boot and pulled out…

'My holdall! You found it!' I gave him a weak hug, my arms still being a bit soggy in the muscle department. Then I frowned. 'So you let me think it was lost?'

'Ah, well, yes, sorry about that. But I did need you to know that sometimes things get lost. Just not, on this occasion, your bag.'

'You bugger.' I took the bag from him and slid the zip. The nylon fabric was damp and there was a strand of seaweed wrapped around a handle. Inside, the newspaper-wrapped parcels looked like ambitious papier mâché. I zipped it back up again. 'Oh dear.'

'Come on, I'm sure it'll all be fine, now. Let's go in. Karen's cooking breakfast.'

He saved my string-arms by taking the holdall from me, swinging easily up the steps with it, where the dogs greeted us as though we'd been gone for a fortnight and left them with empty food bowls. We marched into the kitchen, which did indeed smell of wonderful things cooking.

'You are wasted in that café,' Keenan said, clearly half way through his second plate of pancakes.

'Maybe so, but I love it.' Karen eyeballed him sternly. 'And like I've said before, Rory has to finish school before I am going anywhere.' She widened her stare to take in Neil, who looked a bit shamefaced and I gathered some kind of behind-the-scenes conversations had taken place, hopefully involving a future for the two of them. 'So make the most of your pancakes cos I'm not sure how long the café will be open for. That there nephew won't bide his time much longer, especially if some cheap burger place makes an offer.'

I looked at Davin. He looked at me and shook his head, ever so slightly. Then he hoisted the holdall up and said in an unnaturally cheerful voice, which, for Davin, was slightly cheerful, 'Tansy's got you presents.'

'They, er, they might not be in great condition,' I said, slightly worried by the alacrity with which everyone clustered around. 'They did get a bit wet.'

I unzipped the bag and handed out the soggy little parcels. I'd bought a few extra things, just in case, and so managed to have presents for everyone except Neil, to whom I mouthed 'sorry'. He gave me a beaming smile and looked around the room, indicating with his grin that this whole gathering was more than he could have hoped for for Christmas. I didn't miss the fact that he had an arm around Karen either.

Karen and Rory were delighted with their presents, even though I had my doubts that the headphones would ever work after their soaking, and the lovely fluffy top I'd bought for Karen now had the texture of, well, Brian. I'd bought two little wooden pictures in The Shop of Many Smells, one of which Kee received with a touching gratitude. I put the other aside for Larch, when she came back from her stretch.

I handed the final parcel to Davin, almost embarrassed. It was such a small thing and this man had everything, or, at least, the money to buy anything he wanted. Hadn't he, after all, bought this entire house practically on a whim? And now I was giving him a damp newspaper parcel – it was a bit like giving the Queen a set of IKEA teaspoons.

Davin unwrapped the little carved sheepdog and stood very still for a moment, just holding it. I thought I'd made some kind of faux pas, from his expression. His eyes folded and his mouth twitched, as if he was about to cry, then he put the little dog down onto the side of the sink very, very carefully, almost as though it was a real live creature, and wrapped me in his arms. He held me so tightly that I feared for my ribs for a second.

'Thank you,' he whispered, his breath making my skin shiver. 'Thank you, Tansy.'

His intensity was a bit scary so I was relieved when Rory bounced in with presents for Davin and me – a huge hand-knitted and rather frighteningly hairy jumper for Dav, which would have fitted a gibbon and still left room for the swinging, which Davin received with more charm and good humour than I'd have thought him capable of, and a really rather lovely framed postcard of an old map of Dorset for me. He'd bought a squeaky rubber bone for Brian, which was immediately pounced on and dragged under a chair, from where the occasional half-squeak came for the rest of the day.

And while everyone was admiring their presents, or doing something arcane with a bird so large that it looked as though it might have been taken from Jurassic Park, Davin took my hand and drew me through into the living room. 'Thank you so much for Rook – the dog,' he half-whispered. 'You don't know – I guess you'll never know – what it means to me.' His hand went to my face, gentle fingers curled themselves into my hair and, keeping his eyes on mine, he kissed me. It was the kind of slow, questioning kiss that I wasn't sure I had an answer to, unless the answer was somewhere in the chafing groin of my dried-out jeans.

'I've got a present for you,' he said when we finally broke apart.

'Again with the hoping that this isn't a playground joke.' I fanned my face. It felt from the inside as though we could have used it to roast that turkey.

'This is serious.' From a pocket he pulled out a little box. I stared at it.

'You had better not be contemplating going down on one knee, Davin O'Riordan,' I said, sternly. 'Because I seem to remember a lot of talk from you about taking things slowly.'

'Ah, now you're jumping the gun.' He smiled, and it was the slow, devilish smile he used to such devastating effect on-screen. So I ignored it.

'Just for the record, I am not jumping *anything* just now.' I still had my stern voice on.

Davin gave me a sideways sort of grin and handed over the box. I opened it cautiously, preparing myself for anything from an engagement ring to a jumping spider, but it was neither. At least, it *was* a ring: a fine gold and silver woven band with two hands around a heart and a diamond joining them. 'It's a Claddagh. A friendship ring. Because, whatever we might become, just now we're friends.' He took the ring from the box and put it on my right hand. I had to admit that it did look very pretty. Plus, the diamond glittered. I made a mental note not to put it anywhere Brian could reach.

'Thank you.' I turned my finger to admire the sparkle. 'No, really, Davin. It's lovely.' A thought struck me. 'How long have you been carrying this around? Not, like, years…?' I'd had a horrible vision of Davin pursuing various women with the same ring, although why anyone would turn it down I wasn't sure. And then I remembered his surly irritability and knew why.

Now he laughed. And I realised that the seriousness that came over as a grumpy persona was because he didn't laugh often and I wanted to make him laugh more. In a good way, obviously – not by dropping my trousers or falling headfirst into trifle. 'I got Kee to get it sent over from Ireland for you. He was happy to oblige.'

We stood at the window that looked out over the back of the house and up the narrow, steep street, now shiny with the recently passed rain. A few people, hatted and coated against the December chill, were walking down to the sea, exercising dogs or escorting small children, but the majority of the population seemed to have decided to stay indoors. After the weather we'd just had, I didn't blame them. A weak, sucked-lemon sun glimmered over the hilltop and lit the village for a moment before some left-over tatters of cloud hid it again and I shivered. I was, after all, wearing clothes that had been soaked and dried far more than was trendy.

Davin put an arm around me as we stood, quietly, just watching the village come to life. People greeted each other and stopped to talk; dogs sniffed and ran on the beach. Even the gigantic seagulls had taken to the cliffs and weren't trying to mug sandwiches off passers-by. 'It's nice here,' Davin said. 'D'you think you'll stay?'

I looked at his face. He was keeping his eyes on the little town, but I could feel his heart beating fast under the bulky sweater. I thought of my old business, up in London, of Noah, of the things I'd lost that felt almost within reach. And then I remembered Davin's kindness, his understanding and the promises he'd made. Plus he was an ex-model TV star, which didn't hurt at all. 'Why not?' I tried to keep my tone light. 'Like you said, the café is going to need managing, a brand needs building, all that. If Karen decides to go for our idea… we really ought to discuss it with her.'

Davin inclined his head towards the closed kitchen door, behind which some raucous, and probably alcohol-fuelled, laughter was breaking out. 'Yeah,' he said. 'But let's wait until everyone's sober first, shall we?'

I moved closer to his warmth and put my hands up to cup his face. 'Let's,' I said quietly, and stood on tiptoe to kiss his mouth. 'Yes.'

Chapter Fourteen

VALENTINE'S DAY 2019

'Well, what do you think?' Karen stood back, paintbrush dripping. 'I'll say it, though I shouldn't, it looks pretty damn amazing.'

'We'll need to get some A-frame boards.' I was walking around, making lists on my iPad. 'One outside and a couple further back, up the track, so people know we're here. Oh, Dav's got us some costumes to put on the mannequins in the corner there – ' I gestured towards where two genderless and wigless plastic human figures were laid against the wall, wrapped in plastic sheeting like oddly sexless murder victims. 'And the glass cases for the scripts can go up on that wall, there.' I pointed with the end of my stylus.

Karen looked over at me. There were splashes of paint all over her face. 'So,' she said, and the wiggle of her eyebrows was highlighted by the magnolia, 'what did I tell you, Tansy; he's a decent bloke that there Davin. Have you – ?' She waggled the paintbrush in a thrusting motion. 'Cos I saw you and him up at the house the other day, digging the garden, and he was looking like a man who's at one with his parsnips, if you get my drift.'

'Oy, I'm only in here and listening, you know.' Rory's slightly peeved tone came from the café kitchen. 'I don't have much choice after all, when I'd rather be down on set helping Neil and you've got me in here with a screwdriver and... something, I'm not even sure what it is or what I'm meant to do with it.'

Karen and I giggled silently and then the memory of Davin and the nights in the big new brass bed, where he displayed a whole new level of understanding and a degree of attention to detail, made my cheeks get hot.

'You're blushing! Rore, she's blushing out here!'

'Shut up. We open for business in three weeks; once filming really gets underway, we don't have time to stand around discussing – well. We don't. And now the café belongs to the community with nobody to bail it out, there's a lot of work to put in.'

The community had bought the café, once Davin and I had put our proposal to make it a *Watch Tower*- and *Spindrift*-themed place, and Kee had agreed to film some scenes in there to make it even more of a draw for the public. Karen and I had gone into business together – she was the hands-on element and I was the business brain – and it turned out that we worked very well as a team. I had ideas but Karen wasn't afraid to put her own thoughts forward, and I had high hopes for our future. The crew had held a raffle of items from the series to help raise the money and had even helped sell tickets as far afield as Exeter and Dorchester. The money raised had bought the café and given us enough left over for a kitchen refit and a paint job. It *hadn't*, however, raised enough money to pay for actual workmen to do it so we were putting in the hours ourselves. Or, in the case of Rory, were playing Nintendo whilst hiding in the new store cupboard.

'Brian! Brian! Just… sit over there!' I pointed, although given Brian's level of obedience it was largely unnecessary. Brian was wearing a large plastic cone over his head, following his recent operation to ensure that he and Seelie could occupy the same planet once she'd had her pups, and it meant he kept getting stuck under tables or in corners. He wasn't at all happy about this and kept giving me 'Looks', even though it had been Davin who had taken him to the vet's and collected him. Brian knew where the blame lay and didn't hesitate to let me know. And, as Davin was doing some pre-filming work down at Christmas Steepleton, and some publicity work that would, hopefully, soon start sending some business our way, we were looking after Seelie, who was lying on a bed in the kitchen, looking like she'd swallowed a rocket launcher. Brian kept going through and sitting next to her, where together they looked like a very unlikely advert for love.

I ticked off a few more items on the iPad; we'd got a delivery arriving in the morning and I needed to check that everything was ready. Karen slopped some more paint around the walls. All the tables and chairs had been replaced, the walls, once painted, would be lined with left-over props from *Watch Tower* and photographs from the set and the sinister mannequins – which I'd fought strongly to have taken out and burned – were awaiting their costumes. It was all looking good.

Over at the house, we'd finally finished furnishing the last room. Davin had basically sat with me whilst we flipped through websites, getting me to read out details as we went and 'yes' or 'no'-ing items of furniture. There were carpets on the floors, a heating system in place and it was, in short, a home. Nothing like the smart London flat but I'd got used to that. We were using my rescued linen and crockery, both from expediency and as a sort of 'up yours' to the memory of Noah.

I'd got used to Davin's long work hours and a quick kiss on the cheek as he tried not to wake me when he went down for a four a.m. start, or days when I had to go through a new script with him, line by line. There was a kind of comfortable closeness growing between us that had nothing to do with what happened in bed; it was our friendship deepening into something more intimate.

'Mum!' Rory's call sounded urgent. Worried.

'What's up? Forgotten to save another level on that there shooty game thing? Told you, Rore, we've got to get the kitchen finished!' Karen dipped her brush in the tin again and prepared to put another coat of paint on the far wall.

'No, it's Seelie. Tansy, I think you ought to get Davin. I think there's something wrong with her.'

There was an elbow match as we fought to be first in the kitchen. Seelie was sitting up on her makeshift bed in the corner. She had an unfocused look in her eyes as though she was trying to think of the final clue in a crossword and she was shivering occasionally.

'Oh hell.'

'Is she going to have her puppies now? In *here*?' Karen asked, rather frantically. 'Only we've got the Health Inspector coming round for a second check soon and I dunno what he'll say about that.'

I stared at the little dog. 'I don't know! I don't know anything about dogs. Davin's doing some 'establishing shots' or something today...' We looked at her a bit more. 'She could be ill.'

'Look, she's about three years pregnant and due any day; isn't it more likely that she's having her puppies?' Karen said, and she was staring at Seelie too. Both of us were eyeballing the dog as though we expected her to pop like some kind of alien and spray puppies all over the kitchen at any moment.

'I'm fetching Davin.' I made an executive decision. 'He'll want to be here, whatever it is.'

I drove the car which had replaced the 'submarine' over the clifftops to Christmas Steepleton, a drive that was now imprinted on my memory like an expensive special effect. Up the track, over the clifftops, which were now draped in plastic tape warning about the dangers of collapse all along the edges, giving them a sort of 'cheap lace edging' look from a distance. Down past the turn to the boys' school, down the hill, past the houses and B and B's until I performed a handbrake turn in the car park at the bottom, and squeezed the car in between those of the crew who'd recently arrived. My heart was beating so hard by this time that I almost couldn't hear the gentle wash of the waves over the blood in my ears. *What if something happens to Seelie? I have to keep her safe…*

Davin was out on the harbour wall with Kee, a photographer from the local press and Sharon from costume, who was dabbing at his front with a sponge. I had a brief moment of memory of the chest that lay under that shirt, small scatterings of dark hair and smooth skin, pressed against me in the dark, and then I shouted.

Dav and Kee came over. Larch came out of the Old Lifeboat Station, which they were using as an HQ for the time being, until all the vans arrived. 'What is it?'

'It's Seelie…' Almost before I'd finished speaking, Davin was at the car. Larch and Kee piled in behind us, leaving Sharon standing sadly holding her now redundant sponge on the sea wall and the photographer taking some shots of the cold, swirling sea.

'Back soon,' Kee shouted out of the window. 'Just, you know, stay put.'

'What, *here*?' Sharon looked around her at the incoming tide.

'On set!' Kee yelled back.

I thumped into my seat.

'Come on, come on.' Dav had his arms folded. 'How is she looking? What is it? Has anyone called the vet – call the vet, someone.'

Kee was already dialling from the back seat, as we took off with much tyre screeching and other car protestations.

'I'm sure it will be fine,' I said, rubbing his knee.

'Hmph.' Then he turned worried eyes to me. 'Is she restless? Sicky? Oh, feck, Tansy, she's going to be grand, isn't she? I mean, she has to be… by the way, I got you a present.'

'A what?' The wheel slid between my fingers as the car slid on the road. My heart was sliding about too inside my chest.

'It's Valentine's Day, y'know?'

I stared at him aghast, as the car scraped along some branches, just starting to bud. The hedges had been badly damaged by the winter storms, but the scars were starting to fade now under new growth, like accident victims rehabilitating. 'I'd completely forgotten. I've lost track of the date, what with…' My face went hot again as I remembered what we'd been doing that had driven the need to be precise out of my head. 'I mean, I know it's a Thursday, we've got a new oven coming on Friday, but… oh, hell. Sorry.'

'I was going to cook.' Davin gave me a sudden grin. 'Well, I got Larch to tell me a recipe. It's mostly green, but she was the only person I could think of to ask. Although I could burn you a sausage, if you like.'

'It's delicious!' Larch put in from the back seat and made me jump, because I'd almost forgotten she and Kee were there. Davin tended to do that, make you forget that anyone else existed. 'There's seaweed and algae and it's very nutritious.'

'If you're a carp.'

'Shut up, Keenan.'

'Can we put this on hold for a bit? Only, Seelie, potential puppies, yada yada.' I put my foot down hard to force the car up the steep hill at maximum velocity.

We screamed along those lanes, although it was mostly the passengers screaming. I'd got the hang of the narrow byways up here now, driving them half a dozen times a day had given me the kind of casual familiarity that has people who don't know the road yelling 'what if there's a tractor round that corner!' When you know that the hedge is low enough to see the road for a mile ahead at one point, you can drive quite impressively.

We hurled into the car park by the café and Davin was out of the car before I'd even put the brake on. He dashed inside.

Kee got out more slowly and nodded. 'Yep. I'm thinking we can do your first scene here, Larch, when you meet Matt for the first time since he saved you. What do you think?'

Larch, swaddled in her huge duvet coat, although it wasn't actually that cold, just gave him a look. 'I think there could be puppies,' she said. 'And I want the pretty one, so I think we should go and find out.'

Rory met me at the door. 'She's had three, so far,' he said. 'Mum's in with her. She won't let me go in cos she says it might put me off having kids.'

My head swirled for a moment. My mouth was full of the taste of gas and air and sterile wash. I could hear the nurse trying to cry silently but letting tears fall, feel my body betraying me, letting my daughter slip away.

'Tansy! I need you here.' Davin came back out, saw me standing on the threshold. 'Feck. You all right, love? You don't have to be here if it's hard. Go and...' he looked around for inspiration, 'polish the mannequins or something.'

I took a deep breath. Puppies aren't like babies, Seelie would be fine. *I* would be fine. Without a word I went past him, inside. 'How is she?'

Davin winked. 'All going well. Vet's on her way, just to be sure. Your Karen's doing a grand job of midwifery; she said she paid more attention than she should when Rory was born, in case she needed to send him back.'

Seelie was lying on her bed in the corner of the kitchen, three tiny wet bullet-like things snuggled against her. Even as I watched, she raised her head, nuzzled her back end and began licking another small shape as it lay, inert for a moment, then crawling to join its littermates against Seelie's warm body. Karen bent over them all for a moment.

'She knows what she's doing,' she said, quietly. 'I'm basically just catching them. How many do you reckon, Davin?'

Davin got on his haunches, careful not to disturb the little dog. 'Got to be another three, four, in there.' He kept his voice low too. 'Vet should know better. But it's going all right.'

I could feel the tears now. I hadn't even known I was crying until I felt the trickling tickle down my cheek, but I couldn't tear my eyes away. OK, it was a dog, and therefore less gas and air and screaming, but I couldn't help comparing. Lovely puppies, suckling now, warm and – alive.

I pushed my way past Kee and Larch who were standing in the doorway with the soft, folded sort of smiles that people adopt in the presence of new life. *I never had that.* My parents, my sister, they'd come to visit me afterwards; we'd all felt the lack of those soft smiles. Not for me the armfuls of gifts, not for Freya the new babygros and cuddly toys.

'Hey now.' Davin caught up with me round the back of the café. I was staring out to sea, letting the breeze dry my face.

'You should be in with Seelie,' I kept my eyes on the gentle rippling surface of the ocean.

'She doesn't need me; she's managing just fine.' Davin came and stood next to me. Not touching, for which I was grateful. 'You do.'

'I'm just remembering. Thinking how it should all have been different.' I wiped my eyes with the back of my hand. 'That I should have been happy.'

'Are you not happy now?' he asked, carefully.

'I... well, yes. But happiness feels, disloyal, if you see what I mean.'

'To Freya?'

I nodded. And then sniffed, because, try as I might, I couldn't cry the attractive, stage tears like Larch could and snot was beginning to run down my nose.

'How would your future have been if she'd – ' He stopped. Corrected himself. 'If she was here?'

On the horizon, gulls were swooping. 'I suppose I'd still be with Noah. Have the company. And – ' I thought. 'I'd be looking after her and he'd still be cheating on me with all those girls he pretended not to know. I'd be trying to think of ways to diversify and spread the risk, paperwork at home and buying new premises, Freya would be in nursery and Noah...' I looked Davin in the eye now. 'I'd have Freya, but I don't think I would be happy. Not really. Or I'd have thrown Noah out and be managing on my own. I'd be content, but not happy.'

His eyes, fringed with those telegenic lashes and backed with that mass of dark hair, were gentle. 'Life would be very different.' His voice was gentle too. He took my hand. 'You're allowed to mourn her, y'know. But don't let it hold you back.'

I smiled, a wet and pathetic sort of smile, but it was a smile nonetheless. 'No.'

His other hand went into his pocket. 'You know I said I got you something? For Valentine's Day?'

Not an engagement ring, Davin. This is not the time. Besides, I'm not sure I'm ready… not sure I'm over it all yet. But how could I say that to a man looking at me with such love? I took a deep breath. 'Yes? And I'm sorry I haven't got you anything; like I said, lost track of the date…'

'Ah, it's fine now. Look. I was going to do this tonight, but with the puppies and all, it's going to be a late one, so.' From his pocket he pulled a little box. *Oh god.*

Inside, between my trembling fingers, was a fine gold chain. Very, very fine; so thin as to almost not be there. And on that chain was a tiny gold heart. And on that heart was one word. *Freya.*

Davin put the chain around my neck and the little gold heart nestled in the dip at the base of my throat. 'That way, she'll always be with us,' he said, and kissed me. Not a lascivious kiss but a kind, understanding kiss. Holding me close and comforting me by just being there. And, in his own particular way, understanding how it all felt, as much as anyone could who'd never been through it.

When we went back in to the café, the vet was there. 'Nine and I think that's all done,' she said. 'Pretty quick work, young lady, all told. Four bitches, five boys: all strong and healthy. She's done well.'

'Nine!' Davin looked a bit startled.

'They're so cute!' Larch squeaked.

The vet looked unimpressed, but she did give Davin one of the long looks that I was beginning to get used to seeing on the face of women, and, it must be said, a few men. The look that said 'aesthetically you are most pleasing and I should very much like to gain carnal knowledge of your body', only with a lot more Anglo-Saxon and less politeness. 'Are you going to be able to find homes for them all?' she asked.

'Ah now, that's the easy bit. Half the crew want one.'

'They want the ones that look like Seelie. Nobody wants to be cursed with a Brian lookalike.'

We all glanced over to where Brian was lying with his coned head on his paws, looking deeply sorry for himself. 'Oh yes. The Norfolk terrier that we castrated last week. Good-looking lad. I think you'll find first cross Norfolk whippets will be in quite high demand.' The vet started packing up her stuff.

'Wait a minute. Brian is a real dog? I mean, a proper breed?' I stared at the dog in question, who sighed and shifted about a bit, then stretched out in front of the big range cooker, as though hinting that he 'could be warmer, could you please turn this thing on?'

'Oh yes. Quite a valuable breed; there's not all that many of them about. They're getting more popular now, though, and especially to cross with the whippet for first cross lurchers.' She closed her bag. 'Fabulous working dogs. Good luck; you know where I am if anything goes wrong.' And with only a minimal number of backward looks at Davin she was gone.

We all stared at Brian now. Seelie, practically unwatched, licked her puppies and curled around them.

'Bloody hell,' Rory said. 'He's an actual breed!'

'But why?' I looked at the matted unkemptness and general unwholesomeness that was Brian. 'Why would anyone breed something like that deliberately?'

'Ah, come on now, if he's washed and primped a bit, he'd be quite handsome,' Davin said. 'The vet checked for a microchip before they neutered him and there's no report of a missing dog either. He was just always meant to be your dog, Tansy.'

I opened my mouth to say 'he's not my dog,' then looked around the café kitchen. Larch and Keenan were crouched close to Seelie, admiring her puppies. Karen was washing her hands and Rory was still staring at Brian. Casually I linked my fingers through Davin's.

'Yes, I think he was,' I said.

About the Author

Jane Lovering was, presumably, born, although everyone concerned denies all knowledge. However there is evidence that her early years were spent in Devon (she can still talk like a pirate under the right conditions) and of her subsequent removal to Yorkshire under a sack and sedation.

She now lives in North Yorkshire, where she writes romantic comedies, one or two of which have won awards. Owing to a terrible outbreak of insanity she is now the minder of three cats and two terriers, one of which is a Patterdale and therefore as insane as Jane. Though smaller, and cuter, obviously.

Jane's likes include marshmallows, the smell of cucumbers and the understairs cupboard, words beginning with B, and Doctor Who. She writes with her laptop balanced on her knees whilst lying on her bed, and her children were brought up to believe that real food has a high carbon content. And a kind of amorphous shape. Not unlike Jane herself, come to think of it.

She had some hobbies once, but she can't remember what they were. Ask her to show you how many marshmallows she can fit in her mouth at once, though, that might give you a clue.

You can find Jane on Twitter at @janelovering, and visit her website at www.janelovering.co.uk.

Note from the Publisher

To receive updates on new releases in the Seasons by the Sea series – plus special offers and news of other humorous fiction series to make you smile – sign up now to the Farrago mailing list at farragobooks.com/sign-up.

Printed in Great Britain
by Amazon